1

From where she stood, Jane's attention was entirely focused on him.

The stranger's imposing presence seemed highly inappropriate in her late father's home. Tall and well built, perhaps thirty years old, he was wearing severe black, but he had loosened his plain white stock and removed a leather glove from his left hand. The sun slanting through one of the high windows shone on his curly dark brown hair, springing thickly, vibrantly from his head and curling about his neck. His face was not handsome but strong, striking, disciplined and exceptionally attractive—the expression cool. He was also one of Cromwell's Roundheads and a man who was familiar to her—a man she had once risked her life for.

The tender feelings that had governed her actions all those years ago had vanished when Cromwell's Roundheads had killed her father. And now, finding one of them at Bilborough Hall, his very presence defiling the beloved walls, made her shake with anger.

She continued on down the stairs, finding it difficult to conceal the sense of outrage that possessed her on finding this Cromwellian in her home, treating Bilborough Hall as if he owned it. Sensing her presence, he spun round, all taut muscle, lean power and pulsing strength. His gaze was fixed on her as she crossed towards him.

Helen Dickson was born and lives in South Yorkshire, with her retired farm manager husband. Having moved out of the busy farmhouse where she raised their two sons, she has more time to indulge in her favourite pastimes. She enjoys being outdoors, travelling, reading and music. An incurable romantic, she writes for pleasure. It was a love of history that drove her to writing historical fiction.

Previous novels by Helen Dickson:

THE DEFIANT DEBUTANTE
ROGUE'S WIDOW, GENTLEMAN'S WIFE
TRAITOR OR TEMPTRESS
WICKED PLEASURES
  (part of *Christmas By Candlelight*)
A SCOUNDREL OF CONSEQUENCE
FORBIDDEN LORD
SCANDALOUS SECRET, DEFIANT BRIDE
FROM GOVERNESS TO SOCIETY BRIDE
MISTRESS BELOW DECK
THE BRIDE WORE SCANDAL
SEDUCING MISS LOCKWOOD

Did you know that some of these novels are also available as ebooks? Visit www.millsandboon.co.uk

DESTITUTE ON HIS DOORSTEP

Helen Dickson

First published in Great Britain 2012
by Mills & Boon, an imprint of Harlequin (UK) Limited.
Harlequin (UK) Limited, Eton House, 18-24 Paradise Road,
Richmond, Surrey TW9 1SR

© Helen Dickson 2011

ISBN: 978 0 263 22909 7

Harlequin (UK) policy is to use papers that are natural,
renewable and recyclable products and made from wood grown in
sustainable forests. The logging and manufacturing process conform
to the legal environmental regulations of the country of origin.

Printed and bound in Great Britain
by CPI Antony Rowe, Chippenham, Wiltshire

DESTITUTE ON HIS DOORSTEP

Prologue

The morning mist was thinning when the solitary figure on horseback turned for home. The slender form dressed in breeches and doublet, the shining black hair trimmed to the shoulders and framing a heart-shaped face in soft, natural curls, could be mistaken for that of a youth, but was, in fact a girl.

Suddenly she saw a handful of Roundheads on reconnaissance bivouacked around a fire that glowed like cats' eyes in the gloom. Aware of the threatened danger to herself, she rode for cover into a thicket, just as a large contingent of Royalist soldiers appeared so suddenly that there was no time for the Roundheads to sound the alarm and prepare themselves.

In these fearful days of the Civil War, when it was no simple matter to draw a line between skirmishes and combats, actions and battles, the Royalists, having reached the remarkable conclusion that the King's crown was settled upon his head again, were convinced they would crush the Parliamentarians. For weeks this Royalist troop had ridden about the countryside, harrying enemy patrols. The rising sun reflected upon the pike tips and armour, and except for the differing coloured sashes—red for the Royalists and orange for Parliament—there was little to tell them apart. But the arrogant expression on the face of the man who rode at the head of the Royalists, and the gold chain hanging on his breast, proclaimed him to be their leader.

What followed was chaotic for the Roundheads. The Royalists fought with so much resolution and audacity, and with such a clamour of swords, the butt end of muskets and shot that the surprised Roundheads must have thought they had arrived at Hell's gates. The outcome was inevitable. The Royalists outnumbered them by ten to one, and the Roundheads must have known it was impossible for so few of them to triumph over so many. The fighting was fierce but brief. Roundhead losses were relatively severe, and those who survived were rounded up and bound.

Without so much as a glance around him, the Royalist, Captain Jacob Atkins, sat his mount, impassive and cold, his bloodied sword still clutched in his hand. All his attention was focused on the leader of this bunch of Roundheads, Colonel Francis Russell. Unable to believe his luck in coming upon his sworn enemy unexpectedly, his gaze never wavered. His one remaining eye was a slit of pure venom and something glinted through it, like some predatory fish swimming just beneath the surface. So much hatred emanated from this man that the girl still in hiding nearby shivered as the Roundhead Colonel was seized and led away with his fellow soldiers to await his fate. They were being taken to an immediate holding area—in this case the church in the small market town of Avery.

In his buff coat and carbine and orange-tawny coloured sash— the colours of his captain-general, the Earl of Essex—his proud head bare of the triple-barred helmet, which he'd had no time to put on, the Colonel rode stiff backed and tall in the saddle and not without dignity, looking straight ahead. Nothing showed of the pain and humiliation of defeat which lacerated his fierce pride.

The girl's attention had been drawn to him during the skirmish as he had tried to fight off this Royalist force, confirming her assertions that Parliament might have control of the country, but the Royalists were crushed but not yet beaten. The Colonel must have known what the outcome would be, but despite this he had fought gallantly, wielding his sword as the girl had seen no other do, while his compatriots were cut down. There was a hardness concealed within a ruthless instinct for survival that made him formidable. The girl wondered what demon drove him. The ferocious wildness that had spurred him on to slay his enemies, sparing himself no hardship in the process, had gained him her admiration.

Despite her young age she was an avid follower of the Civil War and the men who controlled both sides. She knew who Colonel Russell was, as did every Royalist soldier present. As one of Cromwell's ironsides he was an impressive figure. Without doubt he was a superb trainer of horsemen and a tactical leader in Cromwell's recently formed New Model Army, having gained a larger-than-life reputation for invulnerability in every battle in which he had fought, demonstrating a valour above and beyond the call of duty.

A supporter of the King and confident that she had nothing to fear from the Royalists—she was well acquainted with Captain Atkins, for he was her stepmother's brother—the girl rode into the open. 'What will they do to him?' she quietly enquired of a young soldier as they watched the prisoners herded off in the direction of the town.

The soldier glanced at the young stranger he took to be a youth, wondering briefly where he had come from and what he was doing there, but then he shrugged and turned away with little interest. 'Atkins will give him no quarter. Russell alone is more dangerous to the Royalist cause than an entire troop of Roundheads. With Atkins it's personal. They've met once before, at Newbury, and there isn't a day goes by when Atkins doesn't curse the injury inflicted on him by this Roundhead's sword. It took his eye out, and it almost cost him his life. Atkins has vowed vengeance. He'll see to it that the Roundhead doesn't live to fight another battle.'

'He'll bring the wrath of the whole Parliament force down on him if he does that. It would not be in his own best interests. Colonel Russell is an active and daring commander, highly thought of by Cromwell himself. An exchange must be negotiated.'

The soldier turned and looked at her grim-faced. 'Not in this case. This is different. Woe be it for me to speak ill of my superiors, but Atkins is an ugly, vicious bastard, a man devoid of any kind of honour. He deals out his own style of justice—thinks he can do what he likes, and if he thinks he can get away with shooting a Roundhead officer, even one as highly valued as this one, he'll do it without batting his eye. You wouldn't want to witness how he deals with his enemies. He inflicts pain first, lets them stew a while, then...' he made a slicing gesture with the side of his hand across his throat '...that's it.'

The soldier moved off, leaving the girl to watch the Roundhead's departing figure. Shock and anger at the injustice of the situation rose like bile inside her. Colonel Russell was a Roundhead and therefore her enemy, but he was too worthy a man to die in such a sadistically cruel manner that was nothing short of murder.

Much of her knowledge had come from her father, a prominent Royalist. He had told her that when officers were captured, on each side it was normal for commanders to negotiate exchanges of officers of equivalent rank, and they could even be paroled on the promise never to fight again, but it would seem Captain Atkins made up his own rules. He was to show no such leniency to this particular Roundhead who had been a thorn in his side for too long. To shoot him would be a flagrant breach of the rules of war, but Captain Atkins, a cruel, sadistic man, would not be swayed from his decision. What hope had this Roundhead of being spared by such a man? And he was such a fine man.

Raising her head and squaring her shoulders resolutely, one thing the girl knew, she would not in all conscience let them kill this brave man.

When she came to Avery she pulled her hat low over her eyes, though with such a large influx of soldiers all taking care of their own needs, no one paid her any attention. She rode up the winding, cobbled street between gabled and thatched houses and made straight for the church, which was set apart from the centre of the town.

It wasn't difficult to find out what had happened to the Colonel. When she saw a couple of men drag him out of a building adjacent to the church, none too ceremoniously, it was evident that Captain Atkins had lost no time in putting his victim to the torture. He was as quiet and still as a dead man, but he wasn't dead—she could hear him breathing; she heard Captain Atkins order the guards to take him to the vestry, to keep him away from the other prisoners until dark, when his fate would be sealed.

The men stood guard over their prisoner, grudgingly, for all around them their fellow soldiers, celebrating their small victory over the Roundheads, were making merry with the liquor, which was in plentiful supply in the town's ale houses.

With a combination of her wits and a goodly amount of this strong brew, which the girl plied on these guards, she soon had them snoring. Even though she knew she was putting her own life in danger, she was determined to get the Colonel out of the vestry. After obtaining the key from the pocket of one of the guards and picking up the discarded jacket from the other, careful not to draw attention to herself, she let herself in.

The interior was dimly lit by light slanting in through a high window. The Colonel was sitting propped up against the wall. Thankfully his eyes were open and clear. The girl was slender and pleasant looking, and her dark eyes, though often defiant, were gentle. In that moment an emotion that was completely alien to her gentle nature almost overwhelmed her as she stared mutely at the slumped figure. She hated Captain Atkins for the cold and cruel calculation of which this Roundhead Colonel had been the victim. He had been treated with savage cruelty. His dark hair, blackened by gunpowder, was soaked in sweat. His handsome face was battered and bleeding, and his burned and bloodied and mangled right hand he held cradled to his chest.

Swallowing the nausea that rose in her throat and gathering all her courage about her like a cloak, she went towards him. Putting a finger to her lips, she said quietly, 'I've come to get you out.' She looked towards the door, her nervousness growing with every minute. 'My plan is simple. But we must act quickly.'

The Colonel's face was as rigid as if it had been carved of stone. 'It is a brave plan and I am grateful for the thought which your heart and sense of justice dictate, but you must see it is impossible.'

In an attempt to raise his spirits, she gave him a grin of confidence. 'Not as impossible as you think.'

'Is it not? Tell me. Why should I trust you?'

'I speak out of respect, not insolence. I am no chivalrous knight in gleaming armour. I saw you fight. I'll not stand by and watch Colonel Atkins destroy you. Are you able to walk?' He nodded. The girl handed him the guard's coat. Out of her pocket she drew a rose-pink scarf. 'Take off your coat and put this on. I'll help you. It may be a tight fit, but it's the best I can do.' She passed him her wide brimmed hat. 'You can wear this. Pull it well down.' Dragging a table over to the wall, agile and nimble on her feet, she climbed on top and shoved open the window. As she looked down at the prisoner, despite her fear her grin was mischievously wicked. 'Don't worry. I don't expect you to climb up here, but when the guards find you gone, they will think this is how you escaped.'

Jumping down, she helped him to his feet and to remove his coat, careful of his injured hand. Assisting him into the guard's coat and grimacing when it came nowhere near fastening over the Colonel's broad chest, knowing there was nothing she could do about it, she passed the Royalist colours over his shoulder.

The girl laughed when she saw the look of disgust that crossed the Colonel's face at having this final indignity forced on him. 'This could save your life and lose it in the same day if you are not careful.'

'How so?'

'It will get you away from here, but if you don't take it off before you reach your fellow Roundheads, they may shoot you for a Royalist without asking questions.'

Tearing a strip of white cloth from one of the vestment robes hanging on the back of the door and concealing the Colonel's coat beneath them, she set about tending the wounded hand as best she could. The mutilation appalled her, not because of the gory sight, but because it was his right hand, his fighting hand, and without it his future as a soldier—if he was successful in escaping Captain Atkins—was over.

The colonel shuddered, groaning. As he watched her bandage his injured hand his voice was harsh with bitterness. 'Dear Lord in heaven! Could Atkins not have dealt me another wound but that? He's made damned sure my sword hand is useless.'

Always practical, the girl said, 'You have another hand,

Colonel, a perfectly good one. If you are half the man you are reported to be, you will learn to use it. There will be other battles to fight before this business is done. Now come. The more important matter of saving your life concerns me now.'

Going to the door, she opened it a crack and looked out. Seeing the guards were as she had left them and the soldiers who weren't clogging the taverns carousing on the village green, she beckoned the Colonel forwards. 'Go round the church to the back. Walk through the graveyard and when you come to the gate let yourself out and turn to your left. Halfway down the street turn left again down an alley way. There you will find a horse waiting for you.'

Wonder, astonishment and, finally, admiration glowed in the Colonel's eyes. Before slipping out he paused to look at the young stranger he fully believed to be a youth. There was a strange intensity in the pale face under its unruly mop of curly black shining hair. 'You've thought of everything. It's a scheme worthy of a master planner.'

The gratitude in his voice took the edge off the girl's fear. 'Promise me you will take care of the horse. His name is Arthur.'

Colonel Russell frowned with concern. 'It is your horse?'

She nodded.

'And yet you are willing to part with it.'

'There is no other way you can get away from the village. All I ask is that you treat him well.'

'I promise you no harm will come to it by my hand. You help me even though you know what will happen to you if you caught. Your age will not protect you. You will be hanged for a traitor.'

'I know that, sir.'

'Why are you helping me?'

'This is war, Colonel. Captain Atkins may be of my persuasion, but that doesn't mean to say that I have to like him. I don't hold with personal vendettas. I could not stand by and watch him kill an honourable man.'

'Thank you. Human nature is full of surprises. You are a remarkable young man. I am grateful. Avery, which is staunchly behind Parliament, has been taken by the Royalists, but it is only a matter of time before we take it back. Can I not persuade you to change sides? We could do with men like you.'

She would have laughed out loud had she not thought he might see through her deception. 'I am not yet old enough to fight, sir. If the war is not over when I am of age, then my sympathies are firmly with the Royalists.'

'And your name? At least tell me that?'

She grinned, a mischievous, wicked twinkle dancing in her dark eyes. After a moment's thought, she said, 'You may call me Tom, sir.' She inclined her shining head in a respectful bow, the smile widening on her lips. 'Glad to be of service.'

'God be with you, lad. I'll never forget the debt I owe you for saving my life.' With that he slipped away.

When he had disappeared round the church and she had locked the door, covering her tracks, she put the key back in the guard's pocket. She was elated, considering all the danger to have been worthwhile to acquire Colonel Russell's esteem and to help him escape the odious Captain Atkins. Thrusting her hands into her own pockets, she left Avery and followed the road that led to her home. Already she missed her beloved Arthur, but, knowing he would aid a brave man escape the clutches of Captain Atkins and that he would be well cared for, she didn't mind so much.

On finding his prisoner had escaped, in his rage Jacob Atkins came to two decisions, which he would never alter as long as he lived. The first was very simple. One day, he would meet that accursed Colonel again—and when he did, he would kill him.

Chapter One

Jane looked with distaste and a cringing fear at the chair Jacob Atkins would have her bend over so he could beat her with the thin cane which he was casually slapping against his booted right leg. His one remaining eye held a strange pin-prick of light that Jane, with a sinking heart, knew boded ill for her. It would not be the first time she had felt the sting of that cane. Red welts usually criss-crossed her back for days following a whipping. He seemed to take special delight in marking her bare flesh.

'Please do not use that on me.' Her voice quavered. 'I have done nothing so terrible that deserves a beating.'

'It is a *punishment* you will receive, Jane, and as usual you are being impertinent.'

Jane hesitated, then, her terror bolstering her courage, though she was sadly aware that it wouldn't make any difference to what was about to happen, she raised her head bravely. 'There is nothing wrong with trying to defend myself. These—these punishments have to stop,' she said haltingly. 'I am not one of your daughters. I will not be beaten into submission.'

Jane watched with dreadful, terror-filled fascination as his face turned a dangerous crimson; the colour of it appeared to leak into his eye. She held his gaze with something like defiance, her proud nature rebelling against compliance to this man. She just hoped he wouldn't notice how violently she trembled, the fear instilling uncertainty of what form of punishment he'd use on her if she openly defied him. While her lovely face seemed almost without expression, her eyes betrayed her inner fear as she stared back at him.

When he moved to stand directly in front of her, her heart sank and her blood ran cold when he raised his hand and she felt his fingers brush her neck. On a gasp she struck at his hand, only to find her own as quickly imprisoned. He seized a handful of her long, thick hair, pulling her head back with spiteful force.

'Oh, no, Jane. You have much to learn,' he hissed, his mouth close to her ear. 'If I want to touch you, touch you I shall.'

She stood rigid and silent, his touch making her skin crawl. A violent shivering shook her from head to foot when he released her hair and his grip tightened around her neck with ever-increasing brutality. With helpless fury she looked into his eye.

Jacob gave a slow, satisfied smile. How he craved to run his fingers over the white skin beneath the dress of this girl while she trembled before him, to look on her nakedness and see her proud, complacent smile turn into a grimace of terror as she cried and pleaded for mercy. Just as suddenly as he had touched her he pulled himself together. The smile faded from his face and his hand released her.

'How dare you question my authority, Jane, my judgement. I would advise you to obey me immediately or go to your room until I give you permission to leave it. I have to go out and will not be back until tomorrow afternoon, at which time we shall continue this discussion and I will consider the punishment you deserve.'

'By all means lock me in my room,' she uttered tremulously. 'I would rather that than be beaten by you for merely riding out alone. I am nineteen years old and what I have done does not deserve a thrashing.'

Jacob watched her closely. As she stood before him, he felt a certain satisfaction in knowing how much she feared him— hated him. She was quite magnificent as she held her head high and her eyes shone with bravely held tears. But she had defied him and he would not have it. He would make a show of his authority. The girl, his late sister's stepdaughter, was full grown, a strong and healthy girl with too much pride, and he would not rest until he had thrashed that pride out of her.

Jane Lucas was a beauty. Her sun-warmed flesh and peach-coloured lips and her warm dark eyes were accentuated by the midnight blackness of her hair.

'Do not think you can escape, Jane. Do you remember what happened the last time you ran away from me?' He laughed, delighting in the horror that suddenly appeared in her eyes, for she had tried to escape him—twice—and each time he had found her and brought her back. Her punishment had been severe, and she had been kept in her room until she was fit to be seen. 'You will take your punishment,' he said, smacking the palm of his hand with the cane. 'I promise you that.'

He stood directly before her, and Jane could clearly see the huge bulge that filled the front of his breeches. He was breathing rapidly, his face suffused with colour. A horror so great, so overwhelming, a thought so preposterous, so disgusting, was running through her mind like quicksilver. Surely he would not subject her to… Dear God, no, but then… Yes. Jacob Atkins was perverted and he could and he would if he had his way.

At fifteen years old when she had come to live in his house, she had been wise enough to recognise that he enjoyed the spectacle of degrading a gently nurtured girl even more than he would enjoy the physical act of ravishing her. Now, one glance at his flushed features laid bare the lascivious nature of his private thoughts, and the humiliation that those thoughts were directed at her was too dreadful to contemplate, but they told her that he intended the second pleasure to follow the first.

All their lives his daughters had suffered pain and fear at his hands. They had always been afraid of him, even when their mother had been alive and she had done her best to interpose between her rage-filled husband and cowering children. Now grown women, they were still meek and obedient and punished for the slightest transgression. The youngest, Elizabeth seventeen and Anne a year older, were vulnerable and weak, whereas Hester could withstand his indifference, his cruelty, for, apart from the beatings, which seemed to give him some perverse pleasure, he barely infringed on their daily lives.

He had made them what they were. They were fed and clothed and slept in warm beds, but they were nervous and terrified of their own shadows, always looking over their shoulders to see if their father was watching them. Nobody could stand against Jacob Atkins—nobody—not even Jane. But somehow, some time, she would make good her escape. She would leave his house for ever and go back to…

There was a place she knew where time went by on widespread wings, a place where she had known nothing but happiness and love and been allowed to grow and flourish as every young woman should be able to do. But here in Jacob Atkins's house time plodded wearily on, slowly, painfully on calloused feet. With her stepmother dead and finding herself now quite alone and increasingly the target for her step-uncle's unwelcome attentions, she knew it was time to leave his house—to go home to Bilborough Hall.

Jacob turned his back on her to show his absolute contempt— or so he would have her believe, but the truth was that he would not be content until he had accomplished what he had set out to do, which was to make her understand the rules she would have to live by in his house, and by the time he had finished with her he was certain she would obey those rules. Moreover, his body's almost uncontrollable desire for her had to be slaked, which was why, when he had triumphed over her flimsy defences, he had decided to take her for a wife.

'You are disobedient, Jane—indeed, you seem to enjoy openly defying me. If you do so one more time, I shall be forced to take further measures.' He turned to face her. 'You have no idea how cruel I can be.'

He was wrong. Jane knew the cruelties he was capable of inflicting on people. The pain his punishments elicited had heightened her dread of him. So great had been her ordeals during these years at his hands that she likened his house to a torture chamber.

Looking at Jacob Atkins now, that was the moment she realised that he had slipped over some invisible line between cruel viciousness and into madness. His eye flickered at her and a fleck of white frothed at the corners of his mouth. Perspiration beaded on his forehead and his face was scarlet with some inner rage.

Repulsed, Jane whirled about and fled the room. Hester met her on the stairs. Her usual pleasant smile was not in evidence as she looked at Jane with concern, seeing not for the first time the signs of distress.

'Are you hurt?' she enquired softly.

Jane shook her head. 'No, Hester—at least no more than usual. I've been ordered to go to my room.' Through the mists of shock and fear she darted a nervous look around to make quite sure no one was listening. 'I think it's time I left this house,' she whispered fiercely. 'I fear for my safety if I remain here any longer.

Your father will not be satisfied until he has beaten me into the ground. He is to be away until tomorrow afternoon. Enough time for me to prepare. I intend to be away at first light. This time I am determined, Hester.'

Picking up her skirts, Jane carried on up the stairs. Hester hurried after her.

'But is that wise?' Hester asked, on entering Jane's room, her concern evident. 'He will come after you. He caught up with you the last time you tried to flee—and—and he hurt you so much, Jane.'

'I know, but last time I had nowhere to go. This time I shall go to Bilborough.'

Hester stared at her and paled. 'Bilborough? But—you can't go back there. Do you forget the reasons why you had to flee your home? The villagers accused Gwen of being a witch. They wanted to see her hanged—and they accused you of conspiracy. You will be in as much danger there as you will be if you remain here. People have long memories, Jane.'

Jane paled. What Hester said was true. 'You are right, Hester, but with no family of my own I have nowhere else to go. It's the only place I *can* go. I truly am between the devil and the deep blue sea—but I think I would rather take my chance at Bilborough than remain here with that man another day.'

'But witches are associated with all that is evil. It is dangerous to be accused of being a witch, as the most common punishment is death.'

'I know. No one liked Gwen. In their ignorance the inhabitants of Avery thought the woman my father married was unnatural. Their prejudice was an emotion that ran deep, twisting their reasoning until they believed she really was a witch. Gwen was just a herb woman and known as a healer. Many benefitted from her carefully mixed potions. She also possessed great beauty and charm. Men's heads were turned when she passed by; driven by jealousy, the women maliciously pointed her out to the witch finder who came to Avery one day in the summer of '48, falsely accusing her of poisoning a woman and her unborn child.'

'I thank God she managed to escape their vindictiveness before she was examined,' Hester said. 'My only regret is that she did not live long when she reached Northampton. Things might have been different if she had. She was the only person I knew who could stand up to my father. If you are set on going back there, Jane, I shall pray you do not have to bear the brunt of the malicious hatred that might still fester in the breasts of those who consider they have been cheated out of hanging a witch.'

'So do I, Hester. But it's a long time ago and I'm hopeful that things will have changed.'

'Then if you're set on leaving, I'm sure I can be of help in some way.'

Jane smiled and clasped her hand. She was deeply touched by the sincerity in Hester's voice. With her soft blonde hair and pale blue eyes, Hester was a modest young woman, with a retiring and wary nature, which was hardly surprising considering the harsh treatment meted out to her by her father.

'Dearest Hester, ever practical and always kind. Ever since Gwen brought me here you have been a pillar of strength. As for helping me—you shouldn't. You know your father will find out. He always does and then you will be in trouble as well as me.'

Hester smiled. 'I'm prepared to risk it. Sometimes I fear what will become of us—but it's right that you go. At least you have somewhere to escape to, whereas we will have to stay under his authority until he finds us husbands,' Hester retorted, in a voice made harsh by the hostility of her thoughts. 'Indeed, Jane,

I cannot wait. Nothing could be as bad as this—no man as cruel as he is. His behaviour is abnormal, deranged. I believe his mind is twisted—in fact, there are times when I am sure he is quite mad. How else can his cruelties by explained?' Tears were glistening in her eyes and on her lashes when she asked, 'Is there always a man to be found behind women's suffering?'

Her words were met by silence, then Jane took out a handkerchief and handed it to her. Jane was worried about what would happen when Jacob Atkins discovered she had left. 'It certainly looks that way, Hester. God help us all,' she whispered. 'I believe there is.'

With her few possessions secured to the back of the horse and Scamp, her little dog, curled up in front of her, with the end of her journey in sight, Jane focused her eyes on the road ahead. With the war not long over, the countryside was infested with footpads, vagrants and displaced soldiers. She was armed with an ancient matchlock pistol, one of a brace that she had taken from the house. She would not be afraid to use it should anyone try to accost her.

After a long and weary ride, having reached the borders of the Bilborough estate in the heart of Cambridgeshire, suffering from aching limbs and a severe headache, she rode slowly. She tried to ignore her discomfort in the joy of being close to Bilborough Hall, telling herself there would be plenty of time to rest when they were home.

She was going home in peace—at least, it was peace of a sort, for although England was now a Commonwealth, the Civil War had ended. She let her gaze move lovingly over the achingly familiar landscape. The countryside around them was beautiful, the land rich and fertile, with ancient woods full of game and huge oaks and elms stretching to the sky like a benediction.

Marsh birds came in flocks to settle on a large lake, wheeling and calling overhead. Corn standing tall and golden in the fields indicated that harvest wasn't far away.

Halting her horse to let a young swineherd cross the road to the next field, she noted sheep and cattle grazing contentedly in meadows; in another, half-a-dozen splendid-looking mares had foaled. She was impressed. Long before her father had died all the horses at Bilborough had been requisitioned by the army. She wondered where all these horses had come from.

There was no sign of neglect here, as had been the case of other manors she had passed through. Despite the ten years of Civil War, it was plain that their steward, Silas Thorpe, had done his work well, and was a good taskmaster in managing the tenants and obtaining from them the requisite labour.

Jane's eyes had been fixed on the horizon for the past hour. At last she was rewarded when the turrets and rooftops of the hall came into view. In recent years she had often thought about the past and now, seeing the pink-and-gold stone walls, with ivy growing around the facing windows, it brought it all back with a strange force. With poignancy she found herself thinking of her father and all he had tried to do for her. Sadly she had never known her mother, who had died shortly after her birth. The memory of her father's death flashed into her mind and brought tears to her eyes. She blinked them aside. Bilborough Hall had been a place of peace and happiness, and she vowed it would be again. It was home, and this was where her heart was, for always.

'There it is, Scamp. Does the sight of it not gladden your heart?'

In reply, the little dog twitched his ears and licked her hand. Her eyes switched to the left of Bilborough, settling on the picturesque rooftops of Avery in the distance. On a note of gravity she said, 'I wish I could say the same for the town.'

She was remembering the last time she had been there, when Gwen, her stepmother, had been attacked by hostile locals, who had accused her of being a witch. Jane felt her heart contract with remembered fear.

'It will be better now, Scamp. What happened was a long time ago. Things have moved on and people forget. Please God the people of Avery have done so.'

Not to let any unpleasant memories mar her homecoming, she thrust them away. Dropping Scamp to the ground, she laughed joyously, gathering the reins firmly in her hands. 'Time for some exercise, Scamp. We are home at last and I can't wait to get there. Let's see who can get there first.' With a tap of her crop and a kick of her heels against the horse's flanks, she took off in a flurry of skirts.

As a child, no one but Jane's father had been able to control this wayward, headstrong girl. In Northampton Jacob Atkins had subdued her spirit and it had lain dormant but for ever simmering. And now, within sight of Bilborough, it was resurrected and ready to fly free.

Jane's father had been killed in a skirmish near Oxford, leaving his widow with not a penny in the house. The country at that time was racked with civil war, plague, food shortages and high prices. Gwen had no liking for Bilborough Hall or the people of Avery, who on the whole supported Parliament and were making their lives at Bilborough a misery. When the threat of being charged with witchcraft became a reality, Gwen had fled Bilborough, taking Jane with her, and returned to live with her widowed brother at the family home in Northampton, much to Jane's disgust, who, despite her fondness for her stepmother, had thought she should do as other women with absentee husbands were doing all over England and play the soldier and stay and defend her home with prudence and valour.

Jacob Atkins had prospered in the provision of trade before the war. He had married the widow of a cloth merchant, who had brought him a small fortune and given him three daughters. He had promised Gwen on her deathbed that he would look after Jane until she married, but having his sights set on Bilborough Hall since the estate was not entailed to the male line and was now Jane's inheritance, he had a mind to marry her himself.

His anger would be fierce when he returned home and found her gone, but Jane had no qualms about leaving. When she'd put the house behind her, she'd felt like a gilded bird freed from its cage. But she feared that he would come after her and threaten her life and her future. Every waking moment from now on she would expect to see him. The picture of him coming after her for revenge was so bright, so vivid—inescapable. But she would not regret her decision to leave.

As she galloped towards Bilborough Hall with Scamp running along beside her, she was unaware of the three mounted men who had paused to watch her on the edge of a copse, their open-mouthed expressions revealing their astonishment and at the same time their masculine appreciation.

'Good Lord! Where the devil did she come from?' one of them exclaimed.

'Wonder who she is?' asked one of his companions.

The third man and the employer of the other two, Colonel Francis Russell, his eyes also following the female rider as she flashed across his sights in a blur of red, her long black hair streaming out behind her like a jaunty pennant on a ship's masthead, replied, 'I'm sure the young woman, whoever she is, must be a stranger to these parts—dressed as she is.' His eyes sparkling with appreciation, he chuckled low. 'If he were to see her, Justice Littleton would lose no time in having her whipped and clapped in the pillory.'

Francis continued to watch the young rider a moment longer before turning his horse and heading for home, for there was something totally distracting about watching a young woman racing a horse across the countryside without regard to how fast it was moving, or how uneven the ground stretching out ahead of her.

Jane rode through the arched gateway and into the courtyard. A single walnut tree gave shade in one corner. As she slid from the saddle, her horse, sensing that he was at journey's end, dropped his head and was twitching his lips in expectation of a bag of oats, while the flies settled on him.

Facing the house, she felt strangely lightheaded. Her whole body ached and she was hot and thirsty. The heat and sun had drained her energy and she was in desperate need of food. Having left so abruptly, she had sent no warning of her arrival, and she wondered what she would find.

Walking to a gate in one corner, she shoved it open and gazed at the garden spread out before her. The gardeners had kept up their work, at least. The lawn was freshly cut, the ornamental hedges trimmed. Sweet-scented roses grew up trellises lining the long terrace. A sundial gleamed gold on its marble column and a fountain sent up jets of crystal into the late afternoon sky, misting the grass brightly starred with meadow flowers.

The quiet and the stillness all around her was profound. She took a deep breath, drinking in everything she saw and felt. To live in such surroundings as these, without the hurly burly of Northampton was luxury indeed. Closing the gate, she turned her attention to the house. Climbing the shallow flight of wide stone steps to the door, she let herself quietly inside.

The spacious, oak-panelled hall was cool, the air scented with a subtle blend of beeswax and herbs. Elaborately ornamented stonework clearly evidenced the artistry of talented masons of bygone years in the fluted archways that set apart the great hall located at the heart of the manor. Two servants passing through merely glanced her way, their voices hushed to murmurs as they disappeared into the shadows. Without moving, Jane watched them go. The warmth and welcome of the house embraced her, bringing with it a sense of well-being. She felt herself begin to relax, the tensions of the journey easing out of her, but her head was aching terribly.

Two large wolfhounds stretched out in front of the hearth. Jane, who had grown up with dogs roaming the house and grounds, showed no fear of them, although these two she did not recognise, which caused her to lift her brow in curious wonder. Smiling, she went to them.

'Hello, you two.'

Sitting up, their tails thumping the floor, they sniffed and then licked her outstretched hand, and then she squatted down to pet them in turn.

Her attention was distracted when an elderly servant, her arms full of fresh linen she was about to take up the stairs, paused to turn and look at her. It was Mary Preston, who had been house-keeper at Bilborough Hall since before Jane was born. The older woman's mouth gaped open in amazement, her eyes opening wide in recognition, and she gasped. Retracing her steps, she carefully placed her burden on a central heavy round table before crossing to the young woman as quickly as her ample frame would allow.

'Mistress Jane? Oh, mercy me! It is you. I thought my old eyes were playing tricks.'

'Yes, Mary,' Jane replied, moving into the centre of the hall and kissing the housekeeper's cheek affectionately, 'it's me, and glad to be home at last.'

'Home? Oh—why…goodness me! You gave me quite a turn.'

'I'm sorry if I frightened you,' Jane apologised.

In her black dress and white apron, her iron-grey hair covered by a white cap, outwardly Mary had changed little in the past four years, but on closer inspection, Jane saw that a look of anxiety had replaced the merry twinkle that had been for ever present in her eyes. She was a good, hard-working woman, and she had served the Lucas family faithfully over the years. On leaving Bilborough for Northampton, her stepmother had dismissed the staff and left Mary and Silas as caretakers until the time came when they could return.

'How are you, Mary? Well, I hope.'

'A few more aches and pains, that's all. Of course I've worried about you, so far away, and I was sorry to learn that the mistress had died. But just look at you. I see you've fleshed out, but you've not changed.' Her eyes suddenly swam with tears. 'You look more like your dear mother.' Jane's skin was unblemished and smooth as the petals of a rose. Her thick black hair fell about her shoulders in a tumble of glossy curls, and her graceful figure was full bosomed and slender waisted, her dark eyes aglow with warmth. 'And I haven't seen a gown that colour since the dreary shackles of the Commonwealth began to tighten.'

As if in defiance of the new laws passed by the Government, Jane was indeed wearing a colourful gown—poppy red, in fact. She laughed, and couldn't help teasing Mary. 'Would you rather I came back dressed like a black crow in Puritan garb? I'm not afraid of Oliver Cromwell, Mary—not him or all his ironsides. Besides, he isn't anywhere near here.'

As Jane did a quick turn to take everything in, she failed to see the sudden pallor on the housekeeper's face and her look of agitation as her eyes darted towards the door.

'And how have you fared, Mary, these past four years?'

The housekeeper shook her head sadly. 'After all the heart-
ache and anxieties that have befallen us since the wars started,
on the whole I can't grumble. I've always had food to eat and
a roof over my head. Too many good royalists have lost everything.'

'We've all suffered,' Jane replied, suddenly sombre, 'and there
are many Royalists still in hiding after Worcester with a price
on their heads. If there's any justice in the world, King Charles
II will come into his own before too long.'

Mary shook her head sadly. 'Dreams, Mistress Jane. That's
all they are.'

'Maybe so, Mary, but without dreams we achieve nothing.
But,' she said on a more cheerful note, 'there'll be no talk of war
today. I'm here now, home at last, and from what I saw on my
way to the house, Silas has done an excellent job. It's so good
to be home, Mary. You can't imagine what it means to me. I
want you to tell me everything that has happened.' Mary opened
her mouth to speak but Jane gave her no time to answer before
ploughing excitedly on. 'I'll just go and take a look around upstairs. I'll need some hot water for a bath—I feel so hot and dusty
after the journey,' she said, skipping towards the stairs.

Mary's arm came out to stop her. 'Wait—there's something I
should tell you, something you should know before...'

Jane was deaf to anything she had to say as she went up the
wide staircase to explore the house, trying to ignore her wors-
ening headache and her aching legs in the joy of being home.
She smiled at the servants as they went about their work. She
certainly hadn't expected to see so many; in fact, the house
seemed fully staffed. Fresh-cut flowers filled vases and the silver
gleamed. Floorboards, oak panelling and furniture were highly
polished, and was she mistaken or were there some pieces she
hadn't seen before?

With no one living in the house for four years, she had expected the rooms to smell fusty with dust everywhere, but they didn't, which she considered strange.

Jane paused in the doorway to her old bedchamber and her expression became one of puzzlement. Tentatively she took a few steps forwards. As she did so she found she was able to distinguish the things around her better and she began to take in the details of the plain but sumptuous decor. The beautiful eggshell blue-and-silver curtains and bed hangings she had chosen many years ago were gone. Now the bed was entirely hung with midnight-blue velvet, quite plain and unadorned, save for the gold cords that held back the heavy curtains. The windows were hung with the same fabric as the bed. A pair of exquisitely carved ivory statuettes along with a chessboard of amethyst and silver, shining in the light, stood on a table by the window. On either side of the table were two comfortable leather chairs, which she had never seen before, and the portrait of her father, which had hung over the dresser, and the miniatures of her mother and herself on its surface, had been removed.

Who was responsible for the alterations and why? On one of the bedside tables was a leatherbound book by the sixteenth-century popular dramatist Christopher Marlowe. A scent hung in the air. It was a scent that was unfamiliar to her, a masculine scent. She was more bewildered than ever, for there was something intensely personal about the scent and the changes. Moving slowly round the bed, on the other bedside table there was a pistol. Holding her riding crop in one hand, she picked the weapon up with the other and gazed at it in confusion. She was curious, but had no time to dwell on the changes, for at the sound of several horses clattering into the courtyard, she hurried to a window and looked down.

Three horsemen had drawn up in front of the house, but only

one dismounted. Turning back towards the stairs she scowled, in no mood for visitors. What did they want? Treading quietly, she paused halfway down the stairs to observe the man who had entered, removing his hat, the heels of his wide-topped boots sounding loud on the stone floor. His presence seemed to fill the hall with authority. He went to the large hearth where a fire struggled to blaze. In an attempt to bring it back to life, he kicked a log into the centre of the dull glow, moving back when it sprung to life.

From where she stood, Jane's attention was entirely focused on him. The stranger's imposing presence seemed highly inappropriate in her late father's home. Tall and well built and perhaps thirty years old, he was wearing severe black, but he had loosened his plain white stock and removed a leather glove from his left hand. The sun slanting through one of the high windows shone on his curly dark brown hair springing thickly, vibrantly, from his head and curling about his neck. His face was not handsome but strong, striking, disciplined and exceptionally attractive, the expression cool. He was also one of Cromwell's Roundheads, a man who was familiar to her, a man she had once risked her life for.

The tender feelings that had governed her actions all those years ago had vanished when Cromwell's Roundheads had killed her father. And now, finding one of them at Bilborough Hall, his very presence defiling the beloved walls, made her shake with anger. Damn them all, she thought. They had descended like a plague of locusts on every Royalist house in England, stealing whatever they could get their hands on, and in most cases abusing the inhabitants and leaving them to starve.

She continued on down the stairs, finding it difficult to conceal the sense of outrage that possessed her on finding this

Cromwellian in her home, treating Bilborough Hall as if he owned it. Sensing her presence, he spun round, all taut muscle, lean power and pulsing strength. His gaze was fixed on her as she crossed towards him. A well-defined eyebrow jutted upwards in what could only have been astonishment, and then his eyes narrowed, half-shaded by his lids as he coolly stared at her. There was a barrier of aloofness about him, an hauteur, which was intimidating. He had the healthy glow of one who liked to be in the open, and the air of someone who was not happy to be confined indoors all the time.

In that moment Jane noticed the startling, intense blue of his eyes, and again she thought how extraordinarily attractive he was. His face was hard, but around his eyes there was the tracery of lines from his ready smile. Her heart seemed suddenly to leap into her throat in a ridiculous, choking way and she chided herself for being so foolish. Their paths might have crossed many years ago, but he was, after all, still a stranger to her, and a Roundhead at that. The hounds had got to their feet and taken up what had every appearance of a protective stance on either side of him. No reasonable explanation could be found for their acceptance of this stranger, at least none of which Jane was aware.

'You are a stranger here, sir,' she said calmly, having no intention of reminding him that they had already met for at that time, despite having helped him, they had still been enemies and she wondered how he would react to her if she did.

He bowed and answered in a deep, rich voice, 'Colonel Francis Russell at your service.' He straightened to his full height and studied her closely, because, apart from recognising her as the young woman he had seen riding her horse earlier, there was also something vaguely familiar about her and he couldn't think what. He was moderately sure they had never met before, and yet… No, surely he would not forget a face as lovely as this. Her beauty fed his gaze and created in his being a sweet, hungering ache that could neither be easily put aside nor sated with anything less than what he desired. It was the natural desire a man felt for a woman, a desire Francis had not felt in a long time.

Jane knew instinctively that he was just as aware of her as she was of him, and she bent her head so that he should not see her confusion or the anger in her eyes.

'Kindly explain why it is that you should be holding a pistol in such a way as it could do much harm,' he said.

She lifted her eyes, not realising until now that she was still holding the weapon. He was studying her closely and she was aware of the tension in herself. 'I am Jane Lucas, daughter of the late Sir John Lucas.'

'And the pistol?' He indicated the gun in her hand.

The amazing eyes were still focused on her as he waited for an answer. She drew a breath. 'I picked it up when I was upstairs.'

'And were you going to use it on me?'

She lifted her chin as her eyes caught him running a surreptitious eye over her appearance, the expression on his face condemning as it settled on the naked flesh at her throat. 'No, I was not, Colonel Russell. I was merely going to place it out of harm's way.'

'Harm being?'

'How would I know that, since I have only just now returned home?'

'Home?'

'Bilborough Hall, of course.'

Francis gave her a long, slow look, a twist of humour around his beautifully moulded lips. He had been aware of who she was from the moment he had set eyes on her. He recognised her from some of the Lucas family paintings he had seen on his arrival at Bilborough Hall, painted when she had been a girl. Her dark beauty had startled him. There had been a plumpness to her features, and in her eyes the artist had captured an over-boisterous girl. With the passing of the years she was much changed. At thirty years of age, he had known many beautiful women, selecting those of fire and passion, and yet he'd had no desire to form a long-standing relationship with any one of them. He had not expected to find the girl in the painting to have blossomed into such an exotic creature.

No man could remain unmoved by this young woman's beauty. With hair as black as ebony and as sleek as silk, high cheek bones and slanting eyes as dark as two shining blackberries, a figure to rival Venus and full, ripe lips that betrayed her sensuality, she was all temptation—a bewitching, exotic creature. Her neck was long and there was a certain grace in her movements that reminded him of a swan. He was conscious of the musical resonance of her voice when she spoke, and when he lowered his eyes he saw tiny beads of perspiration in the V of her dress, open at the throat, and the thrust of her high, firm breasts straining against the fabric.

The smile building about his mouth creased the clear hardness of his jaw and to Jane, it made him appear in that moment the most handsome man in the world. The flame in his gaze kindled brighter, burning her with its intensity. Then, suddenly, his direct, masculine assurance disconcerted her. She was vividly conscious of how close he was to her. She felt an unfamiliar heat flushing her cheeks that she had never experienced before.

Instantly she felt resentful towards him, threatened in some way. The glow in her face now faded. He had made too much of an impact on her, this Roundhead, and she was afraid that if he looked at her much longer he would read what was in her mind with those, clever, brilliant blue eyes of his. She straight-

ened her back, raising her chin in an effort to break the spell he
wove about her with his eyes.

Hearing his companions' horses clattering out of the courtyard, she said, 'If I have offended you in any way by greeting
you with a pistol in my hand, it was not intentional. I ask your
pardon. I should hate you to leave Bilborough Hall thinking I
am lacking in manners.'

A well-defined eyebrow jutted sharply upwards. 'Leave? Why
should you think I am leaving? I am not going anywhere.'

'But—your friends. I think they are leaving.'

'So they are. Without me.'

'But—forgive me if I appear somewhat foolish, but if they are
leaving, why are you not going with them? Excuse me for being
blunt, Colonel, but I find the mere thought of entertaining the
enemy in this house offensive.'

'Enemy?' A soft, amused chuckle issued forth from Francis.
'I am not your enemy, Mistress Lucas. Far from it. War seems
to get the best of everybody, but the war is over and the country
is trying to pull itself together.'

'Not while that odious man Oliver Cromwell is in charge. I
must ask you to be plain, sir, and explain to me why I should
find a Roundhead in my home treating it as if it were his own.
Or do you prefer prevarication to plain speaking?'

'No,' Francis said slowly. 'I always make a point of speaking
plainly.'

'Then why have you not left with your friends? Where will
you stay?'

'Right here. In this house.'

'Oh, no, I think not,' Jane said, a boulder settling where her
heart had been, disquiet dwelling where just a short while before
there had been happiness and joy.

'No?'

'No.'

'Why should I go anywhere when this is my home? The house and estate belong to me now. I purchased it fair and square.'

Jane stared at him in instinctive fear. 'But—how can it? You lie.'

'I do not.'

For a long moment she did not move. She was shocked, and as she sank on to the edge of the settle, clutching its arm, an onlooker might have supposed she had died. Surely it could not be true. She had heard of such happenings, of course, of properties belonging to Royalists being sequestered, but for it to happen to her—to have Bilborough taken from her! She was too shocked to weep and this man's careless indifference to her plight brought her to her feet, and the ill-judged words sprang to her tongue almost without conscious thought.

'How dare you! How dare you be so callous, so thoughtless at what your purchase of Bilborough would do to me, the owner of this house.'

'Not any longer,' he replied bluntly. 'Forgive me, Mistress Lucas, but I did not know you—not that it would have made any difference.'

To Jane his reply was insultingly flippant and she felt the bite of his mockery. She had been so oppressed living in Jacob Atkins's house these past four years that her temper had been subdued. But now, for the time being, those fears began to fade, for she had greater problems at hand. Tired of being at the mercy of Jacob Atkins for so long, she had not escaped his tyranny to find herself at the mercy of another, and she would do whatever it took to claim back what was rightfully hers. As she rose and confronted the Roundhead once more, she felt a deep and abiding anger.

Francis saw the young woman's face turn white and the slender fingers clench on the riding whip they held, and knew a fraction of a second before she raised her hand what she would do and raised his own to avoid the blow, trapping hers easily and twisting it up behind her back, knocking the whip from her grasp and sending it clattering to the floor. His arms were a cage holding her against him.

Jane could feel the heat of him, the hard-muscled strength of him as his eyes looked mercilessly down into hers. Almost immediately his hands released her arm and closed over her shoulders, thrusting her away. Suddenly and unexpectedly he laughed.

'You appear to be remarkably quick with your hands, Mistress Lucas. I can see I must not underestimate you. You might well have been a match for my fellow soldiers. So much for the popular conception of gently bred young ladies being raised like tender plants given to swooning and the vapours.'

The bright colour flamed in Jane's cheeks once more and she bent and retrieved her whip, trying to ignore the pain in her wrist. 'If I am angry, sir, it is because I suddenly find my home, which has belonged to the Lucas family for generations, has been stolen.' She was also feeling increasingly unwell. Her headache was definitely getting worse and she was so hot and thirsty.

He laughed again in the face of her anger. 'Of course, I should be delighted to have you remain as my guest—until *you* have found somewhere else to go. Do you have relatives hereabouts?'

Jane was dumbstruck. And so it was that she looked at the Roundhead Colonel with new eyes. And because it happened so unexpectedly, leaving no time to prepare herself, she experienced a sudden, terrible sense of loss and loneliness so that, for a moment, she found she could not speak. As she went on looking at him in disbelief, almost unseeing, she felt her heart gradually begin to pound, and all the tensions she had been trying so hard to control building up inside her until they came together in a tight knot at the base of her throat. She'd had moments of dejection before, but they had never been so serious. This was a bitter blow.

Chapter Two

It took Jane a moment to find her voice and say, 'No, I do not.
I do not understand you. You talk in riddles.'

Despite her haughty stance, Francis saw that her dark eyes,
which moments before had been hurling scornful daggers at him,
were now glittering with unshed tears. Somehow he found himself unable to move. She looked so unutterably *sad*—was that the
word?—as though she had a troubled mind and he knew that his
dogs sensed it by the way they looked at her with soulful eyes.

'No, Mistress Lucas,' he said on a gentler note. 'It is you who
is lacking in understanding.'

'I don't think so,' she answered, feeling a sudden urge to hurt
him as much as she was hurting. 'Who are you, Colonel Russell?
Please explain to me how this house can be yours? Where do
you come from?'

'From Cambridge.'

'Really. I know Cambridge. Your name is familiar. As I recall
there was a family by that name. They were farriers, I believe.'

His expression tightened. 'You have a good memory, Mistress
Lucas. You are right. My family dealt in horses.'

'So, you took advantage of the upheaval of the war to take
for yourself the house of a Royalist gentleman. You are nothing

but an upstart, the son of a farrier, a man of exceedingly humble birth,' she uttered scornfully. 'You may be deserving with your newly acquired status, Colonel, but you are undeserving of such a prize as this. People of such low quality are unfit to inhabit such a house as Bilborough.'

Anger flared in his eyes at the intended insult. Ordinarily Francis had little difficulty in sustaining the air of cold detachment that was at once his most valuable defence in his dealings with his fellow men. He had had enough practice, but he had learned very soon that the cruel, avaricious world of war equated civility with weakness. And now the regenerated son of a horse breeder was looking forwards to teaching the arrogant and headstrong daughter of a Royalist nobleman a lesson or two.

'I have every right. The Bilborough estate and rents were confiscated,' he stated, his tone carrying more hidden steel than a rapier.

'I had no knowledge of that,' Jane replied, thinking that Gwen must have known and kept it from her.

'That was not my concern at the time. But did it not occur to you that any estate known to support the King would be at risk? You left the house unattended.'

'I did not—or perhaps I should say my stepmother did no such thing. When my father was killed she closed the house—indeed, there were those in Avery, those who supported Parliament who far outnumbered the Royalists, who were glad to see the back of us.'

'There was also trouble of a different kind, was there not? Before you left your stepmother was accused of being a witch.' His tone was light, but he watched her closely. 'Personally I don't believe there are such things as witches, that it's all superstitious nonsense.'

'I'm glad you think so. We did leave for that reason. It was a terrible time for us both, a time of great fear. Dreadful threats were issued against my stepmother—against both of us. At that time all around us women suspected of witchcraft were being brutally tortured and hanged. They used such threatening methods against us that in the end we were left with little choice but to go. We left the estate in the hands of a loyal steward.'

'He was removed from his post when I bought Bilborough. I had no use for him.'

Jane stared at him in disbelief. 'You dismissed Silas? But— you had no right.'

'I had every right. He was your steward, not mine. I did right to dismiss him,' he said, as calmly as though he was discussing the weather. 'He had got above himself.'

'You did not dismiss the housekeeper,' she pointed out as part of her argument.

'Mrs Preston is less quarrelsome than your steward.'

Jane wondered at Silas's fate. She must find out what had happened to him. She had a duty to do that. Ordinary people found that their lot was often worsened with the change of ownership in land consequent upon the confiscations, because the new owners were noticeably less humane than the established proprietors to whom the local inhabitants were familiar.

'By leaving Bilborough you left your home wide open. Wars are not all won on the battlefield, Mistress Lucas. With the men away fighting whatever cause they support, who do you think should protect the property? It's the women who keep the enemy from the door, or stop their home being put to the torch.'

'Or in this particular case to stop black-hearted, conniving scoundrels stealing property and moving in.'

Francis's face had set itself fast into the implacable mould that would have been instantly recognised by the men under his command. It was the face that had won him many a battle for it showed not a flicker of emotion, nor an inkling of his thoughts. It was cool, self-controlled and as smooth and empty as that of a newly born child.

He moved closer and spoke very quietly, but his eyes glittered with curiosity as he said, 'Are you insulting me or Parliament, Mistress Lucas?'

'Oh, much more than that,' she shot back. 'I'm criticising every one of those in Parliament who thinks that by imposing order on the human spirit, no matter how absurd and cruel the order, it has achieved something. I am criticising Oliver Cromwell and his censorship. I despise everything he does. So, yes, by all means I am insulting you since not only have you stolen my home, you are a part of all that is in charge of the rottenness which executed King Charles I.'

'I would advise you to have a care what you say. For your own sake you must learn to guard your tongue more stringently. People have been executed for less. Your words are treasonable and therefore dangerous—for you. The war is over. You must learn to live with its consequences.'

'I shall, just like everyone else, but I believe Cromwell is now presented with a civilian battlefield with as many doubts and perplexities as those of the war.'

'I couldn't agree more, but they will be dealt with. Your reference to the dead King Charles implies the existence of a Charles II.'

Curling her lip with disdain, Jane dared to present a statement not altogether respectful. 'I cannot and will not accept a Protectorate should Oliver Cromwell become Lord Protector. Charles II will take the throne one day. You will see.'

Unable to ignore what had every element of being a disparaging challenge, Francis made a point of elevating his brow to a sceptical level. 'Like it or not, Mistress Lucas, you will have to live under the Commonwealth. And I did not steal your home. It belonged to Parliament. I had the support of local officials and others of purported authority. You are not alone in having property confiscated. Other examples occurred all over England.'

'I am not a delinquent, Colonel,' Jane replied coldly. 'I am aware of that. I also know that when the Puritan Roundhead regime introduced sequestration against the royalists, involving the removal of their estates and rents from their possession, in most cases they were subsequently able to regain them in return for a fine calculated as a proportion of the value of the estate.'

'That is true.'

'Good. I'm glad we agree on something. I shall go to the correct committee and demand that the estate be returned to my possession.'

A flash of annoyance darkened his eyes. 'Demand? Really, Mistress Lucas, to use such language in front of the Committee for Compounding in London would mean certain failure. To *apply* would be a more appropriate term. Do you not agree?'

Jane's cheeks flamed at his attempt to give her a lesson in etiquette. 'Whatever it takes to retrieve Bilborough I shall do. So I advise you not to get too comfortable.'

'You are desperate and desperation should never be underestimated. I am sure you are an exceptional woman in persuading others to do your bidding—but you have no idea what you will be up against.'

'I'm no weakling who gives in at the first obstacle. Women are more resourceful than men give us credit.'

'I know many who are on both sides, but such fire and vehemence—you are a veritable tigress, Mistress Lucas.'

'And you are insufferably rude, Colonel Russell.'

'But always honest.'

Jane stepped back, her eyes flashing with the force of her

anger and the heat that was beginning to consume her body. 'Do not mock me, sir. I am serious. I shall not give up on this.'

'Do as you must, but you will be wasting your time.' He encountered her hostile gaze and smiled.

It was a disconcertingly pleasant smile, and the fact that even through a haze of anger and acute physical misery and social embarrassment she could recognise it as such increased Jane's hostility. 'We shall see. I shall do whatever it takes to have you removed from this house.'

'And fail. Two categories are exempted from applying—those who were the King's top men, and those who are both Catholics and Royalists. Your father belonged to the latter.'

'He was not a Catholic.'

'No, but he was a staunch Royalist. Therefore his estate was confiscated and sold—to me.'

'Aye, with money plundered from the Royalists, I don't doubt.'

His eyes glittered like ice. 'I am no thief, Mistress Lucas. I have got where I am by my ability to succeed. Right now you are distraught and angry—and rightly so, since I can imagine how you must feel on knowing the place you have called home is no longer that, so I shall ignore what you have said. But know this. The money with which I purchased this house was earned in honest occupation, so please don't accuse me of being a thief again.'

Jane stared at him, white and rigid. Something warned her that she dared much with her open disdain. She thought here was a man who revealed nothing of his thoughts and passions, and he ruled himself like steel. Lowering her gaze, she nodded. 'Of course.'

'Just one more thing, Mistress Lucas. You say you will travel to London to face the Committee for Compounding.'

'What of it?'

'Will you have the money with which to pay the fine?
Bilborough is a sizeable estate. Should the Committee consider
your application, the sum will be considerable.'

Jane stared at him. So confident had she been that she would
be able to simply walk into Bilborough and carry on as though
nothing had happened, she had given no thought to any of this.

'No,' he said, taking her silence as assent. 'I thought not.' He
cocked an eye at her, the light from the leaping flames in the
hearth setting strange shadows dancing around them. The lights
flickered over his thick hair, outlining his face. He looked down
at her. She had allowed her guard to slip a notch, showing her
distress. She looked so young, innocent and vulnerable and her
pride was hurting, and for some unknown reason he felt a fierce,
uncontrollable urge to protect her. A gentle smile touched his
lips.

'So, Mistress Lucas, it would seem you are homeless.'

She bowed her head. Though her face did not flinch, Jane
could feel her anger mingled with her distress simmering inside
her, but knowing he was observing her and feeling the indignity
of her position, impelled her to raise her head bravely. 'It would
appear so,' she replied tightly.

'You have travelled from Northampton, I believe.' She nodded.
'Alone?'

'Yes.'

'Then you are more reckless than I thought. Can you not return
to Northampton?'

'No—I cannot do that,' she replied haltingly, lowering her
eyes to hide the painful memories his question evoked. 'It—it
is out of the question.'

He stared at her for a moment, seeing her anxiety, but he did
not comment on it. Biting back an admiring smile, he watched
her struggle to maintain a cold façade in the face of his silent

scrutiny, and he marvelled that she could convey so many things without moving or speaking. She was outrageously daring and untempered by wisdom or hampered by caution, and he wondered why she had left Northampton. Was it merely because she had wanted to come home, or something more sinister than that? Had she been driven out by desperation?

Curious as to the cause of it, he turned his head away lest he be seen with the expression on his face of the deep, welling, growing emotion she aroused in him. Deep, yes, ever since she had hurtled so precipitously into his life just moments before.

'And you have no family you can go to?'

'No. I have no family.' Beginning to realize the true gravity of her situation, an awful lump of desolation swelled in Jane's throat as she folded her hands in her lap and tried to think what to do next.

As if he read her thoughts and not unacquainted with hardship—he had not forgotten the pain of it—he said, 'I am not as heartless or as unfeeling as I might sound. At least let me offer you accommodation. My invitation that you remain as my guest still stands,' he offered, hoping she would, astonishing himself.

'I must reject your invitation. I will not inhabit the same house as a Roundhead,' she replied.

Francis was relieved that her reply sounded more of a statement than a heated exchange of anger. 'No, I though not. So— where are you planning to go?'

'That is no concern of yours.'

'Humour me,' he said drily. 'You have to go somewhere.' When she didn't reply and continued to look down at her hands, trying to hold on to his patience, in exasperation he said, 'Mistress Lucas, are you always this disagreeable and stubborn?'

She glanced up at him. 'My father always told me that I have a unique talent for it.'

Glancing down at her, Francis thought he glimpsed a shadow of a smile curving her soft mouth as she lowered her head once more. 'I'm beginning to realise that. Might I make a suggestion?'

'Please do.'

'Your steward's house is empty. You could stay there for the time being…' A smile touched his lips. 'Rent-free, naturally.'

'That won't be necessary. I may not have the money to pay the fine on Bilborough, but I am not destitute. I can pay my way.'

'So you agree to live in the steward's house?'

'I am left with no choice.'

'But you do have a choice.'

The dark eyes narrowed. 'And I told you that I will not stay under the same roof as a Roundhead.'

'As you wish.' He turned away from her and shoved another log into the fire with his booted foot. 'But I wonder if all that pride of yours will keep you warm at night and your belly full.'

Jane lowered her gaze, too aware of her situation to make any denials. 'One must be practical.'

'My thoughts exactly.' His hard blue eyes narrowed as they took in her uncovered head and gown in one coldly speculative glance, and he raised his brows. 'In which case, might I suggest that unless you wish to draw attention to yourself from the authorities, you remove what you are wearing and dress yourself in normal apparel.'

Burning colour flooded her face, and placing her hands in the small of her waist, she moved closer to him, glaring at him, her eyes overbright with an oncoming fever. 'Dear me, sir, you really are a Puritan through and through, aren't you—condemning those who are given to frivolity and prefer to wear lace and silken-coloured gowns instead of the morbid black of a crow. No doubt you think there is too much laughter in the world, too many people intent on enjoying themselves, no matter what the cost to their immortal souls.'

Francis became still and Jane's breath caught as he stepped nearer.

All his senses completely involved with her, Francis felt an overwhelming desire to take her arms and shake some sense into her, or to drag her into his own. Her soft ripe curves beckoned him, made his body starved of a woman for too long ache with the want of her. Her loveliness quickened his very soul, stirring his mind with imaginings of what loveliness lay hidden from view beneath her provocative red dress. It was a long time since he had felt this need in him to feel the warmth of a woman, to sweep her up in his arms and ease the lust in his loins. Were he to do so, he could well imagine Miss Lucas's outrage.

A lazy smile crept across his face and Jane's heart skipped a beat. Francis Russell had a smile that could melt a glacier. All she was conscious of was a sense of complication and confusion. Everything had suddenly changed. His powerful, animal-like masculinity was an assault on her senses. Moistening her lips, she could almost feel her body offer itself to this man, this Roundhead, this stranger—and yet he wasn't a stranger, not to her, and in that instant they both acknowledged the forbidden flame ignited between them.

Francis drew a ragged breath, wishing he could understand why she seemed so familiar to him. By an extreme effort of will he replied casually, 'I am a man of the Civil War. That does not make me a Puritan who would tell you to cover yourself and say that your appearance is unseemly in the eyes of the Lord—that your breasts are as wantonly exposed as your brazen, flaunting hair.'

The warmly mellow tones of Colonel Russell's voice were imbued with a rich quality that seemed to vibrate through Jane's womanly being. To her amazement, the sound evoked a strangely pleasurable disturbance in areas far too private for an untried virgin even to consider. As evocative as the sensations were, she didn't quite know what to make of them. She glanced up at him, cheeks aflame.

'Then since you are not a Puritan, Colonel Russell, you would not say those things?' He shook his head. 'So my state of dress, immodest as it is, would not trouble you?'

'Not in the slightest, but for your own safety you would do well to heed my words.'

'Oh, I shall, sir, but I will continue to wear what I please. Nothing you may say or do will persuade me to discard this dress. And you cannot force me to do so.'

'Can I not?' He looked at her with that faint amusement that she was already learning to detest. It was the same look that he might give to a bad-tempered, obstinate child. An amused look, but quelling. 'I believe that you know better than that, and since my method of persuasion might be construed as rough, it might be as well, while you reside on this estate, to do exactly as you are told.'

Jane was tempted to tell him that she would reside anywhere but near him, but seeing Mary standing in the doorway, she considered it wise to hold her tongue. Never had she felt so wretched or confused. Later she would break down and weep, but at that moment she was caught in an icy world from which she could not escape.

'The steward's house is habitable. I'll instruct the housekeeper to have some food sent over and some linen.'

His eyelids lowered, masking the expression in his eyes. A muscle pumped along his jaw and Jane felt herself dismissed in a way that she thought was disconcertingly regal—for a Parliamentary man.

'Excuse me. I would like to go and have a word with Mary.'

Her head throbbing, Jane began to cross the hall when suddenly nausea rose in her throat and she stumbled, finding it difficult to breathe. Placing the back of her hand to her forehead as her vision became blurred, she stopped to overcome a wave of dizziness. She summoned her will-power to keep upright, but she had no strength left and her thoughts refused to obey her. Dimly she heard Mary call her name and was aware that Colonel Russell was striding towards her, then she swayed and slumped to the floor with no memory of falling.

From far away she heard one of the servants gasp and say, 'Is it the plague?' and Colonel Russell briskly order the doctor to be sent for.

No, a voice shrieked in Jane's throbbing head. No—not that. Not the plague. It couldn't be. Dear God, no, it screamed as she was swept up into a pair of strong arms, where she struggled before she was enshrouded in darkness.

Jane sensed the presence of someone in the darkened room as she floated in a comfortable grey haze. Always there were hands and voices near her, muffled and meaningless, flowing past her in a whispering stream, but she could not pay attention and was incapable of joining them. She was content to linger in this blissful state, because it allowed her to evade the haunting questions and nameless fears lurking at the back of her mind.

Reason and memory played no part in the timeless vacuum in which she existed. She was living and breathing, but set apart from the world. With a natural buoyancy her mind began to rise slowly upwards, and then there was a tiny aura of light. Voices drifted towards her down a long tunnel, the words muted, encouraging her to respond.

'Jane? Can you hear me?'

The voice was soft and close to her ear and familiar. She felt panic as she was a drawn up into the world of awareness. She felt quite odd, but for the first time in unaccountable days, the fever clouds had rolled back. A great weariness weighted down her limbs.

'Jane?'

She tried to open her eyes, but they were stuck tight. Suddenly she remembered where she was and what had happened before she had collapsed. She also remembered the words the servant had uttered and in her dark world the reality that she might have the dreaded plague hit her.

'Where does it hurt?'

The question was so irrelevant in the context of the discomfort that consumed her that, if she hadn't known she was dying, she would have laughed. Fear, the weakness she despised above all others, spread through her, evading all her efforts to subdue it, and a tremor passed through her at the thought of her life being cut short by such a terrible disease.

'I—I cannot open my eyes. They're so sore,' she whispered. Her voice was weak and hoarse and her throat and lips were dry. Her body was burning hot. Hearing the sound of a cloth being dipped in water, she breathed a sigh of relief when she felt someone bathe the stickiness from her eyes that kept them glued together.

'There, is that better?' Mary murmured.

Jane's eyes flickered open and she nodded and blinked. Painful shards of brightness caused her to close them again and she winced, quickly shading them with her hand.

'It's the light,' a man's voice said. 'Pull the curtains.'

Again she blinked her eyes. The room was darker now. The air in the room was strangely still, the colours in the fabrics muted. The indistinct shadow of the man gradually became clearer. He gained her full attention. Inexplicably a sharp pang of anxiety ran through her even before she saw his face clearly.

Disconcerted, she pressed back against the pillows and eyed him warily as he came closer. Probing her memory, she fathomed the cause of her dismay. The darkly handsome face should have stirred feelings in her woman's breast. Yet there was something about the moment that made her heart lurch and grow cold within her chest.

She opened her mouth to speak, but a hoarse croak was the only sound she could manage. Mary, recognising her need, slipped an arm beneath her shoulders and raised her up and placed the rim of a cup containing cold water to her lips. When she had quenched her thirst, Mary lowered her back on to the pillows.

'There. How are you feeling now?'

'I'm not sure,' she replied. Her clothes had been removed and she now wore one of the two nightgowns she had brought with her. Her gaze moved searchingly around the room that was so achingly familiar to her. This had been her parents' room. She lay in a large four-poster bed with overdrapes of scarlet and green.

The man she recognised as Francis Russell was watching her closely, hands on lean hips, short dark hair slightly tousled. His eyes were bright and vivid blue, as blue as the sky on a summer's day. She frowned, wondering why he was here.

'I'm glad to see you are back with us, Mistress Lucas,' he said, his voice imbued with warmth. 'You were sleeping so soundly we were beginning to wonder if you would ever wake. As it is you've slept two nights and most of three days.'

Francis had been deeply concerned about her. From the moment she'd been confined to bed he'd enquired after her almost hourly. Mary had assured him that although Jane was very ill the physician was confident she would make a good recovery. When Mary had left the room to fetch fresh linen, he'd gone in to see for himself. As he'd stared down at her, her gleaming hair spilling over the pillows, guilt and fear made his chest ache. She looked so ill, but what struck him forcibly was how small she looked in that great bed, tucked around with bedcovers and pillows.

When she'd arrived at Bilborough, she had faced him with all the self-assurance of an educated, prim and proper young lady. But when he'd gazed down upon her face, unguarded in sleep, there was nothing prim about that soft, generous mouth and those long curling lashes that lay like crescents against her cheeks. He realised as he watched her chest rise and fall with fitful little gasps, how vulnerable she was, how innocent she looked. She had told him she had no family. It would seem she needed him more than she realised and the urge to protect he'd felt on their first encounter was stronger than ever.

When Mary had returned and seen the deeply etched lines of fatigue and strain on his face she'd urged him to get some rest—'Otherwise when she opens her eyes the sight of you might frighten her into a relapse.'

'You do remember me?' he asked softly, and as he spoke with a lightness to his words, no one would guess at the terror that had gripped his heart when she'd collapsed and how he'd prayed to God for the first time in years not to let her die.

She nodded, but the movement made her head hurt. 'Yes, Colonel Russell,' she answered tightly, feeling the dreamlike sense of submergence threatening to engulf her again. 'I remember you.'

He moved to stand closer, lending her his undivided attention. She could not take her eyes off him, for never had she seen a man as handsome as he was. His dark hair, curling slightly, was just long enough at the nape to brush the open collar of a shirt that appeared no less than dazzling white in the dimmed light. 'Please don't,' she said, suddenly alarmed that he was about to venture too close. Struggling to raise her head, she was overcome by a dry cough. When the cough had abated she managed to gasp, 'Please don't come any closer. You mustn't.'

He ignored her and came to stand next to the bed, looming over her. 'And why not, pray?'

'You'll become infected.'

'I'm quite safe. I had the illness when I was a lad.'

'Then you were fortunate to survive it. Better if you all leave me to die in peace.'

'Die? Who said anything about dying?' He chuckled low in his throat. 'Dear me, Mistress Lucas, you *are* feeling sorry for yourself.'

Jane's eyes widened in disbelief at his cruelty. 'Sir, you are indeed a callous brute. I know the plague spares very few.'

His eyebrows arched upwards. 'The plague? Who mentioned the plague?'

She stared at him dazedly. 'Why—I—I thought…'

He seemed suddenly amused. 'There is no need for alarm. According to the physician who examined you, you have nothing more serious than the measles.'

Jane looked at him, suddenly feeling very foolish. 'The measles?'

He nodded. 'Show her, Mary.'

Mary produced a mirror. Turning her head away Jane peered into it, unable to believe it was herself staring back. Her face was covered with a red blotchy rash. She was appalled by what she saw. Tears welled in her eyes and she bit her trembling lip. 'Oh—just look at me. I look dreadful. I—I was convinced I had…'

'The plague? No, Mistress Lucas,' Francis said, seeing the

gallant effort she made to bring herself under control before she turned her head on the pillow and looked at him once more. 'Measles can be serious, but the physician is convinced you will get well. He has advised that you remain in bed for a few days. You must drink plenty and he's left medicine for you to take that should ease your cough. The rash should fade in a few days, although your cough may persist a little longer. I'm afraid you will have to stay here for the time being.'

Having just been subjected to several moments of fear and feeling more than a little foolish, Jane reacted with a flash of anger, which had more to do with feeling mortified that he should see her looking so ugly, so wretched—which did nothing for her self-esteem—than anything else.

'With you?'

'I'm afraid so. Unless...' he smiled lazily, mocking her with her own words '...you insist on leaving, since you have an aversion to residing under the same roof as a Roundhead.'

Jane stared at him, wishing she were not confined to bed so she could strike out at him. 'I am sorry to impose on you. I can imagine how my presence must inconvenience you. I shall do my best to get well and be out of here as soon as I am able.'

Francis met her angry gaze with an amused smile, momentarily awed by her eyes as they caught a stray shaft of light penetrating a crack in the heavy curtains. For the moment they looked so dark as to be almost black, emphasising the redness of the ugly rash that marred her lovely face. With some difficulty he dragged his mind to full attention. He knew she was feeling most unwell and upset and pondered how he might soothe her fears.

'You do not inconvenience me, Mistress Lucas. My only concern is for your state of health and your welfare,' he assured her on a softer note. 'You are welcome to remain as my guest for as long as you wish.'

'Thank you. I am indeed grateful,' she uttered tightly. 'But it is a strange feeling to be treated as a guest in my own home.'

'I hope you will continue to treat it as such while you are here,' he replied, ignoring her sarcasm. 'I had quite a struggle getting you up here. If nothing else, I'm glad to see your temper has improved.'

'My temper? Why—did I object when…?'

'You did. The language you used would have made a seaman blush.'

'I—I didn't…'

'Yes, you did—is that not so, Mary?'

From across the room where the housekeeper busied herself, she nodded. 'I'm afraid she always was too outspoken for her own good.'

'Why, what did I say?'

A crooked smile accompanied his reply. 'You have an un-ladylike turn of phrase, I will say that. I have been a soldier for a good many years, Mistress Lucas, and never have I been more slandered—or my parentage for that matter—nor in such colourful detail. Quite frankly, I was shocked.'

Twin spots of colour grew in her cheeks, but the dim light and the rash did much to hide her blush. 'Oh, I did not. I think you exaggerate.'

'And how would you know that? You were delirious. In fact, if I hadn't thought you might be close to death, I would have been thoroughly entertained.'

'I've never been ill before—at least, not really ill. Not like this.'

His smiling eyes captured hers and held them prisoner until she felt a warmth suffuse her cheeks. He answered with slow deliberation. 'Then consider yourself fortunate to have excellent health. Some people are not as lucky. In someone with a less robust constitution, a severe bout of the measles can be fatal. How are you feeling now?'

'As bad as I look.' She smiled, her expression open and direct. 'I apologise for not looking my best.'

Francis marvelled at the fact that she could actually joke about it, which gave him the impression that pretensions were completely foreign to her, which made her refreshingly unique. Unfortunately that realisation led quickly to another one, one that banished his pleasure at her recovery and made him take a step back from the bed. There was nothing natural about the way he was thinking about her. He was the last man on earth who had the right to think about her in any personal way.

'I can see you are tired. I'll leave you to Mary's ministrations. And please don't worry. So as not to upset or anger you, I shall make myself scarce.' He turned and went to the door.

'Thank you,' Jane said quietly.

Francis turned and looked at her. 'For what?'

Those candid eyes were levelled on his, delving, searching, and Francis had the fleeting impression that they could see right into his blackened soul. She obviously hadn't got his true measure because she smiled and said, 'For letting me stay.'

'You were very ill. I was hardly going to turn you out.'

Jane was very much on Francis's mind as he left her. The shadow of the dark days of War and his own personal torment were never far from his tortured mind. War and death was an ugly business, the aftermath of battle always messy and merciless. No matter how he had tried to eradicate what he had seen and done from his mind, it had left its mark on him. Like a wound it was painful, deep and festering. War had hardened him and changed the man he once was, but on that fateful day when Jane Lucas had returned to Bilborough, for the first time he had paused to contemplate his meaningless life.

Something had begun to grow within him. At first it was only a vague restlessness, then it had become interest—interest in Jane Lucas. Had he imagined it? Was it a dream that he had conjured from the depths of hopelessness that Jane Lucas had actually returned to her old home? The haunting image of soft, perfect features and rippling dark hair swirling around her shoulders, and ripe, curving breasts swelling almost free of a provocative red gown was branded on his memory with minute detail, stirring an agonising impatience that could only be relieved when he could hold her in his arms.

In increasing frustration he flung himself on to his bed. Was it possible that where Jacob Atkins's brutality had failed, the illusion of Jane Lucas came close to breaking him? In desperation he held the vision, for when it faded it would be replaced by a gruesome one of a dimly lit room, of being beaten and slowly tortured by a one-eyed sadist.

True to his word Francis kept away, but he did enquire of Mary how Jane was doing. Wearily Jane knew he did so probably out of duty or an unexpected pity, or guilt that he had been the catalyst of the whole sorry business.

Now the fever was gone she was restless and insisted on getting out of bed. After four days the measles rash had turned brown and began to fade, but her cough, though not as severe, persisted.

One week after she had taken to her bed, the world still felt unreal. When she thought of the future a sudden fear threatened to engulf her. However, she was relieved there was no word, no sign of Jacob Atkins.

The hardest and most painful thing of all was accepting that

Bilborough Hall was no longer her home. She begrudged Francis Russell every stone and blade of grass, every fraction of his unearned possession, and she never expected to feel any different.

It was early afternoon and she sat by the window curled up in a large chair, her feet tucked under her nightgown and feeling pretty miserable. Nothing stirred outside the window and the house was quiet. Leaving her perch, she paced the room. Intense boredom was beginning to drive her insane. Crossing to the door, she opened it and peered out, looking up and down the landing, vaguely aware of Scamp scurrying out and disappearing round a corner, delighted to be freed from the confines of the room. Immediately on the heels of his flight, something rattled and crashed to the floor.

Wondering what her mischievous pet had sent flying, she hurried to investigate. Her curiosity went unappeased, for as she turned the corner she came to a mind-jarring halt against an obstacle firmly standing in her path. The following moments became a time of utter chaos. With dazed senses, she reeled away haphazardly. The threat of falling seemed imminent as her bare foot slipped on the highly polished floor. In the next instant, an arm stretched out and clamped about her waist in an unyielding vise. Before she could gather her wits, she was swept full length against a solid human structure that, by rights, should have made her hackles rise. The thin fabric of her nightgown seemed insufficient protection against the stalwart frame, and she had cause to wince within the unyielding embrace of the man who clasped her so tightly.

In an attempt to regain her dignity, immediately she pushed him away, relieved when he let his arms fall and released her. Upon reclaiming her freedom, she stepped away from him, only to find that the object Scamp had overturned was a large vase of flowers, the water having formed a pool around her feet. She slipped once more and found herself completely off balance, her arms flailing wildly about her in a frantic attempt to catch hold of something to stop herself falling. The only thing within her grasp was the front of the leather jerkin the man was wearing and in desperation she clutched at it. Even then she failed to regain her footing and as she went down her shoulder made hard contact with Colonel Russell's loins.

Immediately he choked from her assault. Unfortunately Jane's disgrace was not complete, for as she slid down his hard-muscled thighs and fell at his feet with a bump, her legs went in different directions and her nightgown rode up above her knees. It was difficult to know who was the more shocked or who winced more from the fiasco.

Silently reproaching herself for her clumsiness, carefully Jane sought to regain her modesty. She scrambled to sit upright, bringing her legs together. Upon achieving that position, she pulled her nightgown down as she sought to hide the bare flesh from his eyes.

'I'm so sorry,' she uttered, shoving the heavy mane of her hair from her face as she tried to conceal her mortification and distress, hot colour mounting her cheeks. 'My dog doesn't like being shut in, but I can't have him leaping about all over the place, as you see, for he seems to have knocked over a vase, and—'

'Never mind,' Francis managed to say, the tendons in his face taut as he fairly struggled to surmount his manly discomfort. Reaching out, he took her arm and pulled her up, his arm going round her waist once again as he set her on her feet. Her hair, which he realised had a life and direction of its own, was tumbling about her neck and down her back.

Jane caught a vague scent of the cologne he wore, mingled with an underlying smell of leather and horses. The scent was pleasant and provocative and floated tantalisingly through her senses. A painful grimace was evidence of Colonel Russell's continued discomfort, tightening his chiselled features as he endured the torment.

In complete innocence, Jane enquired, 'Is anything wrong? Did I hurt you when I fell?'

To her shock he smiled at her enquiry, a slow, seductive, secretive smile that made his eyes gleam beneath their heavy lids. Jane was far too naïve to recognise the nuances of it, or she would have seen peril lurking behind that come-hither smile of his. It was the dangerously beguiling smile of a ruthless predator—a predator who wanted her to sense his power, his defiance of any who stood in his path, and to be seduced by what he represented.

'Just a bit,' he replied, diligently adjusting his trousers at the waist.

Realising too late what had happened, Jane let a breathless gasp escape her throat and she suffered an endless moment of excruciating embarrassment. The maidenly blush that mantled her cheeks deepened. Purposefully she focused her gaze on the upper part of his chest. It seemed the only way she could marshal her thoughts. Her response to his closeness was as unwanted as it was lightning quick. She felt a hot pull of attraction deep inside that could not lead to any good.

In the midst of his chiselled features and dark blue eyes, now thankfully devoid of pain, at least enough to convey some evidence of humour, strong white teeth as perfect as any Jane had ever seen appeared in a wayward grin. Feeling as if she were being drawn into a snare, for a moment she found herself susceptible to his appeal.

'Worry not,' he murmured, leisurely observing her beauty to his heart's content, making no effort to curb his amused, all-too-confident grin. 'To see you thus and hold you close—to share such a moment—was well worth it.'

The warmly mellow tones of his voice were imbued with a rich quality that seemed to vibrate through Jane's whole being. But his casual statement ignited her temper. 'Share? We did not *share* anything,' she railed at him. Accustomed as she was to the admiring glances of gentlemen, there was nothing gentlemanly about this man's insolent, lazy perusal of her body. 'Are you quite finished?' she asked tersely, very nearly slipping again as she took a step back. Laughing deep and shaking his head in chiding reproof, reaching out he took her elbow, but she jerked it free. 'Don't you dare touch me again, you—you buffoon,' she shrieked.

His unhurried gaze lifted to her eyes and a wry smile quirked his lips when he heard the outrage in her voice. 'That's quite a temper you have,' he said, meeting her furious glare with glowing, wicked eyes. 'I am surprised to find you wandering about my house in your night attire. I would like to think you might be looking for me.'

'Why, you—you conceited jackanapes! I most certainly was not. I merely came to see what scrape my dog had got itself into.'

His amusement dwindled to a slanted smile, but a teasing light still danced in his eyes. 'Is that all? Then I am disappointed.' He shrugged casually, openly savouring the delectable details of her womanly curves, admiring her intriguingly round, delicately hued breasts, and remembering how sleek her limbs were—far more admirable than any he had ever seen—fully aware of his responding body. 'Little did I imagine when I first saw you that I'd be so completely vexed by my desire for you. You can't blame me for hoping you were looking for me—now can you, Jane?— and in a state of undress. I have to say you flaunt yourself with such grace and style the mere sight of you stirs my blood.'

'Flaunt?' she cried in outrage, thoroughly incensed by his audacity to accuse her of enticement. 'You lecher. I am guilty of no such thing and you know it.' Her brow arched at a sceptical angle. 'Am I to understand that you are soliciting me for my favours?'

'I would not insult you by doing so,' he answered lightly, trying to make his words sound convincing while offering no apology for allowing his gaze to ogle her so blatantly. 'The sights are much too enticing for any man to ignore. If you must know, I enjoy looking at you as much as I like looking at any beautiful woman.'

Aware of the fact that he really was grinning like some hopeful lecher as his gaze lingered overlong on her breasts, belying his words, Jane crossed her arms over her chest in a protective manner. The audacity of the man! Her dark eyes narrowed as she fixed a malevolent glare upon him. 'You are far too bold and too sure of yourself. Have you no shame?'

'None whatsoever. Whatever the truth of it, I make no pretence about my vulnerability as a man or that I find you the most enticing, fascinating woman and as perfect as I've seen in—well, in a long time.'

Sharply elevating a brow, Jane considered the handsomely chiselled visage for a brief moment before replying. 'And you jest with me, Colonel. There are enticing and fascinating women in every bawdy house,' she stated caustically. 'I suggest you go and look for one there.'

'Come now, Jane,' he said with a mock, pained expression, making use of her given name too loosely for Jane's liking. 'Have you no sympathy or pity for what I've just suffered—what your mishap has put me through?'

'Absolutely not,' she declared flatly. 'I've done nothing to kindle your ardour. But since it seems to bother you overmuch,

Colonel, I'll remove myself from your sight and go back to my room and leave you to ask one of the servants to clean up the mess.'

And so, finding his brazenness too much to bear, her cheeks aflame and her chin raised in an attitude of haughty displeasure, after scooping an unrepentant Scamp up into her arms she turned about and stalked away with as much haste as cat whose tail was on fire.

The colonel's lips stretched leisurely into a rakish grin as his gaze ranged the length of her retreating back, lingering admiringly on her delectably round derrière well defined beneath the fabric of her nightgown, and not until she had disappeared from sight did he turn and with a soft chuckle walk away.

Chapter Three

Behind the closed door of her room Jane paced the floor, tossing her head with each change of direction so that her long dark hair swung about her face and shimmered with reflected light. Had the situation been less dire, she would have fled the house. Indeed, after what had just happened she had to fight the urge to do so now. It nettled her sorely that Colonel Russell had seen more of her than she cared to contemplate, but with her future at stake there was a limit to her patience, determination or guile.

But on reflection, when she thought of Scamp bounding about all over the place and setting off a train of events that had been unavoidable to escape, causing Colonel Russell considerable discomfort when she had bumped into him had finally battered down her wall of cold indifference. Playing out the scene in her mind and how comical it would have looked to an onlooker as they floundered around, seeing the funny side she laughed out loud. She suddenly felt very foolish and bad tempered. True, Colonel Russell had behaved outrageously just now, but considering the things she had said to him and her hostile attitude since arriving at Bilborough, she hadn't behaved any better.

Perhaps, she thought, a mischievous and cunning and what she hoped would be a profitable plan beginning to take root in her mind, if she tempered her attitude towards him and used her female powers of persuasion to batter down his defences, it might go some way to helping her get her home back.

When the house was quiet and the last flickering flame was snuffed, Jane fell into a troubled sleep. Her unconscious mind had a will of its own and she was thrust into that nightmare world where dreams become reality and she relived those awful years that she had spent at the mercy of Jacob Atkins. Trepidation seized her and she retreated into her own mind to seek some secure haven where she could find relief for her distress. Her mind was filled with chaotic visions, and rising to the fore of these was a one-eyed face bent on hurting her. She cried out and began to shake uncontrollably and writhed on the bed, keeping her eyes tightly shut to bar the alien from her sight.

Through the haze she heard someone speak her name and the tone was somewhere between a plea and a command. But the voice did not belong to the villain of her dreams and it only confused her more. She mewled and cringed away, wanting to escape the nightmare that pressed down upon her. It was then that she felt herself drawn into strong arms that embraced her and held her tight. Someone's cool hand smoothed her hair from her brow.

As Jane half-woke her eyes fluttered open. A single candle burning on a table cast a glowing light and she could see Colonel Russell's face bent close above hers. Sensing she had nothing to fear, she did not pull away, but nestled closer still, looking at him with fear-glazed eyes.

'Hush. No one is going to hurt you. It was just a dream. It is not real.'

Weak and exhausted, she clung to him, unmindful of the fact that she had swept the quilt off the bed. Her skin was moist with perspiration, and she welcomed the cool air that seeped through her cotton nightgown. It clung to her clammy skin, boldly revealing the womanly curves of her body.

'Could I have some water, please?' she whispered.

'Indeed,' he replied and reached for a glass.

She took it into her shaky grasp and sipped from it slowly and then gave the glass back to him. She did not resist when he drew her back into his arms and held her and stroked her hair. His shirt hung open to the waist and she felt his hard, furred chest pressed against her cheek. She felt his nearness with every fibre in her being. Her eyes flickered downwards as the warmth of his breath touched her ear.

'Was the dream very bad?' he asked softly. What had she found in her dreams that was so distressful to her? He was completely undone by her obvious terror and he could find no plausible explanation for it. Gently he placed his lips on the top of her head, the fragrance of her hair filling his head. She nodded, but did not speak. 'Would you like to tell me about it?'

'No,' she whispered. Acutely conscious of the brush of his hardened thighs against her own and the manly feel of his body branding her through her nightgown, realising her weakened condition made her extremely vulnerable to his whims, spurred into action at the idea of being caught in such disarray, she pulled away from him and looked up into his eyes. 'I was very frightened, but it has gone now. I'm sure I shall be all right.'

Francis stood up and considered the pale features, noting the dark shadows around her eyes. Her head was tilted back and the loosely curling tresses spilled free down her back. She really was very lovely. Her beauty filled his hungering gaze and lighted a fire in his blood. The need to gather her to him once more was overwhelming but now, when she was in such a distressed state, was not the time to think of seduction. How could he even entertain the idea? Picking up the quilt from the floor, he tucked it around her and contemplated her from beneath his brows.

'Was the nightmare about something that has happened to you—something unpleasant?'

'Yes.'

He smiled gently. 'Would you like me to stay with you? It might come back.'

'I know.' He was looking down at her with an expression so intensely caring that she felt a softening in her heart towards him. She managed a tremulous smile. 'If it does, I shall have to deal with it. There's no need for you to stay. Thank you for coming to wake me. How did you know?'

'I heard you cry out. I was worried and came to see what the matter was.'

'I'm sorry if I woke you. I'll be all right now—truly. Go and get some sleep.'

When he'd gone Jane lay back on the pillows, reluctant to close her eyes lest she succumbed once more to the dream. How many times must she endure these nightmares? Would she never be free of what Jacob Atkins had done to her?

The following day she left the house dressed in the grey gown Mary had insisted on putting her in that morning. Apart from her red one she had no other. She slipped out of her room and down the back stairs. If she didn't get away from the sickroom, from the house even for a little while, she would go out of her mind. At the prospect of some freedom, an excited Scamp bounded along ahead of her as she went in the direction of the stables.

Finding Jane's room empty, and glancing out of the window, Mary saw the object of her concern heading across the park on horseback at full gallop in the direction of Aspen Wood. Without more ado she went in search of Colonel Russell.

'Mary, is something wrong?' he asked the irate woman, who was quite beside herself.

'Indeed there is, sir. Mistress Jane has left her sickroom with that dog of hers and gone galloping off on her horse—and it will soon be dark.'

'Is she well enough to go off by herself?' he asked, frowning with genuine concern, especially when he remembered how distressed she had been during the night.

'Certainly not—at least, not in my opinion. She is still not herself and she should not be gallivanting off like that.'

'You saw her ride off?'

'Most certainly, sir—and without her cloak. She should be wrapped up.'

'In which direction was she heading?'

'Towards Aspen Wood.'

'Then I'll find her and bring her back safely.'

Francis rode off in the direction indicated. Jane was sitting on a low stone wall when he found her, the mare tethered to a post and her dog sniffing about in the undergrowth. She was gazing out across the panoramic view. There was a purple hue in the sky, in which a skylark was singing its heart out without a care in the world.

Dismounting some yards away from her, she did not seem to hear his approach, even though her dog turned and bristled, its paws splayed, for Francis had his own dogs with him. He took a moment to watch her, hoping there had been no recurrence of her nightmare when he'd left her. He understood exactly how it would have affected her, for he had nightmares of his own, nightmares of being chained and beaten that left him shivering with terror.

He was quite taken aback by his feelings as he had been taken aback by the sight of her when he had first set eyes on her. He was also bewildered by the emotion he felt in his heart. He couldn't really describe what he felt for her because he didn't have any words. All he knew was that he felt strange, different from anything he had ever expected to feel. It was something that had happened suddenly, not there one moment and there the next, as if it had always been there or as if he had spent his whole life waiting for her to be there, and now that she had appeared he suddenly felt the urge to live again.

There were no women in his life, no mother, no sisters, and the only females he had anything to do with were his brother's wife and the wives and female relatives of his friends. There were the women who sold their favours to any man with the money to pay for them, but the relationship with any of them was anything but romantic, giving release to his body while touching his emotions not at all. But Jane Lucas was different. Never having seen her before, he did not know her, but this strange thing that was working inside him was something new.

The light was just fading as Jane sat in the warm shadows and watched the river in the far-off distance beyond the wood. She had enjoyed riding through the long grass, with poppies, clover and the air heavy with the cloying scent of meadow sweet. The gauze bushes on the edge of Aspen Wood were a vivid yellow against the darkness of the trees. She thought there was no one about, then she heard a soft footfall behind her and the whicker of a horse greeting her mare. She knew without turning that it was her tormentor of yesterday and her saviour of the night. Instead of being annoyed that he should disturb her solitude, she smiled secretively and a peach tint suffused her cheekbones as she half-glanced around, experiencing a tingling rush of excitement that affirmed his presence.

'Jane.' He spoke to her profile, his voice gentle, for this young woman, he knew, was grieving sorely—although he sensed she would rather die than admit it to him. She turned her head when he sat beside her. When his hounds would have given chase to a wary-looking Scamp, Francis clicked his fingers and they slunk away and lay beneath a tree, their eyes never leaving their master. The dark liquid of the young woman's eyes deepened as she became caught up in the disturbance of his presence.

Even as she struggled to subdue her feelings the blush that had stained her cheeks on his arrival—stirred by the memories of when she had slipped on the water and stumbled into him, damaging both her dignity and her modesty, of his low, exacting perusal and his bold solicitation—deepened. She lifted her gaze to meet the translucent blue eyes now gleaming back at her, a slow, mischievous smile curling her lips.

'Why, Colonel Russell! Have you come to torment me some more?'

He stared at her in amazement, wondering at this change in her. She was smiling as if she was genuinely pleased to see him. Why? he asked himself, suddenly wary. 'Nothing could be further from my mind. When you arrived here you argued so eloquently about losing your home, and not content with that, yesterday you gave me a dressing down the like of which I haven't had since I was a lad. Have you no mercy?'

'None whatsoever.'

'I ask your pardon if I offended you yesterday. Tell me I am forgiven.'

She laughed softly, her eyes shining with humour. 'I forgave you last night when you came and woke me from my nightmare. What happened when I slipped on the water meant nothing. I suppose you behaved much the same as any man would when confronted by a woman clad only in her nightgown. I apologise for my dog breaking your vase. I can only hope it wasn't valuable.'

'Think nothing of it. I trust you are feeling better today and your nightmare did not recur?'

'There are no after-effects if that is what you mean. Thank you for what you did.'

His eyes narrowed as he gave her a suspicious look. 'Pardon me for asking, but I am asking myself if this is the same angry young lady who arrived at Bilborough and accused me of being a black-hearted, conniving scoundrel.'

Jane raised her eyes to his, and Francis basked in the unconcealed warmth and laughter lighting her face. 'I meant every word—although since my illness you will be pleased to know that I've mellowed somewhat—although don't go thinking I'll take back what I said. I'm sure you are all the things I accused you of being and more.'

Francis threw back his head and laughed out loud at the contrast between her tone and her words. 'You are probably right, although I have to say that your change of attitude warms my heart.'

'You have no heart,' Jane quipped, smiling dazzlingly at him. 'If you did, you would give me my home back.'

His gaze, soft and inviting, settled on hers. 'Never—but you could try persuading me. It could be highly entertaining and I always enjoy a challenge.'

'What would be the point if, in the end, you deny me my triumph by refusing to give it back?' she said good-naturedly.

'Which is my prerogative.'

'I suppose then I would have to surrender my claim.'

Her words seemed to hang portentously in the silence that followed. 'I was hoping you would say that,' he said quietly, 'but I do not believe the word surrender—at least not in the sense you mean—is in your vocabulary.'

'I see you're getting the measure of me, Colonel Russell.'

'I think so. As for yesterday, I apologise if my conduct offended you when we met on the landing. It's not every day a scantily clad female falls into my arms.'

'Don't be. It couldn't be helped,' she said, knowing he was watching her intently and surprising him, for her tone held no trace of rancour. A rueful smile lit her eyes to a glowing warmth as she held his gaze. 'I have been rude to you and I'm sorry. I'm not usually so bad tempered or outspoken.'

His eyes smiled approval at her sudden change of attitude, but he was in no way fooled by it. He raised a dark brow and considered her flushed cheeks and the soft, trembling mouth. He knew what she was up to and he wasn't in the least put out. To have Mistress Lucas flirting with him could prove highly entertaining and desirable. He would see her efforts weren't wasted.

'I can understand why you behaved as you did and I cannot blame you for being angry. I would have felt exactly the same.' In the spirit of relaxed affability which they'd begun to enjoy, he said, 'May I sit down?'

'Of course you may.' She smiled a quiet puckish smile that could have been construed as provocative. 'I won't bite.'

'I'm relieved to hear it,' he remarked, a slow, roguish grin dawning across his features. Sitting on the grass close beside her, he stretched out his long, booted legs, supporting himself on his elbow and looking up at her.

Jane studied him lounging beside her and looking for all the world like a gentleman of leisure. And yet she sensed that beneath his relaxed exterior there was a forcefulness, a power, carefully restrained. There was intelligence and strength of purpose in his features, together with assurance and confidence. Looking into his eyes she detected neither cruelty, conceit nor dishonesty, and he had the air of a man who succeeded in all he sets out to achieve.

'What are you doing here?' she asked softly. 'Were you looking for me?'

'Mary is in a fearful state over your disappearance.'

'Is she? I'm sorry about that, but I knew if I told her what I intended she would have stopped me. I had to get out—if just for a little while.' She watched him sit up and reach for her cloak that on Mary's insistence he had brought with him. She felt his chest brush her arm and peered aslant into the opening as his shirt fell away from his chest.

Francis became momentarily engrossed in spreading the cloak around her shoulders. Considering his actions outrageously bold and wanting to avoid a repetition of his behaviour of yesterday, feeling altogether far too vulnerable by his close proximity and the brush of his fingers on her naked flesh, Jane was tempted to snatch it from him and do it herself, but remembering her decision to temper her attitude and finding his nearness in no way displeasing, she let him continue.

Heartened when she didn't object to his ministering, Francis's teeth flashed white in a lazy grin and his gaze dipped lingeringly to her soft lips. 'According to Mary you shouldn't be out without a cloak. I agree with her that you are not fully recovered and should be kept warm,' he admonished softly. 'I would not want you to come down sick again.'

'I won't,' she answered, touched by his concern. Conscious of his stare, she lifted her head, but did not look away.

Something about the way she held her head, about her voice and dark eyes, stirred the ashes of some vague memory. Forgetting that his eyes were locked on hers, Francis continued to gaze at her, trying to grasp what was eating at him like a worm at the back of his mind.

Jane cocked her head to one side and eyed him quizzically. 'What is it? Why are you looking at me like that?'

'I have this strange feeling that we have met before—before you came to Bilborough. It's a feeling I've had ever since I laid eyes on you. Perhaps you can enlighten me.'

She smiled slowly, a mischievous light twinkling in her eyes, deciding to have a little fun while she kept him guessing. 'If we had, I hate to think you had forgotten it.'

'I am positive that if we had, I would remember.'

'Maybe it's because of the picture of me you saw in the house—when I was younger.'

'Mmm,' he said, not convinced that was it. Jane felt a *frisson* of alarm when his eyes continued to gaze down at her. When they lingered on her lips she had the strangest sensation that he might kiss her, but she quickly dismissed that notion as some stupid fantasy of her own and admonished herself for having such mistaken illusions.

A raven brow lifted wonderingly as Francis perused her face. 'You are feeling better, I can tell. You certainly look much improved since I last saw you.'

'Much better. I shall not impose on you for much longer.'

'You may stay here as long as wish. I am only sorry you have no family you can go and stay with. Will you accept my offer and stay on here in the steward's house, or have you changed your mind and decided you will return to Northampton?'

Jane looked bemused, but something was coming alive in her eyes. 'I'm not sure of your meaning.'

He smiled. 'It's simple enough.'

'To you, maybe, but not to me. Do you want me to leave? Do you want the house for someone else?'

He shook his head. 'Not at all. It would please me greatly if you were to stay on. The house is yours for as long as you want it.'

With grudging reluctance, she said, 'Thank you. Just now there is nowhere else I can go.'

'Why can you not go back to Northampton?' he asked, curious as to what her life had been like living in the house of her stepmother's brother and wondering if this might have had something to do with her nightmare.

Her eyes shot up and fastened on his, and for an instant a flame burned in their depths along with a deep and abiding fear. 'No. I will never go back there.'

Francis had his answer. 'Why? Is there something—or someone—there you are afraid of? Was your stepmother's brother such a tyrant?'

Her brows drew together and she wondered why he was speaking so slow and deliberate and looking at her in that penetrating manner. She nodded. Fear set her hands a tremble and she clutched them together to keep them from transmitting their weakness to the rest of her body.

'Won't you tell me about him?' he prodded gently.

She took a deep fortifying breath before saying, 'Only that he wanted me for his wife.'

'You are an attractive young woman of marriageable age. It is quite normal for a man to feel that way.'

She kept her eyes and face down so he would not see her despair and her fear. 'I know that,' she said quietly, 'but he is also a cruel and fiercely ambitious man. Now the war is over all he wants is wealth and land, lots of it, and then he can sit upon it like a giant spider and enjoy it.'

'Did he hurt you?' he asked, his voice gentle, looking at her bent head.

'Sometimes,' she admitted, her voice so soft her answer was almost lost on him.

Francis looked at her steadily. Her brave face was masking something and he would like to know what, but he would not press her. He hoped she would tell him in her own time.

'I—I despised him,' Jane went on hesitantly, 'and I know that if the two of you should meet, you would share my opinion of him.' She spoke quietly and with much conviction, for the enmity between Jacob Atkins and Francis Russell that had been established long ago was not forgotten.

'He has children?' Francis queried, hoping his question would rouse her from her unhappy recollections, while feeling an unexplainable surge of anger at this unknown man. Deep inside, he felt a stirring tenderness, a protectiveness towards her that surprised and disturbed him.

'Three—all girls. I do miss them—especially Hester, who is my age. They live in fear of him. They are like counters in the games he plays, to be shoved forwards as bait, to draw rich husbands into his web.'

'In this present climate, there are not so many wealthy husbands available. Did he fight?'

'Yes, for the King.'

'His rank?'

'Captain. Unlike you he failed to make it to Colonel. He was wounded twice, once at Newbury and again at Naseby. When he was captured in '45, he was released on parole after giving his word never again to take up arms against Parliament. He was also a weak man who used brutality to gain authority. He left the army with a legacy of torture and plunder. I would not have shed a tear had he been caught and hanged.'

Distracted by the light glinting on her dark head, Francis considered her a moment before saying, 'I see. That bad. And he allowed you to leave his house?'

'No. He was absent from home when I decided to leave. He will not be pleased—in fact, he will be infuriated that I have gone.'

'Will he come after you?'

'He is ambitious, greedy and he has an enormous sense of

revenge, so I imagine he will. He is not a man to give up anything without a fight, and in his own mind Bilborough already belongs to him. If he does appear, he is going to be disappointed when he discovers Bilborough no longer belongs to me, but to a Roundhead.'

'And he will return to Northampton and leave you alone?'

She looked at him askance. 'I can't say.'

'Then little wonder you are afraid.' His eyes became soft with concern and, placing his finger gently under her chin, he tipped her face up to his. 'Do you think that while you are here, under my protection, I would let anything happen to you, Jane? I would fight man and beast if necessary to keep you safe. So would you trust me enough to let me help you as I want to do? I know you are frightened and I believe I can help if only you will trust me.'

She gazed directly into his eyes. 'I do trust you, but you should look to yourself. When he finds out you are the new owner of the estate that he coveted and how rich you are—for you must be a man of considerable means to have purchased Bilborough and I have seen for myself how well it prospers despite the hardships imposed on the country as a result of the war—he will lose no time in running you through.'

'And why should he want to do that? I have done him no wrong.'

Jane merely smiled secretively and looked away. 'Of course there is another scenario,' she prevaricated on a note of humour. 'He might introduce you to one of his daughters.'

'And will I be tempted, do you think?'

'Oh, no, Colonel Russell,' she replied with conviction, 'you won't be. Of that I am quite certain.'

'Why, is there something wrong with them?'

'No, nothing. They are warm and friendly and very pretty—

and indeed I became fond of them all, but there are reasons why they would not appeal to you.'

'Reasons? What reasons?'

Directing her gaze away from him, she spoke quietly, almost to herself. 'I would rather not explain. Just believe what I say.'

'Then I shall not be tempted. When I decide to take a wife, I shall be most particular in the woman I choose.'

'The same can be said when a woman takes a husband. Life's too short for a person to be bound to one man or one woman unless they have a liking for one another.' She glanced uncertainly at him. He was watching her intently, but without a trace of rancour over her earlier ill humour. Something about the softening in his eyes and the effortless ease in which he lounged beside her made her curious to know more about him.

'Do you have family, Colonel Russell?'

'You needn't be so formal,' he teased with a devilishly wicked grin. 'Will you please call me Francis—my dear, or any endearment of your choice. I find it tiresome to be addressed so formally. And I shall continue calling you Jane—providing you have no objections.'

Jane shrugged. 'I have no objections one way or another—but I think I shall stop at Francis.'

His eyes smiled their approval. 'Thank you. In answer to your question, my parents are both dead. I have two brothers, Richard and Walter.'

'And did they fight alongside you?'

'At the beginning of the war Richard was with me, but he was wounded out in '44.'

'And your hand?' she asked, looking down at the black leather glove he wore at all times on his right hand that rested on his knee. She recalled the terrible wounds, the pain it had caused him, and how she had tended and bound it as best she could. 'Did that happen in the war too?'

He looked down at the glove, remembered suffering tightening his features. 'Something like that, except that it is not a battle scar. It was inflicted as an act of revenge by a man by the name of Jacob Atkins, a Royalist, who held me responsible for the loss of his eye.' He fell silent as he tried to shut out the memory and when he next looked at Jane he saw her face was white. 'I'm sorry,' he said with concern. 'Are you unwell?'

'No,' she replied, her hands clenched by her sides. 'What a terrible tale. How you must have suffered.' She tried to smile, but she could not. Jacob Atkins's name was enough to make her tremble with nameless terror. It was foolish of her to feel such terror. It was dangerous to be out of control before her companion's eyes. What would he say, she wondered, if she were to tell him that the same Jacob Atkins was her step-uncle? She could imagine his rage, and that in that rage he would be blinded to all reason. She realised that Francis had his own demons to fight, and it would matter little that she had been attacked. They were still strangers so why should he believe her? He would order her to leave Bilborough forthwith, and she could not risk that. Oh, sweet Lord, be merciful, she prayed, for she could not bear the thought of it.

'I was not so badly injured that I had to give up the fight and managed to see the war out to the end. I have that to be thankful for.'

Jane heard the same lazy sound in his voice, saw the same mild amusement in his face that so strangely affected her. For she was able to sense that this idle indifference to what had happened to him at the hands of Jacob Atkins thinly concealed a temper at once relentless, fierce and cruel. She was conscious of wanting to break through that veneer of urbanity, to see for herself something of the stormy power that hovered just beneath the surface, not dormant but carefully concealed.

'And Walter?' she asked, drawing the conversation away from his injury.

His eyes clouded as they looked into the distance. 'His allegiance was for the King.'

'I see. That must have caused a rift in your family.'

'At first it did, but he did his duty as he conceived it must be done.'

'And where is he now?'

'In France, with other Royalist fugitives.'

'And will you hold it against him—that he chose the other side?'

He shook his head, his voice low and steady when he spoke, but there was an unconcealed pain in the depths of his eyes when he remembered the heartrending moment when he had watched Walter leave their home to fight for the King.

'No. He is my brother first and foremost. There were many things in which he and I could never be in agreement, but his politics are his affair and I respect that. He is a good soldier and a man of honour. The decision he took was a difficult one, but both Richard and I understood that he fought the war because, like us, he believed in the principles for which it stood.'

'I can see how close you were as a family for it not to come between you. Did you ever meet in battle?'

'No. I thank God we were spared that.'

'And your father was a farrier.'

Francis laughed at her ignorance. 'No. The farrier, John Russell, was my uncle. I was brought up at Russell House not far from Cambridge. My father was a horse breeder—indeed, he had some of the finest horses in England.'

Jane looked at him with sudden interest. 'And is that what you do? I saw some fine horses in the paddock on my way here. I confess I was curious as to how they came to be there. Most of our horses were requisitioned by Parliament at the onset of the war. Others were stolen. We did not have the means to replace them. I suppose if we had, while ever the war continued they would have been seized, so what was the point?'

'It is true that horses were always in short supply and were an extremely attractive item of booty. Cavalry and carters needed them. Horses were stolen, by both Royalists and Parliamentarians, and they were hard to identify and almost impossible to recover.'

'I thank God the war is over, but I am saddened by the outcome. So many lives were lost. The King made mistakes,' she went on quietly, 'but our loyalty was to him to the end. The day Englishmen murdered their King is a day to remember for ever. God save King Charles II,' she murmured under her breath.

Soft as her voice was, Francis heard her. 'My brother in France will share your sentiments—and I, too, in some ways. I had no desire to take the King's life. In the beginning thousands of young men set off for the Civil War full of that innocent enthusiasm with which so many before, and will do again, have welcomed the prospect of battle. Few had much idea of the reality of war. Brought up in a relatively peaceful society, they were totally unprepared for the military discipline, the physical exhaustion, the divided loyalties, the emotional strain, the loneliness, and, above all, the violence of combat. War is not some glorious adventure. It is a ruthless, bloody business inflicting suffering on thousands of people. I hope never to endure the like again.'

'I'm sure you do, and I imagine you hope your brother will eventually find his way home from France so you can be united as a family again.'

'If he were to do so now, he would be arrested, so it is my hope that he remains in France for the time being. He will be safe enough there. Tomorrow my brother Richard and his wife Elizabeth will arrive to spend some time at Bilborough. I have not seen them for some considerable time so it should be a joyous occasion. Elizabeth was Elizabeth Merton before she married Richard. I think you will remember the family. The Merton family still live in the manor house outside Avery.'

'Yes, I do remembered the family, although I am not acquainted with them. I recall Samuel Merton's name cropping up in conversations between my parents from time to time. He was an old man then, a man who, over the years, had not only become a wealthy miller but also a well-respected patriarch among the citizens of Avery. Elizabeth Merton and her younger sister must be his granddaughters.

He nodded and smiled. 'That's right. You have a good memory. Tomorrow night I would be honoured if you would dine with us—if you are feeling well enough. The physician tells me you are past the infectious stage now. You will like Elizabeth, I promise you. She is a warm, kindly soul and devoted to Richard. So, Jane, what do you say? Will you dine with us?'

'I—I'm not sure,' she answered hesitantly, taken by surprise by his invitation.

'Elizabeth's sister Alice is to accompany them,' he added, seeking to ease the qualms she was apparently suffering, and thinking that another female for company might help her to decide. 'She still lives at home with her parents. Elizabeth thought that while she is at Bilborough with Richard, it would be nice to spend some time with her sister.'

Still Jane hesitated. 'Given the circumstances, I—really don't think that would be appropriate.'

The softness vanished from Francis's expression. 'I don't see why not,' he said. 'Unless it is beneath you to share a table with a horse breeder. The war is over, Jane.'

The silence that fell between them was as heavy as the executioner's axe. Francis had not blinked an eyelid and did not speak. He just looked at her, his mouth compressed into a stern arrogant line, and there was more intensity in his eyes than a thousand others.

She got to her feet quickly, drawing her cloak around her in a protective manner, despite the warmth of the evening. 'I'm sorry, it's just that I'm finding it difficult coming to terms with not being able to call Bilborough my home any more.'

Francis stood up, brushing off the bits of grass that clung to his breeches. 'Jane, had I not taken Bilborough someone else would have done, and if I were to walk away right now, someone else—another Roundhead, who would be less tolerant towards you than I—would take my place.' His expression softened. 'So, Jane, what do you say? Will you eat supper with us tomorrow evening?'

They faced one another, the Royalist's young daughter and the Parliamentarian, and although neither abated one ounce of their dignity, or their unspoken opposition, the attraction between them was almost palpable. Jane was shaken to the core by the bewildering sensations racing through her body. She tried to turn her head away, but his extraordinary eyes drew her back. After a moment of deliberation, she decided that she would dine with him and his family.

'Yes,' she agreed quietly, 'very well—although—I have nothing suitable to wear.'

'That can be overcome. There are trunks in the attic bursting with clothes. They belong to you. Take a look. I'm sure you'll find something.'

Together they rode back to the house, the mellow stone walls glinting golden as the sun went down on the horizon. Francis approached it with a deep affection for its elegance and grandeur, and he could well understand Jane's reluctance to let it go. But he hadn't been thinking of her when he had learned that the house had been sequestered and was looking for a new owner.

Glancing sideways at her companion, Jane could almost detect what he felt as he gazed at Bilborough. There were little lines of tiredness around his eyes, but they were bright, not from the dying sun, but from something else that lit them from within. There was also a tight, leashed excitement she sensed in him. It flowed from him in waves so that she could almost feel it. Why, she thought, Bilborough means a great deal to him. He loves this place just as I do. But he could never love it as much as she did.

Chapter Four

While the house was quiet in those empty hours following the midday meal, Jane climbed to the upper floor of the house where Gwen had set up her stillroom. With windows on two sides, the room was filled with light.

When she entered she took a deep breath, surprised that the air in Gwen's sanctum was still thick with the familiar spicy odours of herbs and roots and fungi. Peering around, she half-expected to find her stepmother pounding away with her pestle as she prepared some concoction or other.

Gwen had always kept the stillroom pristine. Now it was untidy and in need of a thorough clean, but otherwise little changed. Dozens of glass vials, bottles and jars in orderly ranks in the cupboards and on shelves gleamed in the light from the window, along with pestles and mortars, drying frames and stacks of bandages and dressings. On a writing desk in the corner were the black ledgers in which she had written down her recipes and notes for an assortment of symptoms and diseases. Even her apron was still hanging at the back of the door, and the basket she had used to collect the plants was on a stool. It was as if Gwen had just slipped out and would be back any moment.

Slowly she walked around the room, touching and caressing

Gwen's precious things. She could almost feel her presence. She breathed in and sighed deeply. Memories! At least she had them and could keep them in her heart, knowing that in the fullness of time, wherever she was, they would bring consolation. She stood and gazed out of the window, with no real sense of time. The scene was familiar, unchanged and pastoral. More than anywhere else in the house, it was here in the stillroom that she felt transported back in time. Despite the myriad of uncertainties of the future, despite the unpleasantness of her situation, for a moment she was content.

The silence lasted no more than a few moments before she sensed that she was no longer alone. Turning her head, she saw Francis, with his shoulder propped negligently against the door frame, his arms folded loosely across his chest. He smiled and she found herself smiling, too, and she knew her face was alight with pleasure at seeing him. She knew she should hate him, but Francis Russell had charm as potent as any magic.

'I thought I heard a noise,' he said. 'It isn't often anyone comes up here so I came to investigate. I hope I am not intruding.'

'Of course not. If Bilborough is indeed your home, then it is I who intrude.'

'You are my guest, Jane,' he said quietly. 'I sense that this room brings back many memories for you. Would you like me to leave?'

She shook her head and again fixed her gaze out of the window. 'No. That is not necessary. No matter how busy she was, Gwen would never turn anyone away who found their way to this room.'

Frances smiled in the sudden knowledge that for the first time since coming to Bilborough, she wanted to share her solitude. Shrugging himself away from the door frame, he moved across the room to share the space at the window. The quiet of the room and the beauty of the spreading countryside invited silence. He looked down at his companion. There was an aura of peace about her. Her expression was relaxed and serene. He was unable to tear his fascinated gaze away. Her shining hair tumbled over her shoulders in a glorious black mass, framing a face of heartbreaking beauty. Her skin was creamy smooth, her dark brows delicately arched, her lashes thick and curly. Pride and courage showed in every feature of her face, from her high cheekbones and stubborn chin. And yet her mouth was vulnerable and soft, as soft as her breasts that swelled beneath the bodice of her plain gown.

Aware of his scrutiny but not perturbed by it, Jane looked up at him and smiled. 'I've spent many hours looking out of this window while Gwen mixed her medicines. The view is exactly as I remember it. I'm glad you haven't changed things.'

'It is obvious to me that your stepmother spent a great deal of time and trouble setting it up. I wouldn't dream of changing a thing—not when it can be put to practical use in the future. She must have spent a great deal of her time in here.'

'Yes, she did. When I came in I half-expected her to see her standing at the table mixing her potions or writing in her ledger. I suppose it's hardly surprising, with so many of her things still here, just as she left them. I could almost feel her presence.' She laughed lightly. 'I'm sorry. You must think I'm quite mad to be talking like this.'

'Not at all. You were fond of her, I can tell.'

'Yes, I was. I don't remember my real mother—she died when I was a baby. When Father married Gwen she became the mother I never had.'

'You must miss your father very much.'

She nodded. 'And Gwen. Everything was so happy then...' She bit her lip, feeling a wave of sadness. She had spoken of a time when she had been safe, when she hadn't known that people and events could harm her. 'Gwen was an attractive, tall woman, always laughing—more often than not at herself—and she didn't suffer fools gladly. I should wish nothing but to be like her,' she murmured wistfully. 'She was so kind and lovely, and she knew so much about herbs and things with healing powers. When she first came to Bilborough she was respected for her skills and she was as likely to be successful as any doctor in the curing of the sick—or at least in alleviating their discomforts. I wanted to know all she could teach me.'

'And I imagine you were a good pupil and a great help to her,' Francis said, distracted by the myriad emotions at play in her expressive eyes.

His words, spoken softly, struck Jane with a sense of desperate longing for the woman who had shared her knowledge with her and shown her so much affection. 'I'd like to think so,' she replied reflectively. 'She was a well-educated woman who learned her skills from her own mother and grandmother. She hated any kind of conjuring and would not even have her fortune told by the gypsies at the fair.'

Francis gazed down at her, sensing her sadness. 'Can I ask what happened to her?'

'We hadn't been living in Northampton very long when she contracted a fever. Sadly her medicines couldn't help her and she died within days.' A feeling of bitterness and anger replaced the sorrow and regret she felt for the loss of her stepmother. 'We should never have had to leave Bilborough. It was so unfair, so unjust—and so very painful that you could not imagine. But we had to get away, otherwise Gwen would have been taken—as so many women were at that time who were knowledgeable about herbs and things.'

'Yes, I remember, and you are right. They were times when people were anxious about witchcraft—fearful.'

'Stories began to spread about her—about how she had a more sinister intent than mixing medicines to make people better— that she would light candles and like some kind of priestess cast spells and curses and summon ghosts and spirits to do evil things. It was all nonsense, of course, but people were suspicious and the stories got a deal worse after my father died.'

Francis was watching her seriously. 'I can imagine how unpleasant things would have been had you stayed.'

'The people of Avery were nothing but a lot of barbarians then, who would as soon kill her as look at her if they thought her a witch—and they did, but all the accusations against her were false. And the worst of it all was that she'd helped so many of them when they had fallen sick. So much for gratitude,' she finished softly, unable to conceal the bitterness she still felt to this day.

'And yet you weren't afraid to come back,' Francis said.

'What had I to fear?' she replied, tossing her head back, almost as a gesture of defiant pride. 'They could no longer persecute Gwen and I had every right. Besides I could not stay in Northampton any longer. Bilborough was my home. Where else would I go?'

Francis was not prepared for the sharp stab of pity he felt as he met her gaze. He saw beyond her words to the truth and recognised the heartless malice of those who had caused her so much pain. He felt a sudden, overpowering desire to ride into Avery and smash his fist into the people who had driven her from her home. 'Where else indeed,' he murmured.

'Had she not had me to consider, I think Gwen would have stayed here and faced the consequences, even though she knew she would never be able to convince those who would examine her that she was not possessed of the Devil. As things turned out, she died anyway.'

'And you remained in Northampton for four full years,' Francis summarised, his voice filled with hoarse gentleness.

Jane stared at him, while a startling discovery slowly revealed itself to her. The man who she had accused of being ruthless was something quite different—he was, instead, a man who was capable of feeling acute sympathy for a woman who was a stranger to him—it was there in the softened lines of his face. She was momentarily mesmerised, her eyes imprisoned by his hypnotic blue gaze.

'I have given you reason to dislike me and I regret that, Jane. Do you dislike me?' he asked, putting his gloved and bare hands either side of her face, turning it up to his.

Jane was still and he held her gaze steadily, as if he were trying to will words he wanted to hear into her mouth. 'No,' she said softly, lowering her gaze. 'Of course not. I may not like what you have done to me, but I neither like nor dislike you.'

'And you will allow me to call on you at the cottage when you move in?'

'It is your cottage. It's not my place to deny you.' Under his fingers her cheeks were tingling. He smiled down at her and she looked at him, fascinated, powerfully aware of his charm, which was so strong it seemed to be a physical force. As his blue eyes met hers her head began to spin.

'So you do like me then?' he demanded. With his bare hand he touched her cheek and her forehead, smoothing the tense flesh and caressing her temples with gentle fingers. The sun through the window made a spatter of light on her face and throat. Her lips were moist and parted and her teeth shone white between them. Her dark eyes held his insistently.

Placing her hand over his that cupped her cheek, she murmured, 'Francis, what are you afraid of? You can kiss me if you like.'

There was no mistaking his ability to accept her offer, and before Jane knew what he was doing, he took her face in both his hands once more and kissed her, one soft kiss, full on the lips, as confident as an acknowledged lover.

Raising his head, he gazed down at her soft features. His face was taut, his eyes smouldering with a desire so intent it scorched her. Losing himself in the soft liquid eyes that held him, he was barely conscious of his actions as he lowered his lips to hers once more, his free hand slipping through her hair to the nape of her neck. He felt her lips slacken and begin to tremble and then open as his mouth moved upon hers. He tasted response, sweet, warm and clinging, and was aware of the rapid beat of her heart pressed close to his chest. The kiss sent the hot blood rushing to his loins. His arms curled about her, gathering her close. A low moan slipped from Jane as his hands slid down her slender back to her buttocks, pressing her against his body.

This was not what she had intended when she had invited his kiss, but as she shivered with suppressed longings every fibre of her being cried out for him to take her. It was an agony to think of denying him, but deny him she must. Placing her hand upon his chest, she turned her face aside, trying to avoid another of his heady kisses before they besotted her mind.

'We mustn't—we mustn't do this,' she pleaded softly. 'I only invited you to kiss me the once. Anything else you take will not be with my consent.'

Francis lifted his head and stared down at her with hungering eyes, feeling his body begin to throb as it always did when he was near her. He was bewitched by her loveliness. She held such a powerful allure that he found it hard to remain in the same room as her. The thought of removing her clothes and dragging her down to the floor and burying himself in her enchanting body beckoned him like a strong spell. The visual image of her naked and writhing beneath him, her long slender legs clasping him tight, brought him to a pulsing arousal.

He knew the game she was playing, which, if she did but know it, was a dangerous game for her, and he had made up his mind to play along with her from the beginning, but more kisses like that and he knew they would both be out of their depth.

The hunger in his eyes turned to laughter. 'My dearest Jane. It is my fondest wish that we share the cup of passion, but when it happens it will not be a matter of taking. Until then I urge you to take better care of yourself. Your strength has not fully returned after your illness, and should you persist in this activity by inviting me to kiss you, you will at the very least delay your recovery.'

Sensing she had nothing to fear, she breathed a trembling sigh of relief. 'I think,' she murmured, her face still upturned to his, 'that you have a softer, more caring side to your nature than I gave you credit for, that your legend plays you false. All the things your adversaries say about you and about the things you've done—are not true.' She spoke softly, her beautiful dark eyes searching his face as if she could see into his soul.

'Don't ever doubt it, Jane. They're all true,' Francis contradicted shortly, as visions of countless bloody battles he'd fought and the men he'd slaughtered paraded across his mind in all their lurid ugliness.

Jane knew nothing of his bleak memories, and her gentle heart rejected his self-proclaimed guilt. She knew only that the man standing before her was a man who had valiantly tried to fight off a Royalist force headed by Captain Jacob Atkins, and how he had suffered the horrendous tortures inflicted on him when he'd been taken captive—and how he had gained the admiration of the young girl he still thought to this day had been a youth, when he had expressed his gratitude for her aid in his escape.

'I don't believe it,' she murmured.

'Believe it. You of all people must agree that it is so. You have cast me in the role of a bestial conqueror who has had the audacity to steal your home, so do not deceive yourself into casting me in another role. I am no virtuous knight in shining armour, Jane. Believe what you have heard and what your heart tells you. Most of it is true. But I ask you to believe me when I say that I do not wish you harm. I will protect you with my life if others come here to threaten you. Bilborough was your home before it was mine. When I bought it I did so because I wanted to live here and with no malicious intent towards you. Please believe that I only wish to do right by you.'

Her answer was said without thought, as if it had suddenly been born in her heart and not her mind. 'Badly enough to return it to me?'

'No.'

He said the word dispassionately, without hesitation, without regret. Jane sighed. 'Oh, well, you cannot blame me for trying.'

'No—it is your right.'

'As for the kiss—well—I don't know what came over me,' she murmured, her eyes tender as they caressed his face, and her lips curved in a wistful smile.

'Perhaps it was the heavy scent of Gwen's herbs—of lavender, sage and rosemary that still permeated the air of the room—that bewitched you, or maybe it was the very essence of her spirit casting a spell on you so that you would have welcomed the Devil himself had he stepped through the door.'

'Yes,' she laughed, 'perhaps that's what it was. But I will never know.'

His eyes fastened on her lips once more. 'You might, if we were to repeat the kiss.'

Jane stepped back, shaking her head and laughing lightly. 'I think enough kissing has been done for one day. Now if you will excuse me I have to go and have a look in those trunks you told me about, otherwise I shall be forced to shock your guests by sitting down to dine in my red dress.' Without another word she walked away from him and down the length of the room, her slender hips swaying with unconscious regal grace.

Despite the fact that she'd only glanced at him in passing as she went to the door, Jane had registered the odd light in his eyes and the indefinable smile lurking at the corner of his lips. She had no idea what was behind it, she only knew his smile completely eclipsed the unhappiness in her heart.

Jane was apprehensive about the forthcoming evening. She now knew how it felt to be an outsider in her own home, for ever longing to belong and to be secure and safe. To be denied. She had considered staying in her chamber but then, taking hold of her pride, she braced herself. She would have to face people sometime, and a Lucas never cowered. By the time she left her room to face everyone, she was sufficiently wrought up to do battle.

Moving gracefully down the stairs, on reaching the bottom step she paused to rearrange the folds of the deep blue gown she wore. She had found it in one of the trunks in the attic along with several others she had not taken with her when she had left Bilborough. She had gone to great lengths over her appearance, and it was all on account of Francis Russell and his guests whom she had never met, but she was determined to put her mark on the night.

She had a moment to observe Francis conversing with his guests. He was so attractive, exuding the kind of strength and masculinity that women found extremely appealing. And he looked as if he had the perfect knack of making a woman feel special. He was bending close to the younger of the two women, listening attentively and watching her with those deep blue eyes—the same eyes that had smouldered when he had looked at her in her shift on the landing when she had almost knocked him over, and again when he had kissed her.

Attired in black, the only relief a startling white neckcloth, he looked so poised, with dark hair feathering the nape of his neck. A slow half-smile curved his lips, and she saw him give a careless shrug. He was finally alerted to her presence when the woman he was speaking to glanced beyond him to where she stood. Francis looked in her direction as she rested her slender hand on the wide staircase's heavily carved newel.

Momentarily transfixed, he stood watching her in silent fascination, his gaze missing nothing. Her body was rounded and disturbing in its femininity, the swell of her hips outlined softly beneath her gown, the curve of her breasts beneath the bodice hinting at their firm shapeliness. How she had looked when she had collided with him in her nightgown and how sweet her lips had tasted beneath his own had been dwelling on his mind ever since. Now, persistently, that memory in the dark of the night haunted him like some wilful, tormenting apparition determined to haunt his sleep. From that moment he suspected that his mind had been seared for evermore with an image of her delectable form.

Their eyes met and he excused himself, quickly striding forwards to meet her, a slow smile of admiration sweeping over his face.

Jane was delighted with the effect produced. Though he offered her a warm smile, she regarded him coolly. He held out a hand invitingly, desiring to have her near. When she remained where she was, he went to her and his hand reached towards her. He took one of her own, which she had folded in front of her, and by greater strength alone won it. Smiling casually, he brought it halfway to his lips.

'Playing host has its rewards,' he murmured, placing his lips lightly on her fingers.

'Play the host all you like, Francis,' she murmured, slowly withdrawing her hand from his grasp, 'but I am apprehensive about sitting down to dine with your family. I am doing so with as much enthusiasm I would feel for a public flogging.'

He grinned. 'That bad!'

'I'm afraid so.'

There was something about the amused tilt of his eyebrows, the sudden mischievousness in his eyes, that a tentative smiled tugged at her soft lips as he led her forwards to be introduced to his guests. 'Try not to worry,' he murmured quietly. 'They will not judge you because of your allegiance to King Charles during the War.'

Colonel Russell's brother and his wife were not at all what Jane had expected. Richard Russell was tall and sandy haired with a pleasant demeanour. His gait was awkward and he walked with the aid of a cane, which indicated that he was just another wounded participant from the Civil War.

Elizabeth, his wife, was extremely pleasant and went out of her way to be friendly. Her eyes were clear grey and calm under perfectly arched eyebrows. She was sympathetic about Jane's situation and most interested in knowing all about her background and upbringing at Bilborough. In no time at all it was as if they had been acquainted for years.

Alice, Elizabeth's sister, was another matter entirely. She was about three years older than herself and there was much about her to admire, for she was overflowing with physical assets. She was of medium height and neatly built, with pale gold hair and liquid green eyes, and though her firm mouth turned down at the corners it lent no hint of dejection to an expression that looked habitually pleasant. Wispy curls framed her youthful face to good advantage beneath a white lace cap.

But Jane was certain that the green eyes were calculating. It was as if their owner was impersonally taking note of all her smiles, gestures and mannerisms and listing them to be ticked or crossed—more often than not crossed, she was convinced, at her leisure. It was plain to Jane from the first that here was a woman who wanted Francis for herself, and saw Jane as a rival. Jane didn't like her in the least, but she gave no hint of this.

'This certainly is a beautiful house, Jane,' Elizabeth remarked, 'and I can well imagine your resentment when you found out it had been sequestered—a resentment I am sure you must have felt for its new owner. I would have been quite devastated.'

A moment of strained silence passed. Half-smiling, half-frowning, Francis considered Jane carefully. 'Resentment? Yes, it is to my regret that Jane had every right to feel resentment, Elizabeth. Considering that when she arrived I shocked her out of her wits, I feel responsible for her present condition.'

Jane smiled benignly. 'Please don't let there be any argument on my account. A man can hardly find favour in being reminded that he purchased a property which the owner had no idea was up for sale.'

'Well I can't say that I'm in favour of Parliament taking people's property. What say you, Richard?'

'Whatever I say will not change the way things are, Elizabeth,' her husband replied. 'This is a fine house, I grant you, Francis, but Russell House hasn't been the same since you moved out.'

'It would seem Bilborough, with its rolling acres, is his preference, Richard, for him to rear his horses,' Elizabeth remarked, smiling fondly at her brother-in-law. 'I fear I've never felt confident about them myself, and prefer to ride in the carriage. Although I can understand, with your vast equestrian skill, why you joined the cavalry. You certainly proved your worth many times—just like your dear brother before his injury.' She patted Richard's arm affectionately.

Richard tossed a grin towards his younger brother. 'I'm afraid you put me to shame with your many exploits and daring-dos, Richard. I wish I could have been there at the end.'

'Let us hope that Worcester was the end of it.'

'By all reports, your troop of horse proved itself as valiant in the battle as any in the Model Army.'

'I was fortunate to command men of exemplary courage,' Francis assured his brother. 'Whatever tribute has been laid on me, I owe the greater part to them.'

Richard flipped a hand towards his brother's gloved hand. 'I observe you still cover your hand, Francis. How did you fare in battle? It must have been difficult—hampered with just the use of one hand.'

Francis glanced at the injured member. It had taken months for it to heal—as much as it was possible for a hand that had been crushed and badly burned to heal—but it had continued to pain him for longer. It was so badly disfigured he would never be able to use it properly, and, conscious of its deformity, to spare people's sensibilities he wore a glove whenever he was in company. He had closed his mind to the torture inflicted on him by Jacob Atkins, who had set about it with an intent look on his face—lit up, like when a man is looking at a pretty wench he's attracted to. Francis had blocked out his bitter hatred of the man and devoted himself to learning how to use his left arm.

'It was, at first, but I followed some sound advice given to me by a very brave lad who risked his life to help me escape my torturer—who, I have no doubt, would have become my executioner.' His expression was sombre as he spoke, his eyes cast down at his gloved hand. 'The lad—Tom, his name was—reminded me that I had another hand, a good hand, and that I should learn to use it. I took that advice and I shall be eternally grateful to the lad. He also gave me his horse to make good my escape.'

Jane was all attention, though she tried not to show it as she asked casually, 'And what happened to the horse?'

He looked at her and smiled. 'He's in the paddock. His name is Arthur. He served me well and is deserving of a long retirement.' He could not know what joy this knowledge brought to the young woman, who truly thought her beloved Arthur must have perished long since on some battlefield or other, as he said on a more cheerful note, 'Now please come and be seated, or we shall find ourselves eating dinner at breakfast.'

Favouring Jane with his attention, he escorted her across the hall. Alice walked with small, mincing steps and demure little smiles, and glided along beside her sister and brother-in-law. When Jane glanced behind her and met her steady gaze, she sensed Alice's antagonism, which she was determined to ignore.

They entered the dining parlour in which Jane's family had dined for generations. It brought back so many memories for her. It was a room where they had enjoyed conversation and restful pleasantries, a mug of ale or a small draught of a stronger beverage. It was a room where Gwen had stitched her tapestries, or played a tinkling melody on the harpsichord. Now it glowed golden from the lighted candles in sconces around the room, and strangers sat at the table.

It was these tender, cherished memories that tore into her consciousness and rekindled all the resentment she felt for this usurper, Francis Russell.

The customary place of honour for the Lord of the Manor had

always been at the head of the long dining table. It had been that way during her father's time, and it seemed destined to be so under Francis Russell's authority. Jane hardly expected him to escort her to a place immediately on the right of his chair, but that was indeed where he led her. Richard was directed next to her, Elizabeth and Alice seated across from them, Alice, by design, next to Francis.

It was not until they had all taken their seats that Jane glanced around the room and saw that the painting that had been a favourite of her father's—an equestrian scene, the artist having used Bilborough Hall as a backdrop—was still hanging in a prominent place on the wall above the fireplace, between two silver sconces. The tapers cast a warm glow on it, setting it off to perfection.

Her surprise was so complete that she gasped and turned to look at Francis. 'I see you kept the painting. It was my father's favourite.'

'What can I say?' He grinned as he shrugged. 'You father had excellent taste. I liked it well enough to keep it. Of course I shall be happy to reimburse you—or return it to you if you so wish. There are other paintings I had removed to the attics, which I consider still belong to you. You may go through them at your leisure.'

'Thank you. I will.'

'This is indeed a comfortable house,' Richard remarked, looking to his wife for agreement. 'I certainly envy you the solitude—unlike Russell House, which is far too close to Cambridge for my liking.'

'I would think that it is more comforting to live here than chase Royalists up and down the country,' Jane said with sudden impudent defiance as she tried to fight the power of their host's charm. He seemed amused as he studied her.

She saw the twinkle in his eye, the twist of humour about his firmly shaped mouth. 'Each to his own, Jane. There are more discomforting experiences than chasing Royalists. Here, for instance, in this very house, is one that could prove to be far more dangerous and troublesome than a whole troop of Royalists.' His eyes narrowed with mockery and more than a little humour.

Jane stared at him, wondering if she should take offence, then, seeing the teasing expression in his startling blue eyes, allowed herself to smile. 'I do believe you jest with me, Francis. Since you are so clever, I am surprised you did not make it to major and buy a house to equal that of Whitehall Palace.'

For a fleeting second an expression she did not understand flashed through his eyes, then was gone. 'It was not for want of trying on my part, I assure you. We are not all as fortunate as you and your kin.' His voice was thickly edged with irony, his cool eyes resting on her face without a trace of self-pity.

As she regarded him, Jane felt a stirring of respect. 'I am not so fortunate now.' Food and drink as always had their effect. The atmosphere mellowed a little as the evening progressed, but the tension inside Jane was unappeased. Because she had made up her mind that she wasn't under any circumstances going to be ignored or condescended to, she joined in the conversation, smiling and talking about anything that occurred to her, while maintaining a cool and formal manner.

The meal was almost over when Richard turned to his brother in serious vein and said, 'You can't imagine how relieved we are to have you back with us, Francis. Alice insisted I keep her abreast of the battles in which you were engaged and was most concerned when you failed to come home immediately after Worcester. The awareness that you were constantly in the midst of conflicts in which so many lives were lost filled her with an enormous dread.'

'Then I am mortified that I might have been the cause of any suffering you might have felt, Alice,' Francis replied, glancing a smile at the simpering young woman on his left.

'Lives were lost on both sides,' Jane pointed out sharply. 'Good, honest Englishmen, fighting for what they believed to be right—be it for Parliament or the King. We must never forget that.' In spite of the distance between them, she could feel the heat of the glare that smouldered in Alice's green eyes. It hinted strongly of an unreasonable jealousy that revolved around her. Several times throughout the meal she had looked directly into the woman's eyes and smiled in an attempt to make some kind of contact, but though Alice had returned her smile, it was malicious and her eyes continued to pass judgement.

'You are right, Jane,' Elizabeth interceded lightly. 'Far too many fine Englishmen died and will be for ever in our thoughts and prayers. But enough of this talk of war. It is over, and I for one thank the Lord for it. This is not, after all, a political occasion, but a celebration that we are all together at last—albeit without Walter, but no doubt he will find his way home in time. Actually today's ride from our home was my dear husband's first since the physician pronounced him fit to mount a horse. Is that not so, Richard?'

'It is, indeed, and I have to say that it feels good to be back in the saddle.'

'Then it would seem I couldn't have picked a better time to invite you to Bilborough, Richard,' Francis said to his brother. 'Tomorrow I shall enjoy showing you the estate—and I have some fine horses I think you will be interested in seeing. Several mares have foaled and others are due any time. All in all the stud is prospering. I have some good quality horses—two of the stallions from our father's stable, which were from good breeding stock. When I made it known that the Russell strain was still being bred, some of the horses sold at excellent prices. I have orders for future sales.'

'Father would have been glad to know that. Horses were important to him. You are like him, Francis.'

Observing the ease with which Francis played the host at her father's table, Jane asked herself what was this extraordinary aura that this man had? He was like a monarch, she thought. His eyes seemed to possess a comprehensive intelligence—above all there was about him an astonishing sense of power. He had perfect manners, yet he said and did exactly as he liked, and everyone obeyed him.

Around him people who had lost everything in the war that had racked the country for ten long and miserable years were struggling to bring back some kind of normality to their lives, to put their houses in order and put food on the tables for their families, while Francis prospered. For though aged no more than thirty, Francis Russell had grown accustomed to the idea that if he chose, there was almost nothing he could not do. This knowledge when combined with intelligence, could make even the son of a horse breeder into a prince.

When there was a break in the conversation, Alice fixed Jane with a sly look. 'What made you leave Bilborough, Jane? I seem to recall it had something to do with your stepmother. Indeed, at the time the whole of Avery was humming with talk of her being a witch.'

An uncomfortable silence descended upon the table. Elizabeth shot her sister an angry look of disapproval, while Francis merely looked at Jane and raised his eyebrows, challenging her to respond to Alice's provoking words. It only took a moment for him to realise she would do just that, for with a ready wit and an amused and cynical smile, Jane threw back her head and met Alice's challenge head on.

'That is quite right, Alice. What a good memory you have. They did say that Gwen, my stepmother, was a witch,' she said, widening her smile. 'But my father was an important man in Avery so they didn't say it too loud.'

Her answer drew laughter from Francis and Richard, which was fuel to Alice's ire. 'If my memory serves me well, your father was no longer around when the accusations were made. Are you saying there was no truth in the accusations?' she persisted.

'Of course there wasn't.'

'And she didn't spend her time poking about under bushes and crawling on the ground?'

'She did—most days. She was very knowledgeable about plants and herbs and their medicinal uses—as are a lot of women, but that doesn't make them witches.'

'A lot of people said she was,' Alice argued petulantly. 'After all, everyone knows there are both good and bad properties to be found in plants—especially one that can get rid of an unborn, unwanted child.'

Apart from a hardening in her eyes, Jane's expression remained unchanged. 'What are you saying, Alice? What are you accusing her of?'

'Did your stepmother not supply a woman—Mrs Cooper, her name was—with such a drug which, if given too late, kills not only the unborn child but the person as well?'

'No she did not, but unfortunately my stepmother was blamed for it. I remember Mrs Cooper and I know from what her husband said in his grief afterwards that she wanted the child. She became ill after eating something that disagreed with her, which brought on her labour early, killing both her and the child. It had nothing to do with Gwen. When Mrs Cooper asked Gwen if she could give her something to help her sleep, she was given nothing more harmful than a chamomile infusion.'

'Everyone believed it was something more than that. Wasn't that the reason why you fled Bilborough so suddenly because she was about to be questioned about Mrs Cooper's death, and that she was afraid of being charged with witchcraft?'

'Yes—which was quite ridiculous but true. Somehow it came to the attention of Mr Fraser—who as you all know was as detestable as Mr Matthew Hopkins, who had been busy persecuting women in and around Essex a couple of years earlier. Like Mr Hopkins, Mr Fraser was also a self-appointed witchfinder who used the turmoil of the war to his advantage to torture and kill many innocent women. Had Gwen fallen into his hands, she would have found it impossible to prove her innocence and he would have killed her also.'

'Mr Fraser was paid handsomely by the local magistrates, who let him do his work unmolested for fear his eye would fall upon them,' Francis provided. 'So without any challenge from local authorities, he was allowed to ride roughshod over this part of East Anglia for a couple of years. There was no legal counter-argument against the charge of witchcraft. I believe the man died in '51, shortly after his last hanging.'

'I suppose that could be seen as retribution on behalf of all the women he murdered,' Jane said, smiling at him.

'Some would say their deaths were justified, since they all bore the devil's mark in one way or another—and kept a dog or a cat,' Alice remarked haughtily.

'Aye, and so do most people. Boils and birthmarks and any such mark are common enough—and cats and dogs. I have a dog—and Francis has two,' Jane pointed out, meeting Francis's amused gaze with a teasing smile, 'which makes him doubly cursed.'

Having heard quite enough and afraid of where Alice's questions might lead, when her irate sister opened her mouth to make further comment, Elizabeth said, 'Enough, Alice. All this talk of witchcraft will upset Jane.' Over the years, Elizabeth had tried her best to curb the excesses of her sister's malice, but to no avail. Alice was selfish enough and conceited enough to try to make a fool of anyone she took a dislike to, and it was plain she had taken a dislike to Jane who, in Elizabeth's opinion, was undeserving of such rudeness.

Jane glanced at Elizabeth and smiled broadly. 'It's all right, Elizabeth. I don't mind. It's a long time ago now and forgotten.'

'People have long memories,' Alice retorted acidly. 'Some never forget.'

Jane gave her a look of patient indulgence. 'No, I'm sure you're right, Alice, and there is nothing I can do about that. I used to help Gwen with her herb gathering, which made me something of a herb woman. I suppose you could say that made me an accomplice.'

Alice shrugged. 'Only you can answer that. So where will you live now, since Bilborough is no longer your home? You will have to live somewhere, and it is inconceivable for you to continue living here.'

'Why do you say that?' Jane asked calmly.

'Why—with Francis alone, of course. At least there should be someone else present. It is hardly proper for the two of you to be here alone.'

'You have no need to fear, Alice,' Francis said with a trace of sarcasm. 'Jane has been ill. I haven't ravished her in her helpless state.'

Alice was nettled by his mockery. 'I wasn't implying that you had. But, really, Francis, you know how the gossips are. Your character would be lambasted from here to London if it were known that the two of you are living together—in a manner of speaking, of course.'

A mildly tolerant smile lifted a corner of his lips. 'Of course. But you are here now, Alice—you and Elizabeth—so that should silence the gossips.'

'I am sure it will, although it was indeed generous of Francis to offer you his hospitality while you have been indisposed,' Alice said, looking at Jane once more. 'However, I can understand how awkward this situation must be for you, and now you are feeling better, I am sure you will soon find somewhere else to live.'

It was said in a tone designed to put Jane in her place. Already she felt a strong aversion to Alice, as she disliked all women when they were assured and tried to manipulate and insult her. So she ignored the tone and said impulsively, 'I already have. Francis has kindly offered me our old steward's house here at Bilborough until I have settled my circumstances. For the present I have decided to live there and,' she murmured, glancing sideways at their host, 'I shall do my best not to be a troublesome neighbour, giving you no cause for complaint.'

Francis took it with a smile that had more than a trace of condescension in it, which Jane found exceedingly irritating.

'And is there no young man in your life, Jane?' Elizabeth asked, her tone one of consideration rather than interference. Alice's rudeness angered her, and she would make a point of speaking to her about it later. 'I can't imagine a young woman as pretty as you to be without an admirer.'

Jane smiled across at her. 'There is no one—although there was once—a long time ago,' she said light-heartedly on remembering a childhood sweetheart, a village boy, who had kissed her cheek and gone off to fight for King and country without a backward glance or a thought as to how she might feel. 'I have not heard from him in years and I doubt I shall. The last I heard was that he fought at Worcester. What happened to him after that I really have no idea.'

Francis felt a *frisson* of dislike for this unknown youth who had remained in Jane's affections to this day, even though he knew there was nothing to substantiate his jealous imaginings. His expression did not change, nor did his eyes even flicker in her direction. All he said was, 'One of Charles Stuart's faithful, I have no doubt. Indeed, then if he survived and escaped the aftermath, he will probably have made his way to France. If not and he has been taken prisoner, then I have heard that Barbados is a pleasant island with a fine climate for those who have an aversion to the English weather.'

His callous remark earned him a withering look from Jane. 'I sincerely hope that he is in France with Charles Stuart. Better that than transportation, which is Cromwell's brutal solution to dispensing with prisoners.'

'I have heard that some of London's prisons are still full of Royalist prisoners,' Alice remarked quickly, before Francis could reply. 'There is a tendency among them to submit to the powers that be, if they are shown leniency.'

Jane received her words with derision. 'I have not seen any evidence of Royalists becoming reconciled to the Commonwealth, especially among those whose estates were confiscated and put up for sale.'

'I understand how resentful you must feel but, nevertheless, it was most kind of Francis to invite you to be his guest.' Alice had used all her feminine wiles on Francis throughout the evening, but had managed to extract nothing from him, for his attention lay in the woman with her high-and-mighty ways and more than a little resentment for her reduced circumstances across the table. 'You must feel much indebted to him.'

Jane looked across at Alice coldly. She would not be the object of anyone's pity, least of all this woman's with her malicious jealousy. 'Indebted? Why, I do not feel in the least indebted to Francis. Why should I? Bilborough was my home before it was his, and I *still* consider it to be my home. It is difficult not to.' Shoving back her chair, she rose. 'Now if you will excuse me, I will retire. I fear I am not yet fully recovered from my recent illness and I can feel a recurrence of a headache.' When Francis gave her no more than a slight inclination of his head, she took a careful breath and looked away from him.

His brother rose to bid her goodnight. When they had arrived it had been a disagreeable shock to discover not only that Francis had another unexpected guest, but that it was the daughter of the man Bilborough had belonged to before sequestration. In Richard's experience, such things were productive of more head-aches than it cured when the person was a Royalist and no doubt a footloose and flighty piece. His opinion had quickly changed on meeting Jane Lucas, and now he was absolutely charmed by her. A slow smile of admiration swept over his face as he beheld the regal young woman.

'It has been a pleasure making your acquaintance, Mistress Lucas, and I hope you will soon feel better. I also hope that you will continue to favour us with your presence for the time we are at Bilborough.'

His words threw her off balance. Her big dark eyes flew to Francis. She thought she saw his lips twitch, but when her nar-rowed gaze searched his face, he seemed to be regarding her with polite concern and nothing else. Her artificial smile faltered, but she recovered quickly enough to say, 'Thank you. You are most kind.' After bidding Elizabeth goodnight and nodding stiffly to Alice, holding her head high, she swept out of the room with all the dignity of a young queen.

Without appearing to do so, Francis had watched Jane all evening, amusement often tugging at his lips. Her manner had been alarmingly superior, so much so that he had begun to think her eyebrows had taken up permanent residence halfway up her forehead. She had been behaving in an exceedingly ladylike way, her manner sometimes demure and sometimes gracious, her smiles looking very much like they had been stuck on with pins. And she had been more than a match for Alice's barbs.

He was no less awed by her beauty than his brother was, he was simply more skilled in hiding it. Unfortunately he was not nearly so good at concealing his feelings from himself. To be sure his increased pulse rate whenever she was near affirmed his deepening infatuation.

Pushing back his chair he rose. 'Excuse me. I'd better go after her.'

Chapter Five

Before Jane reached her chamber she paused before a mirror fastened to the wall and stared at herself. In the light of the candles' glow she scanned her pale, strained face and her eyes, which were filled with a new expression, a kind of hunger, a hunger that had nothing to do with Bilborough. She desired Francis, she thought bitterly. In her innocence and naïvety she'd had no idea this would happen when she'd decided to temper her attitude towards him, when she'd smiled and flirted and told him he could kiss her. In her arrogance she had thought to keep herself immune, that she was strong enough to keep herself safe.

Then she had met Alice and seen the way she looked at Francis, and that was all it had taken. She knew jealousy for the first time. She was trapped. He had caught her. She must leave Bilborough, go somewhere to gather her thoughts and rebuild her defences.

Outside her chamber a sound made her pause and turn and she saw Francis approaching her, his tall figure dark in the shadows. It was impossible not to respond to this man as his masculine magnetism dominated his surroundings, but she would not show it. For her own preservation she must not.

He cocked an eye at her, the flames of the candles wavering

and setting strange shadows dancing around them. Her lithe graceful form was more tempting in her simple gown than any woman he'd ever seen dressed in velvet and adorned with jewels. Yet somehow simply looking at Jane robbed him of caution, and perhaps a little of the uncompromising honour he prided himself on.

'I'm sorry you decided to leave us so soon. I hope the evening has not proved too taxing for you.'

'Not at all, but I am tired and my head is aching.'

'So it had nothing to do with what Alice said about your step-mother being a witch, or about you feeling indebted to me?'

'No, not at all, although I did find her remarks offensive. I did not intend my response to be so verbose, but I could not over-look the offensiveness of her remark.'

She had her back to the door, and when she half-turned to push it open, Francis leaned past her to do it for her. But his hand brushed against her arm as he did so, and a tremor ran through her. He was aware of it and smiled, moving closer to her as she pressed herself against the door that he had failed to open. A curious sharp thrill ran through her as the force between them seemed to explode wordlessly.

'I am sure that was not her intention.'

'I beg to differ. Alice has a vicious tongue. She meant every word. I am an outsider here—a Royalist, to boot—and while I thought I would be treated as a guest, I am sure I saw her sur-reptitiously make the sign against evil when we first met.'

His eyes captured hers. 'You are my guest, Jane, and you will be treated as such while you remain here. So, if I were to ask you to have done with this war you have against me, you would?'

She stared at him uneasily. 'War? What are you talking about. I—thought we were friends,' she remarked.

'It is my dearest wish, but I am no fool, Jane. I know what you are playing at. I know you have set yourself a strategy to batter my defences with an assault on my emotions in order to regain Bilborough. Do you admit it?'

Defeated, she lifted her chin, and unable to tell a lie, she nodded. 'Yes—I do and I do not regret it. But that does not mean that I am not ungrateful for all you have done for me.'

'So if I were to beg for a truce you would consider it?'

'Beg?' She met his eyes levelly. 'You, beg?'

A smile tugged the corners of his mouth. 'Why not? It is not beyond me—and neither is this.'

Without giving her the chance to object he put his gloveless hand under her chin and forced her mouth up to his, placing his other hand against the door at the side of her head to prevent her escape.

Taken completely off guard and in no mood to be mollified following Alice's rudeness, Jane was outraged and resisted. 'Please let me go! I may have given you leave to kiss me earlier, but that was then and this is now.'

He chuckled low in his throat. 'It's time you had a lesson in playing games, my sweet, one that will make nonsense of all your false declarations to stand against me. If you play with fire, you must be prepared to get burnt.'

'I'm willing to take the risk, now please let me go.'

'Then there's only one way to stop you, little Miss Wildcat,' he said under his breath, and his lips covered hers, stifling her voice with a demanding insistence that stunned her into immobility.

Like an alarmed rabbit captured in a trap, her body struggled against his as he held her pinned to the door, her lips clamped as tight as a vice, but he was hard-muscled, tall and vital and in perfect physical condition, and in no mood to be crossed. They were both stubborn and she fought as if her life depended on it, until her strength began to fail and she found herself not wanting to fight any longer.

For no good reason, a warm melting pleasure spread through her, and all tension and will-power were drained out of her as she became lost in a haze of nameless longings. When she ceased to resist, his arms settled more easily around her. He raised his head from hers and looked down into her face. Her cheeks were flushed and her eyes were closed, the long and curling lashes dark against her flesh. Sliding his bare fingers through her hair on one side of her head, he set his mouth on hers once more, his parted lips crushing hers, sliding insistently back and forth, urging hers to part—the moment they did, his tongue slid between them, plunging into the sweet, soft recesses of her mouth.

Passive and exhausted, Jane lay in the circle of his arms as her whole being seemed to burst into flames, sensations she had never imagined overwhelming her. The feel of him, the warmth and the smell of him, all combined to transfix her, to reassure her and his lips became softer and more eloquent, hungrier and more insistent, moving against hers with his accomplished, persuasive mouth, and then sliding softly down to touch the skin above the neckline of her dress, moving over it so gently that she felt no more than the harmless whisper of a caress. She had no experience of men, especially one as powerful as Francis Russell, and she was lost.

And then he found her lips once more and she felt her body begin to tremble, quietly, independently, in a way that was completely strange to her, as if all her muscles were melting inside and out. The kiss was long, deep and measureless, a kiss unrelated to time or space, past or future, something magical and mystically complete. Neither of them had any idea how long it lasted, but it was Francis who had to find the strength to end what he had dangerously begun. Lifting his head, he dropped his arms and stepped back, once again in perfect command of himself.

Jane opened her eyes, shining black in the dim light. She was horrified by what had just happened, shocked and bewildered by the feelings he had evoked inside her, feelings she had never known existed. There was, it seemed, an alchemy between them, and she was certain it could only lead to disaster. She should never have let things go this far.

Fixing her hostile gaze on him, she glared at him, fully expecting him to lay the blame for this entirely unseemly kiss at her door. 'How dare you kiss me like that? How dare you take such liberties? You might have taken my home, but I did not come as part of the property. Perhaps forcing me to kiss you makes you feel better and in control.'

He drew a long, audible breath, holding it a moment before he said, 'You kissed me back.'

'Reluctantly—and I might have known you would say it was my fault,' she said angrily. His mobile mouth twisted into a grim smile and Jane had the fleeting impression that he was struggling for composure. 'Although after being a soldier for so long and starved of decent female company, perhaps you could not help yourself so I suppose I must feel some compassion for your need. And I am not a wildcat. If there is anything that resembles an animal here it is you. I struggled because I was trying to protect myself from you.'

'How noble of you,' he jeered, 'to sacrifice your precious lips to me. But contrary to your opinion, even a beast like me is capable of some discrimination and restraint. Contrary to what you think, Jane, you kissed me with the same passion I kissed you.'

Drawing herself up straight, as if to fend off Francis's remark, she stepped aside from him since the door prevented her from stepping back. 'I've decided to leave tomorrow. After this I think I must. But however long it takes I shall be back—as mistress of Bilborough Hall.'

He was facing her again, much more closely than she liked, and as she turned slightly, intending to open the door, his hands once more clamped down on her shoulders.

'That will never happen,' he said, his eyes glinting down into hers. 'It is not possible, so give up this madness before it destroys you and turns you into a hard and bitter woman. Where Bilborough is concerned, I have the upper hand—as I do in everything.'

Jane's eyes, her face, her whole being fighting him, she said, 'Have a care, Francis. You are too sure of yourself and the people who depend on the estate for a living. They may not tolerate for long being ruled by a Roundhead upstart.'

Francis smiled thinly at the intended insult and when he spoke his voice was like ice. 'Is that a threat, Jane? Does the once-proud owner of Bilborough make so bold as to threaten me—to put a spoke in my wheel?' He laughed. 'It will be interesting to see you try. I did not realise you are of a vindictive kind.'

'I wasn't, until I came here and met you. It would seem you bring out the worst in me. Vengeance is mine. I will repay what you have done to me and mine—though they are dead.'

Francis felt his heart turn. The fire in her rose. He could see it in the colour in her cheeks and her flashing eyes, and suddenly the charade ceased to be tolerable. And then he had her in a grip that pinned her against him once more, so that she could feel him hard and avid against her, so that she would remember him in every detail.

'Enough,' he bade sharply. 'You have verbally insulted me for no other reason than I bought an empty house. That it once belonged to you is unfortunate, but it's time you accepted the loss fate has dealt you and got on with your life.'

Jane struggled against him. 'Never. Let me go, you—you brute.'

'Not until I'm ready.' His embrace tightened about her until she thought he would crush her, and as his mouth clamped over hers once more, she fought frantically to free herself. But this time the contact was brief. Francis put an end to the embrace as suddenly and decisively as he had begun it, removing his lips from hers, though his body not so suddenly. 'Arm yourself, Jane. No amount of protests or young girl's wiles will keep you safe from me. If I want you, I will have you. I promise you that.'

Anger rose within her, the dark eyes flashed at him. 'I will not give up on what is mine,' she said stubbornly.

'You challenge me?'

'What is life without a challenge and what greater challenge can there be than to pursue that which rightfully belongs to me and achieve the greatest reward of all—total victory?'

'*That* you will never do.' Francis thrust her from him and stepped back. His voice was mocking and his eyes gleamed sardonically though he was still white-lipped with anger. 'I bid you goodnight, Jane,' he said, bending over in the mockery of a bow, 'and sweet dreams. Make the most of it, for this will be the last night you spend at Bilborough, and just in case you have the idea of taking independent action of any kind against me, then I shall be compelled to take action of my own. You will not like it. That I promise you.'

By the next morning, Jane still had not been able to put Francis's earth-shattering kiss or the anger that had erupted between them out of her mind. Sitting in the window seat beside Scamp, she stroked his head while he wagged his tail with the pleasure of it. Watching him, she thought again of Francis and her stomach knotted as she compared her own innocence to his hard worldliness. She was like an unweaned babe against a man like him. How could he have held her and kissed her as if he were trying to devour her one moment, and then be so cold and angry the next? She didn't understand him and nor, she sighed, did she understand herself. She told herself that what had happened had not been her fault so she had no reason to feel angry or guilty. But she did, and she shuddered with shame for her willing participation in the kiss. Her jealousy of Alice had angered her and because of it she had directed it at Francis, which was something she regretted, but she would miss the easy camaraderie that had developed between them in the short time she had known him.

On coming face to face with Jane when she was crossing the hall from the kitchens, Francis was abruptly reminded of the feeling of those soft lips against his. He remembered her responsiveness to his kiss and the incredible surge of hot desire she had ignited in his body. Remembering how it had felt to hold this beautiful, idealistic, intelligent yet headstrong girl in his arms, he tried to deny the feelings coursing through him the memory revived. This was insane, he told himself. He scarcely knew her and he was no young swain who fell for a woman at first sight. And yet that was exactly what he had done, and there was not a damned thing he could do about it.

His weakness made him angry, and when he looked into her eyes, that lazy, mocking grin of his, which seemed naturally inclined to curve across his handsome lips, had not diminished in the least. 'Why, Jane, I see you haven't gone yet,' he remarked, his eyes casually flitting over her. 'I thought you were in a hurry to leave my sight and my house.'

'My house,' Jane stubbornly reminded him, all her antagonism revived by his goading mockery. She would have screamed it at him in fury and called him every foul and insulting name in her limited repertoire had she not thought he would merely laugh at her and make her feel foolish. Glowering at him with dark eyes fairly snapping fire, raising her skirts, she stalked up the stairs.

When she thought of the way he had treated her last night, she was reduced to speechless fury. When he had kissed her, all her pride and her resolve had fallen before the wild surge of feeling he had stirred within her, and it had been a kiss with a greater, deeper and more perfect meaning than any she could have imagined. Then he had released her and told her in no uncertain terms that she wanted him to kiss her as much as he did. She would not allow that brute to break down her defences ever again.

Later that same morning as Francis and his brother rode out of the stable yard and passed beneath the arched gateway, the two hounds loping ahead, Jane watched them from her window. Not until they were out of sight did she say to Mary, 'It is time for me to leave.'

And so, with her few belongings packed into bags and secured on her horse, and Scamp, she left Bilborough Hall to live in the steward's house. She had to make it work. It was only a matter of application and determination and a careful tending of the fires that burned, hidden but persistent within her.

In her haste to leave the house, Jane was unaware of the man who watched her with carefully hooded eyes from some distance away beneath the shelter of the trees. Francis had dropped any pretence of ignoring his guest, yet only the pulse that throbbed in his temple attested to his own disquiet as he stared after her departing figure with mingled feelings of regret and concern.

If not for his damnable pride, he might have broken his guise of stoic reticence and gone after her, letting the servants and his family think what they would.

But Jane, too, was proud, and he knew she would reject his offer, which was why he'd dispatched a couple of servants to make the cottage ready for her earlier. Isaac, one of his elderly retainers, was to take up residence above the stable. He had arranged this for her own protection for he was deeply concerned about her living alone in an isolated cottage. No doubt she would resent it if she knew the truth, which was why he'd told Isaac to assure her his presence was to look after the horse and do menial tasks about the place, such as keeping the cottage replenished with firewood and carrying water from the well.

The steward's house stood in the grounds of Bilborough Hall, about half a mile away and screened from the main house by a high wall. It was a thatched house with mellow stone walls, golden and inviting in the sunlight. A yard at the back was enclosed by outhouses. Inside Jane had been pleasantly surprised to find it well furnished with all the requisites she would need for her comfort.

She had accepted Isaac's presence without argument, for she had not relished the thought of living alone. She still had nightmares that Jacob Atkins would come and find her and that the punishment he would inflict on her for daring to run away would be severe.

She had been living in the cottage for a week when she told Isaac that she was going into Avery to purchase provisions. It was something she had been putting off for days. Because of her father's loyalty to King Charles during the Civil War and the people of Avery on the whole being supporters of Parliament, aware that she would still have enemies in the town since many retained a deep hatred for anyone with the Lucas name, there would be those who would rate her appearance among them unwelcome. There were also the accusations of witchcraft against Gwen, which Jane's sixth sense told her had not gone away.

For the occasion she groomed herself carefully and wore one of the dresses she had taken from the trunk at the Hall, a dark green day dress of the finest linen. Isaac, having been instructed by Colonel Russell not to let her out of his sight, would not hear of her going into Avery alone. Luckily there was a small cart in the stable and after harnessing her horse to the shafts, they drove into Avery together.

The small town nestled cosily round the village green, where the pillory was set up. This instrument of torture was a wooden contraption that stood on a square stone plinth. The court house, the building which had been the scene of a wide spectrum of trials over the years from poaching, witchcraft and murder, doubling as the Town Hall, was set back from the square. The church was the first thing Jane's eyes sought, for it evoked so many memorises of that day when Francis had been Jacob Atkins's prisoner. Who would have thought then that he would return and settle close to the town where he had been so cruelly treated?

Swallowing down her emotions, she looked towards the green, which had seen the training of the militia at the beginning the war, the pike men and the musketeers striking out at imaginary opponents. How soon their training had turned to reality and their opponents had become human targets.

Avery was busy today, it being market day, when farmers came in droves from the surrounding countryside to sell their fresh produce. The usual gathering of townsfolk was present. Wagons and carts and pens filled with pigs, cattle, sheep and poultry filled the market square. But it was strange to her now. The air still vibrated with the same familiar smells. Rancid tallow from the candle makers assailed her, and she could hear the noise of the knife grinders and the hammering of the blacksmith from across the green. But the people were different and so was the atmosphere. It was oppressive. No one wore bright colours any more. Women dressed in plain black, brown or grey, their hair hidden under linen caps.

There was no longer the carefree laughter as the tumblers, the morris dancers and minstrels performed amongst them. They were no longer allowed to perform. As Jane got down from the cart her feeling was one of deep regret. What a dull place England had become, she thought. The whole country was drowning under the Puritans' yoke.

'While you order the provisions we need, Isaac, I'll try and find out what's become of Silas. You know what we require and I'll try not to be too long.'

Isaac gave her a concerned look, not sure what to do. 'If you like, I'll go with you.'

Jane smiled with assurance she was far from feeling. 'I won't hear of it. Don't worry about me. I shall be quite all right.'

Dispensing with a few small coins to a crippled beggar and glad to leave the ranting preachers in the market place behind, she headed towards the street where she knew Silas's sister lived, thinking that he and his wife might be lodging with her. On arriving at the house, she was told that Silas had taken a position as steward on a large estate in Norfolk.

It was with a feeling of disappointment that she headed back to the market place. She would have dearly liked to have seen her father's steward for one last time, to let him know that his dismissal had come as a shock to her and that she'd had no idea that the Bilborough estate had been sequestered.

Word had spread of her return, making her the object of pitying glances, some malignant, for they remembered how she and her stepmother had flown one dark night while the town slept. Now they quietly rejoiced in the fact that her family had been ousted from the Bilborough estate and brought low. A group of apprentices threw jeering insults at her, and some of the men looked her over carefully as they parted for her, and the grins that spread across their faces made her think that their minds were running far afield. Their ogling stares made her feel unclean.

Jane kept looking straight ahead, her eyes narrowed, and her anger seethed anew, for before she reached the market place the air was buzzing with whispered conjectures. But as long as she had life left in her body she would hold her head high and pretend it didn't matter.

Unfortunately before she managed to reach the end of the street, to her horror she found herself seized from behind. She gasped when she was hauled around to face a bearded man whose shape and size resembled that of an overfed mule.

'Not so fine and hoity-toity now, are you, miss?' he sneered.

'Let me go!' she gasped. 'How dare you lay your hands on me?'

She struggled in earnest to preserve her dignity while avoiding the flabby red lips that eagerly sought her mouth. His breath was sour and smelled of ale, and his hands rudely pawed her and brought her ever nearer to his ugly face. 'I demand that you release me,' she cried and braced her arms against his chest, trying to get some leverage in order to gain her freedom. His arms tightened and fear coursed through her as she felt the breath being squeezed out of her. She shivered in revulsion as his slobbering lips touched her cheek.

'Ye smell so nice and sweet,' he chortled. 'If you know what's good for you…'

Suddenly a large presence loomed over them and his words

were lost in a feral growl, and as quickly as Jane had been seized she was freed. She had a fleeting impression of her assailant's eyes widening in sheer terror as he was lifted straight up from her and swung aside as effortlessly as if he were stuffed with feathers and not lard. It was only then that she realised who her rescuer was, who it was that caused the awful terror in his eyes. Francis held the man by the scruff of the neck with one gloved hand while the other fist made contact with his belly, actions that engendered in Jane feelings both of horror and blessed relief. For what seemed an infinite amount of time, she remained unable to move, before forcing herself to take a step back and pressing herself against the wall.

His attention diverted by her motion, Francis paused as he was about to throw another punch. As he slid his gaze from the man in his grasp, the look of abject fury on his face gave way to something else, something equally dark and dangerous, but in a very different way. The man took full advantage of his distraction and wrenched free.

'You'll regret that,' he uttered sneeringly. 'The wench is a Lucas—a malignant—and some say a witch. The people of Avery don't forget.'

A mildly tolerant smile touched the handsome visage, but the glint in the blue eyes was as hard and cold as steel. 'The war is over and Mistress Lucas has committed no crime. Now if you do not wish to meet your maker before your time, I suggest you make yourself scarce,' he warned in a calm tone of reproof.

The commotion had attracted a small gathering, and when one of the oaf's friends sidled up to him and pulled him back, quietly informing him of the gentleman's identity, realising his mistake in trying to take on the new owner of Bilborough Hall, he eyed him warily. 'I meant no harm—just my bit of fun with the lady. No harm done, eh?'

'In that case go and have your fun somewhere else.'

Not so cocky now, the man backed away from the menacing figure of Colonel Francis Russell and made a hasty retreat back down the street. He was later to say to his fellow drinkers in the White Hart that he had feared for his life, and what the devil did the man expect when he had found himself confronted with the most fetching wench in Avery?

With her arms wrapped tightly around her, Jane watched him go, along with others who had stopped to witness her humiliation. She felt more hurt and degraded than she cared to admit and trembled in every limb.

Francis looked at her in silence, then he stepped forwards and put his arms around her. 'Are you all right?'

Burying her face in his chest, she nodded. For a moment she clung to him, aware of his strength and the nice male small of him. She realised with a small jolt of surprise that she wanted to stay like that, savouring the feel of him, the safety of his arms. His hand lightly caressed her back through the fabric of her dress, and though she stood unmoving, every nerve in her body tightened. Forcing herself to move, she pulled away from him.

'I'm fine now,' she said, smoothing down her skirts, her hands still shaking.

Francis raised a wondering brow to Jane, who flushed beneath his bold inspection. 'And none the worse for wear, I hope. I can well understand why the man made the attempt. You are a rare prize indeed, Jane.' He presented an arm gallantly. 'However, he could have hurt you had I not appeared in time. Allow me to escort you safely back to your carriage?'

'No, thank you,' she replied tersely, ignoring his offer. 'I told you, I'm all right. I'm grateful to you for what you did, but it is over. Good day to you. Please don't let me stop you going about your business.' More shaken by the incident than she cared to let him see, she walked quickly on, sincerely hoping he had gone on his way.

Francis stood a moment and watched her go, the full realisation of her plight filling him with a mixture of sympathy, disbelief and concern. He hesitated, torn between the male's instinctive urge to avoid any scene involving a distressed woman, and a far less understandable impulse to offer her some sort of strength, support and much-needed protection. The latter impulse was much stronger and it won out.

He headed slowly and purposefully after her, slapping his riding crop against his leg as he observed her stiff back and the indignant sway of her skirts. Increasing his stride, he was soon directly behind her. Knowing why she had left Bilborough four years ago, he wouldn't blame her if she ran away now. But apart from leaving Bilborough when left with little choice, he doubted she had run away from anything in her life—although he felt some disquiet as to the causes that had forced her to leave Northampton and return to Bilborough and would dearly like to know more.

Now he had come to know her he knew how she valued her dignity, and as a result of the accusations of witchcraft aimed at her stepmother all that time ago, her dignity had taken a public flogging. In her place, not many young women would have the courage to show up again in Avery. Only her pride, her outraged pride, would force her to appear and face them all down, for pride was all she had left right now, and her pride would demand that she appear in Avery with her head high.

Earlier he had seen her horse and cart halt in the market place. When she'd alighted and left Isaac to go off by herself, he'd observed the hostile glances some of the townsfolk cast her way as she calmly passed by, and seen one or two skulk after her, as if they were rats after just one piece of cheese. Concerned for her safety, he had followed on her heels.

On reaching the horse and cart, still shocked and affected by what had just happened, Jane stood for a moment before going in search of Isaac. She was outside one of Avery's ale houses, which was always well patronised on market days. The noise from within was loud and raucous. The slight breeze flirted with the cluster of soft curls escaping from her bonnet and played with the hem of her skirts while it brought a fresh flush to her cheeks. She was a fetching sight for any man, many of whom who were new to Avery and, unaware of who she was, paused after passing and openly glanced back for a second look. One such was a man she was already acquainted with.

Francis halted a moment before crossing the green to the blacksmiths where he had left his horse. Jane stood stiff and rigid beside the coach, her finely boned profile tilted obstinately to betray her mutinous thoughts. He could not help but wonder at the grit of Jane Lucas. He had known no other quite like her, and the disturbing fact was that she seemed capable of disrupting his whole life.

The fact that she continued to be cool towards him only spurred his interest. He also had an overwhelming desire to protect her, to befriend her and gain her trust. He felt most deeply the burden of her present distress and accepted that it was in the greater part his fault. He was concerned by what had just happened to her and he realised her vulnerability. He would have to keep a closer watch over those he perceived to be a threat.

Moving forwards to stand close behind her, he smiled his appreciation at her trim back. Jane sensed his presence but, thinking it was Isaac, was slow to respond. As she glanced around, her gaze caught sight of a pair of wide-topped brown boots, and her wonder became questioning surprise. Her head snapped up, and she found herself staring into the handsome and pleasantly smiling face of the man who disturbed and angered her all at once and more than any other.

'Oh, it's you. I thought I'd sent you on your way.'

'I'm not so easily got rid of.'

'No, it would appear not,' she retorted, scanning the crowd, hoping to see Isaac.

Francis observed her closely, looking for any ill effects from her unpleasant encounter. 'Are you sure you're all right after your ordeal at the hands of that ruffian back there? He was ready to drag you to the ground, and I assure you, Jane, he had nothing honourable in mind.'

Averting her gaze and staring bleakly at her hands, she finally managed to utter with grace, 'I know. I am grateful to you for what you did.' Raising her head, she gazed listlessly at the many people milling about. A long sigh that was oddly broken in the middle lifted her narrow shoulders. Futilely she shook her head slowly, and her voice was barely heard over the noise of the vendors. 'I suppose I'll have to get used to that kind of behaviour from people who used to be our neighbours, although I'll never accept it.'

'You shouldn't have to.' He studied her for a long moment before saying, 'You're a rare one, Jane Lucas. Many young women could not have borne what you have, and not surely with such spirit. You may encounter trouble again in the future, so I feel I must caution you. After what has just occurred, without proper escort it would not be advisable for you to wander beyond the immediate area of Bilborough. For your own safety, I urge this. I advise you to stay at home and send Isaac into Avery when you have any purchases to make.'

'I'll be careful,' she reassured him quietly.

He pondered her reply for a moment as his gaze lightly

caressed her. 'Of course I could always offer my services as your escort.'

A crisp, cool smile was briefly bestowed upon him. 'You seem to have it well planned—except for one thing.'

'Which is?'

'I have no intention of going anywhere with you.'

'You will not have a more capable chaperon,' he argued with a broad, rakish smile.

'Thank you for your offer,' she replied primly while struggling to keep at bay the effect of that smile, trying to keep something of the old bite in her tone. 'But I would rather take my chances alone. I believe I would be safer.'

He seemed undismayed. 'Then please don't worry. I doubt anyone will trouble you out at Bilborough, and if they do you have Isaac and they'll soon find they have me to reckon with. At least let me see you home before you find yourself in more trouble?'

The image of him prowling round the cottage to make sure she remained unmolested was definitely not to Jane's liking, although she was secretly touched by his concern for her safety, but she would not give him the satisfaction of letting him know it. Her mouth came open with her surprise, and she searched the handsome visage, taken aback by his nerve. 'Who do you think you are, my guardian angel or something? Be assured that I can take care of myself. And I don't need your help getting home. I have Isaac.'

He grinned in the face of her rising ire. 'As if I could forget.'

Jane almost expected his teeth to sparkle with the same devilish twinkle she now saw in those blue eyes. His garments were a sombre brown—the colour suited him well. A tremor of excitement tingled down her spine. 'So you see there is no need for you to concern yourself, Francis.'

'Presented with such a charming neighbour as you, my dear, I'm afraid I must,' he said, tipping his hat with a flamboyant flourish and grinning down at her. Even his blue eyes smiled at her, touching her everywhere.

The blush came quickly to her cheeks, mounting high as she recalled how it had felt to be in his arms and a shiver ran down her spine as she remembered their kiss—a simple contact, but the memory of it lingered far too long for her to be able to discount its effect on her. As a gentle breeze blew around them, short heavy wisps of his hair curled about his face, accentuating the lean, hard features. His grin widened, his teeth gleaming with startling whiteness. Jane admitted that apart from his injured hand, he appeared in remarkable health. Indeed, there was a vitality about him that was almost mesmerising.

Clasping his hands behind his back, he gazed up at the flawless blue sky. 'A pleasant day for an outing, don't you agree, Jane?' he commented.

Jane's eyes met his, and if any excitement remained, it was immediately dispelled as she looked beyond thick, black lashes into those deep blue eyes burning with silver lights. She glared at him, holding her temper on tight rein. 'So it is. But there is a purpose to my outing and I have little time to indulge in idle banter—unlike you.'

'Actually, I do have a purpose for coming into Avery today,' he answered smoothly, 'although I do have the time to admire the sights.'

Jane did not miss the meaningful gleam in his eyes as they appeared to devour her face, and asked crisply, 'And what is your purpose?'

'I have escorted Elizabeth and Alice into Avery. They're off shopping somewhere. I've also brought my horse to be shoed by the local blacksmith. I had been visiting the shops myself and was on my way to get him when I saw you.'

'Really! Then don't let me keep you.'

'You won't. I enjoy your company.'

'That's a shame. I don't enjoy yours. And I'm surprised. With so many horses at the Hall, I would have thought you'd have your own blacksmith by now.'

'I intend to, in time,' he replied, ignoring her intended sarcasm. His expression became serious. 'Have you settled into the cottage?'

'Perfectly. I've always held myself adaptable to the circumstances. Scrubbing floors and scouring pans hold no horrors for me,' she uttered drily.

'And it is adequately equipped?'

'Yes—thank you,' she said, tempering her tone and remembering her manners. 'I am relieved that the cottage is well supplied with everything I need.' She glanced at him from beneath her lashes. 'I know it is down to you, Francis, and I am grateful.'

'It was the least I could do. Despite your avowed dislike of me, Jane, you did not have to leave Bilborough so hastily, and I offered you the steward's house with the kindest intent.' He was wearing a contrite expression, completely at odds with his square shoulders and confident, upright bearing. 'Would you not find my company more enjoyable to that of Isaac—a man past his prime and poor company for a young woman? The hall is certainly more comfortable than a draughty old cottage.'

'Draughty?' Her eyebrows rose sharply. 'If it is draughty, Colonel, then it is the landlord's responsibility to put it right—at least that was how it was in my father's time. Isaac is a good person and I am well content with his company. And what, pray, would you require of me to stay at Bilborough Hall?' she queried with cold sarcasm.

He disregarded the sardonic edge to her voice. Indeed, his smile would have been one of compassion were it not for the leer in his eyes. 'Why, if it is rent you speak of I would charge no rent at all.'

'I would not be able to give you any. I've precious little coin to squander. I am not wealthy, that you already know, but I shall pay what debts I knowingly incur. I shall decide what I am to do in the future as soon as I can—a few weeks, no more.' She sighed deeply. 'You must know that I am sorely put to task with having to beg your indulgence until then. If I were to accept your offer and move into the Hall, it would only extend an obligation which I am already at heavy odds to pay. I am quite capable, otherwise, of taking care of myself.'

Francis leaned forwards so that his face was close to hers, his eyes all knowing and mocking. 'Were you wise enough to do that, Jane, you would not find yourself in the situation you are now in.'

Her face burned with the truth of his statement. She had little left to be proud of. Her independence had been stripped from her, and it goaded her that she must rely on Francis Russell, of all men, for her support.

'The offer for you to take up residence at the Hall still stands, Jane. I would require nothing more than to talk with you now and then.'

Jane gave him a glare that would have melted rock. Her voice was thick with disgust. 'Talk! Ha! To keep me as your doxy, more like. What do you take me for—an imbecile? Talk indeed. Why, I had been at Bilborough no time at all and only recently left my sick bed, when you accosted me and forced yourself on me like—like that oaf back there—' Cut short by his laughter, she glared at him. 'Why are you laughing?'

'Because, my dear Jane,' he said, regarding her from beneath hooded lids, humour dancing in their depths, 'I could not resist the encouragement I got from you. Do you not recall how you invited me to kiss you? Or perhaps it's slipped your mind.'

'No, it has not, and if you were a gentleman you would not mention it. You amaze me. You really do. How do you imagine the people of Bilborough would judge our relationship—me in particular, if I were to live with you openly at the Hall? I would be arrested and in no time at all,' she said heatedly, pointing to the contraption of torture close by, 'I would be pilloried and pelted with everyone's unwanted garbage.'

'Come now, you are upset. You exaggerate. That would never happen.' He sighed, shaking his head. 'Are you always like this, Jane, or is it me that brings out the worst in you?'

'I don't know what you mean.'

'You mean you're always like this?'

'No, I am not—and, yes, you do bring out the worst in me.'

'Then perhaps a little libation here in the White Hart will settle your nerves.'

'My nerves?' The words were lashed out. 'It is your nerve that must be reckoned with—and your lusts.'

He grinned, completely unperturbed by her anger. 'Come, Jane, I insist. Let us at least be civil to each other.'

'Insist! You would force a lady?'

He cocked a dark brow, a crooked smile curving his firm lips. 'You rate yourself highly.'

'My father did his best,' she replied primly, tossing her head, 'but I have a mind of my own.'

'You mean he indulged you so much that you are wilful, stubborn and proud,' he said with firm conviction, an amused chuckle accompanying his reply.

'I care not for your opinion of me—not one jot, as it happens.' She was about to move on, but casting a brief glance over his shoulder, she espied Alice emerging from a dressmaker's shop. She forced a smile to her lips, even as she tried to subdue a feeling if irritation.

'Why, see who we have here,' she remarked, her voice dripping with sarcasm. 'I trust she has kept you well entertained at the Hall.'

Chapter Six

On seeing them, Alice hurriedly joined them, not wishing to lose her tenuous grasp on Francis. Reaching them, she clung to Francis's side, wrinkling her nose as the stench from the animal pens assailed her nostrils. Her fair hair was dressed in ringlets that fell to her shoulders beneath a high-crowned hat. Half-turning her back to Jane, she tossed her head coyly, and her wide eyes touched him everywhere. Boldly she placed a hand lightly on his arm.

'I'm so delighted to see you are still in Avery, Francis,' she warbled. 'I was afraid we might have missed you and that you would have returned to the Hall.'

Smiling lamely, over Alice's head he caught Jane's brittle smile. Absently he brushed Alice's hand aside.

'My business here is not yet finished, and the way it looks— for Jane has the looks and the temper to cause pandemonium in the streets,' he said, giving Jane a meaningful look with a mischievous twinkle in his eyes, 'I might be here long enough to escort you back to Bilborough.' He drew a quick, challenging glare from Jane and grinned lazily in the face of it.

Jane held her silence. She would not chide him openly, but

she was firm in the belief that if he had not come to her rescue, things would be very different now.

Turning to face Jane, Alice studied her, smiling as though she had a lemon in her mouth. 'So, Jane, I hope you are settled in your little cottage and that it is not too—uncomfortable.'

'It is perfectly comfortable—for the present,' Jane replied, knowing her words must seem as stiff as her smile. 'It is, after all, only a temporary residence,' she remarked, casting Francis a meaningful look. 'I trust you are enjoying your visit to the Hall?'

'Very much, but then,' Alice purred, bestowing on Francis a winsome smile, the temptation to slip her hand through the bend of his arm nearly beyond her ability to resist, 'how could I not when blessed with such a charming host.'

Francis was immensely amused as he eyed the two women. Jane stood majestically proud and haughty. Sparks flashed in the dark eyes as she glared at Alice. He glanced askance at Alice, unable to ignore the fact that she was encroaching unusually close. 'You appear to have lost your sister, Alice.'

'I left Elizabeth inside the dressmakers,' she said, pressing a nosegay to her face and inhaling its perfume. 'She is unable to make up her mind about some ribbon she wishes to purchase.'

'Then might she not value your opinion? Perhaps you should go back to her,' Jane suggested.

'It is rare that Elizabeth and I share the same opinion, so I think she will do better without me breathing down her neck. We are dissimilar in so many ways that it's often difficult to believe we are sisters. The simple fact is that she resembles our mother and I, our father. Is that not so, Francis?'

Francis, who had initially welcomed Alice at Bilborough, now found the woman's clinging nearness burdensome. She had been outrageous in her pursuit of him and he had found himself in some tight corners where it had taken all his tact and diplomacy to extricate himself. However, he had trouble curtailing a grin as he witnessed this innocuous confrontation between the two women.

'It certainly is, Alice.'

'And you, Jane,' Alice went on. 'Are you here to shop?'

Jane felt a tightening she couldn't explain, but quickly asked herself why on earth she should feel slighted that the handsome Francis Russell would welcome Alice's presence. Later she would sort out her feelings, but for now she fashioned a bright smile.

'Why else would I be in Avery?' she answered. 'I have to eat. I have to buy provisions like everyone else.'

'I'm sure Mary can fit you up with what you need, Jane,' Francis offered, genuinely concerned about how she and Isaac were managing at the cottage.

'I wouldn't dream of asking her. Why on earth should you provide our food? We buy our milk and eggs and cheese from Farmer Burns at Hall Farm, and whatever else we need we shall get from the market today—which is what Isaac is doing this very minute. I shall have to go and find him and give him a hand.'

Alice sidled nearer to Francis, hoping to remind him of her presence. Even then, her attempt to claim his attention from the other came to naught, for he gave every indication that he had dismissed everyone else from mind when he told Jane he would ride over to inspect the cottage himself, just to make sure everything was in order.

Elizabeth emerged from the dress shop, and after greeting Jane warmly, much to Alice's chagrin, who was looking forwards to Francis escorting them back to the Hall, she whisked her away to visit their parents.

The heat of Alice's angry glare was felt by Jane as she took Elizabeth's arm. She smiled pleasantly. 'Goodbye, Alice.'

Alice clamped her mouth tightly shut; in a huff, she allowed Elizabeth to lead her away.

'Richard and Elizabeth will be returning to their home to-morrow—Alice to her parents,' Francis informed Jane. Looking down at her, he looked mockingly woeful. 'I shall feel quite bereft when they have gone—all alone in that great house.'

Jane laughed, a touch of irony in her remark when she said, 'To think that a house the size of Bilborough and its immense staff caters to the whims of one man seems most extravagant, and I can only wonder at the wealth that can afford such luxury. But, really! You are a grown man. Are you not hoping to mirror your brother's good fortune in finding a wife whom you can love and cherish—a woman who will love you in return? Unless, of course, your tardiness in marrying is because you have so many smitten ladies at your heels you are finding it difficult to choose.'

He managed a laconic smile. 'I want a wife—and children. Given time I will marry.'

'Given time? How much time do you need? Of course there is always Alice,' Jane suggested, a mischievous gleam lighting her eyes. 'Should you not wish to go to the trouble of a long court-ship, I am quite certain she would be amenable to a perfectly proper offer of marriage.'

The blue eyes flared. 'Alice is merely an acquaintance—my brother's sister-in-law. Nothing more—and she never will be.'

'I don't think Alice would like to hear you say that,' Jane joked provocatively. 'I'm sure she would like to be more than a mere *acquaintance*—much more.'

'Then she is going to be disappointed. And you should have a care.'

'I should?'

'Alice has a sharp tongue—when she has a mind to use it.'

'Which is often—given the fact that I have only been in her company twice, and on both occasions she has tried to put me down.'

A low chuckle preceded Francis's reply. 'I didn't think she was putting on a show of affection. I also noticed you couldn't resist deflating her a bit.'

'She deserved it.' Tilting her head to one side, she looked at him gravely. 'Going back to what we were talking about, perhaps you should marry. Men of your age have usually a wife and children. Someone needs to take you in hand.'

Francis looked down at her and his eyes danced merrily as he searched her face. 'Are you offering, Jane?'

She stiffened. 'Heaven forbid! I was merely offering you some advice.'

'Do I actually detect some concern for me in your advice?'

'When you're so cavalier about taking a wife, someone needs to try to get you to listen to reason,' she retorted impatiently.

'I take heart that you care.'

'I don't—and don't be conceited,' she responded drily.

'Conceited? Nay, Jane. Like your barbs, your reproach wounds me to the quick.'

'I doubt it,' she scoffed. 'You have a hide thicker than an ox.'

'Come now. Don't be mean,' he coaxed, his voice as soft and smooth as silk. 'An occasional smile from you would not go amiss.'

Tossing her head haughtily, she glowered at him. 'You have done nothing to earn my smiles. And as for yours—save them for Alice.'

His amused laughter took the sting from her words. 'When I have expended so much energy on you, my dear Jane, how can you possibly imagine I have any interest in another woman? And why should you care, anyway, when you're not interested?'

'You're right, I'm not,' she snapped.

His lips twitched with ill-suppressed amusement. 'I just thought you needed reminding.'

'And I am not your *dear Jane*,' she protested with the sudden sweet pang of pleasure his endearment caused as to discourage him.

'But you are, Jane—to me,' he murmured warmly. 'Your antagonism always cuts me to the quick. At least can we not be friends?'

Her expression softened and, as had happened before, her attitude began to melt towards him. He was so attractive, so compelling, it was impossible to stay angry with him for long. 'Friends? Friendship is too strong a word. People situated as you and I cannot be friends,' she informed him sadly. 'Friends have to like each other, and any liking between us is constrained by the vast chasm of difference my changed situation imposes.'

'It needn't be like that between us—not if you don't let it.'

'And I was under the impression that I was a problem.'

Francis's gaze was direct, challenging, almost insulting, raking her from the hem of her skirts, and passing over the narrow waist, and then more leisurely over her round bosom. The neckline of the bodice was demure with a white fichu at her throat. Still, Jane felt undressed beneath his stare. Feeling her cheeks flush scarlet, self-consciously she averted her eyes, focusing them on a rather noisy vendor selling chickens, but without really seeing him.

'I don't regard you as a problem. Quite the opposite, in fact.' His countenance grew more serious as he met her gaze. 'For the greater part, I regard you as a lovely young woman. You are very beautiful.'

'And you have a silken tongue,' Jane chided him in verbal defence, for he was pushing the boundaries of their relationship and she would be as susceptible as she had been when she had arrived at Bilborough.

His lips spoke no word, but his eyes clearly expressed the truth of them. The bold stare touched a quickness in her that made her feel as if she were on fire. It burned in her cheeks and started a trembling in her stomach. He was bathed in a light cast by the sun behind him, and was aglow with deep golden colour that softened his hard, lean frame. Those glowing eyes burned into hers, suffusing her with a growing aura of warmth. How could she claim uninterest in this man when the very words he uttered, his mere presence, could so effectively stir her senses. Angered by her sudden weakness, she turned from him.

'Go away. The mere sight of you is beginning to offend me.'

Francis grinned broadly and swept her a low bow. 'As you wish, Jane. Since I perceive that Isaac is on his way back with his arms full of provisions, I shall leave you and be about my business.'

Jane caught a glimpse of Isaac across the market square just as he described. She was moving away when she heard his next comment.

'If you should change your mind about an escort into Avery in the future, you know where to find me.'

Jane refused to gratify him with a retort, but it was a dire struggle she made for composure as she reached Isaac and took some of the provisions from him.

The mists hung stubbornly in the low spots as Jane walked down the lane towards the paddocks where Francis kept his horses. Hopefully everyone would still be abed, which was why she had chosen to come at this early hour.

She was so overwhelmed to see Arthur again that tears filled her eyes. Nearly black, with his powerful chest and huge shoulders above lean, strong legs, he was in good condition and silky smooth. She was pleased to see he had been well looked after. Climbing over the fence and calling his name softly, she walked towards where he was grazing. Suddenly alert, Arthur raised his head and listened, his ears twitching and turning.

'Hello, Arthur,' she said, smiling with pleasure as she advanced, holding out her hand. On seeing her, the horse snorted and whickered and tossed his head and came to meet her. 'Hello, boy.' She laughed when he stretched out his neck and nibbled her sleeve—an old habit of his that told her he had not forgotten her.

While Jane was becoming reacquainted with Arthur, Francis was walking away from the adjoining paddock where he'd been checking on one of his mares. She was due to foal any day. He would instruct one of the stable hands to have her brought inside where they could keep an eye on her.

Pausing to glance across at Arthur, his eyes lit on a scene that brought him up sharp. He frowned on seeing him being ridden around the paddock by a young woman who straddled his bare back, a young woman he immediately recognised as Jane. As she urged the powerful mount on with a confidence that astounded him, the hem of her skirts blew back above her knees and, holding on to Arthur's mane, she bent low over his neck.

Completely bemused, Francis's frown deepened. She was the last person he would have expected to see at this early hour, and what in God's name was she doing in the paddock riding such a powerful brute as Arthur—and without a saddle? The breeze snatched at her hair, the long curling shiny black tresses flying riotously behind her. Vivid beauty was moulded into every perfect sculpted feature of her face, but her allure went much deeper than that. There was something inside her that made her sparkle and glow like a flawless jewel.

Bringing the horse to a halt and throwing her arms around the stallion's neck, she laughed gaily, the sound drifting towards where Francis stood. It was the first time he'd heard her laugh and the sound was like the sweetest music to his ears. This girl was full of surprises, full of promise, he thought, watching her surreptitiously.

For some reason he remembered his long-held dream of having a woman to light up his life and his home, a woman to fill his arms, a woman who would love him and the children he gave her. Recollecting himself, he smiled at his naïve, youthful dreams and unfulfilled yearnings, which he had carried with him into adulthood and hoped would bear fruit. He thought it strange as he realised Jane Lucas had rekindled all those old yearnings.

Jane was about to dismount when a shrill whistle pierced the air. Arthur's head came up and he whickered low in his throat. The whistle came again, and without a bridle to enforce her commands on the horse, she found herself being carried towards the edge of the paddock where the new master of Bilborough stood watching her. With his hands resting casually on his hips, he wore an expression she did not recognise.

All her grievances where he was concerned were never far from the surface. She looked at his too-handsome face and knew that she should hate him as her enemy, but Francis Russell had charm as potent as any strong wine. She looked at him and knew that her own face was alight with pleasure at seeing him. He walked towards her, offering his hand to Arthur. The horse snorted and came willingly.

'It is plain to see who is his master,' Jane remarked, still clutching Arthur's mane and making no move to dismount. 'Does he always come to your whistle?'

'Arthur is a smart stallion—none smarter,' he replied, his eyes averted as he rubbed Arthur's nose. 'Whoever he belonged to before me taught him well. I taught him to come to the whistle—which was useful when we became separated during battle.' He grinned, looking up at her with hooded eyes, and when he spoke his voice was soft and provocative. 'I have often thought of trying it out on the female sex, but I doubt they would appreciate it. What do you think, Jane? Would you come when I whistle?'

'Certainly not,' she snapped, most affronted by his bold and inappropriate question. 'And if you think I would, then you are more half-witted than I thought.'

He laughed out loud at her outrage. 'I thought not, but Arthur does not often trust a person as readily as he so obviously trusts you, Jane. And I know of no other who has managed to climb on to his back without a saddle and ride him as you have just done.'

Jane shrugged, having no intention of telling him that Arthur had been her father's horse, and that she had ridden him when he'd been hardly more than a foal. 'I like to ride, and I've always been good with horses,' she said by way of an explanation. 'They do seem to trust me.'

'Clearly.' He smiled slowly. 'But I hope you haven't ruined a good mount with all your petting and patting.'

Jane's glare bored into his amused and mocking stare as he continued to caress Arthur's nose while his smouldering eyes boldly roamed her bare legs. 'I most certainly have not,' she retorted, pulling down her skirts. 'And will you please stop staring at me like that. It's indecent,' she reproached angrily, feeling devoured by those burning eyes. 'Being an early riser, I was out taking a walk when I came upon your horse in the paddock. We quickly became friends and he did not resist when I climbed on to his back. I will get down now.'

Without a word Francis moved to stand beside the horse and before Jane knew it, with one quick athletic movement he was up behind her. She gasped in outrage, but before she could struggle his arms were round her, his hands grasping hold of the mane.

'Will you please get down?' she protested crossly, trying to twist away from him, but to no avail. 'This is outrageous. Dismount at once.'

His breath was warm on her cheek and his voice sounded soft in her ear. 'Not a chance. Now be still and enjoy the ride. I will escort you to the cottage.'

'I would rather walk than ride with you in such a manner,' she cried, her mind invaded with the feel of his stalwart chest pressed so close to her back, and his thighs resting lean and muscular alongside her own, and his loins pressed intimately against her buttocks. 'What if we are seen? What then?'

He chuckled lightly. 'I doubt there's anyone about at this hour. And if it is your reputation that worries you, fear not. Your virtue is quite safe with me.'

'I don't think so,' she derided. 'Whenever you are near me you can't resist pawing me. You are a rogue, Francis Russell. I think there is but one thought on your mind.'

'And so there is, Jane.' The words came close to her ear as he smoothed the tumbled, sweet-smelling hair out of her neck. 'When I am with you I can think of nothing else. But enough. Today I promise that you are quite safe. I merely wish to escort you to your home.'

Touching Arthur's flanks with his heels, the horse moved on. Francis leaned forwards, and Arthur quickened his pace, responding to his master's commands as if they were one. Jane was amazed as she felt the movements of man and horse, and as Francis's knees tightened, Arthur stretched out along the path in the opposite direction to the cottage, as if they rode with the wind.

She turned slightly and looked into his face. 'Where are we going? This is not the way to the cottage.'

He shifted her closer to him. 'We're taking a slight detour. You're not afraid, are you, Jane?'

Glancing into the brightness of his eyes, Jane saw a soft, smiling warmth there and felt no fear. Her pique was softened by her curiosity, for this man seemed to have an ability to turn every circumstance to his advantage.

'I am at your mercy, sir.' For safety's sake, she had to submit to the arms laid about her and she resigned herself a bit more happily than she had intended. Pressed against him, she felt the heat of his body through her clothes, smelled the clean fresh smell of his linen, his sweat, and his knee pressing against her thighs was as intimate as if they were naked. 'I can only hope that the poor horse doesn't collapse beneath so much weight.'

Behind her, Francis gave a lopsided smile. 'Fear not, Jane. Arthur has carried heavier burdens than this. He has weathered many storms and come through no worse for wear.'

'Does he get much exercise?'

'As much as he wants, galloping around the paddock. Why do you ask?'

'No reason. I—was wondering if I might ride him sometimes—while I am still here.'

'Why, are you thinking of going somewhere?'

'I don't intend living in the cottage for ever. I shall have to decide what I am to do some time. So what do you say? Will you permit me to ride Arthur?'

'If you wish.' He drew her closer still, her round derrière

tucked snugly into his loins. 'He seems to like you, which is strange since he doesn't usually take to strangers. Perhaps I could ride with you—unless you have an aversion to my company.'

Hearing the gentleness in his voice, Jane turned her head and stared at him. Uneasiness coursed through her, inexplicable but tangible as she gazed at his proud, handsome face. It was as if he was trying to persuade her to put aside her resentment, and she didn't know how to react. As she gazed into those fathomless blue eyes, some instinct warned her that his offer of a truce— for she thought this was what he was angling for—could make him more dangerous to her than he had been as her adversary. Was it possible that she could benefit from some kind of surface friendship between them, for, in truth, she did rather enjoy their light-hearted banter?

She opened her mouth to accept his offer, then stopped and looked ahead, for pride and honesty and desperation were waging a war inside her. It seemed a betrayal to become *too* friendly with this Roundhead who now owned everything she held dear. And yet if she wished to retain any hope of retrieving Bilborough by whatever means—if such a thing was possible—it might be prudent to gain his trust and secure his friendship with a degree of sincerity and honesty. However, still confused and unsure of herself and feeling that she would be plunging into uncharted territory, when she next spoke her answer was evasive.

'What? Like this? I think not.'

'That wasn't what I meant—although the idea does hold some appeal. To hold you like this occupies my mind so completely I can think of nothing else.'

'Please,' Jane chided breathlessly. She was becoming too aware of his body, the heat of him, of the nestling seat his thighs provided. She could not miss his insinuations. 'Behave yourself. Shame on you, Francis!'

He chuckled, his arms tightening, content to ride wherever Arthur might lead to hold her like this. He pressed a cheek against her hair, somewhat awed by her closeness. 'Why? There is no one to hear us—only Arthur, and he won't tell.'

'Perhaps not. But it is not appropriate that you should talk to me the way you do.'

'Humour me a little longer, Jane,' he murmured close to her ear, warming her cheek with his breath, 'and allow me to enjoy being close to you a while longer. I sense that you are learning what it's like to give in to your heart's desire. You cannot hide away in your little cottage for ever. I have known many women and I know the signs. You do desire me, though you hardly know it yet. You are like a little fish swimming against the current. You have seen the bait and want it, but you try to resist the temptation. But fear not, Jane. I shall land you eventually and you will come to me and never be free again.'

Held within the circle of his arms and unable to move, Jane felt the heat of him all around her and heard the whisper of temptation in her ear. Closing her eyes, she turned her face up to the sun and knew her desire.

As light as a breath of wind he brushed his lips against her neck, raised his head and looked at her flushed profile with his smiling blue eyes. He smiled at her, his wicked, careless smile. 'Don't you long for a taste of what I can offer, Jane? Don't you dream what it would be like? All these forbidden things could be yours. I could give you more than you can dream of—more than a taste.'

Jane opened her eyes, hazy with desire, but his words brought her back to reality. 'I'm sure you could—and more besides. But the shame of bearing a child nine months from now is not for me.'

She wriggled forwards, but Francis clamped his arms more

tightly about her and pulled her back, and whispered, 'Stay where you are, for should we meet anyone, I shall embarrass us both should I have to dismount.'

Gasping and unable to turn her head and look at him, she settled back against him. She was glad he couldn't see her face, for the heat of it nearly stifled her. Yet she felt a strange, delicious contentment that her nearness could affect him so.

Francis kicked the stallion and he leapt forwards into a gallop. They sat easily atop the powerful horse as he surged beneath them, riding harder, his hooves sending up clods of grass and earth. Jane remembered the times when she had given him his head, and how her father, worried for her safety, had chastised her most severely. With the impetuosity of youth she had laughed, telling him that never had she felt as safe as when she rode on Arthur's back. Yet now, with Francis's strong arms encircling her, never had she felt so secure. On reaching the lane which wound its way to Avery, he slowed Arthur to a gentle trot.

Turning in the direction of the cottage, on reaching the gate, with a click of his tongue and a tightening of his knees, Francis brought Arthur to a halt. Jane remained where she was until Francis jumped down. When he turned to assist her she put both hands on his shoulders. He lifted her down and held her close to him. She shuddered as she slid down every inch of his body, and smelled the open-air smell and the warm maleness of him. As his firm hands gently set her on her feet she lifted her face.

He stood looking down, holding her eyes in a wilful vise of blue. His voice held an undertone of huskiness as he asked, 'Well? Did you enjoy the ride, my lady?'

Feeling the warmth of his gaze wash over her, she lowered her eyes. 'You certainly have a way with horses. Arthur clearly knows his master.'

In thoughtful silence Francis watched her open the gate and

walk up the path to the house. He continued to look at the door through which she had disappeared a moment longer, before mounting Arthur and returning him to the paddock.

They rode together several times after that, Jane on Arthur and Francis on his big hunter. They rode through fields and woodland, never staying silent for long for lack of things to say. Jane often flared up in anger, for Francis had a knack of igniting her temper, but she never stayed cross for long and Francis would quietly accept her mood, which was one of the things she liked about him—that she could give vent to her temper and in no time at all it was quickly forgotten. When they had both had their say the matter was closed.

It was early afternoon, a quiet time in this peaceful place at the border of the woodland and pasture. On reaching the paddock, strangely it came as no surprise to Jane to find Francis there, his own horse saddled and in the process of saddling Arthur. He paused in his task, distracted by her appearance and by the sunlight glinting on her raven-black hair drawn from her face and secured at her nape by a ribbon, the thick tresses cascading down her slender spine almost to her waist.

'You were expecting me?' With the sun warm on her face and the usual excitement coursing through her at the prospect of riding Arthur, Jane favoured him with a bewitching smile.

'I always enjoy our rides. It's a fine afternoon and Arthur would benefit from the exercise.'

'Then who am I to disappoint him.'

She burst out laughing when Arthur nudged her with his nose, almost toppling her over, and Francis found himself captivated by the infectious joy, the beauty of it. It glowed in her dark eyes and lit up her face. She was unforgettable. He realised it as clearly as he realised that if he were to take her in his arms and lift her into the saddle there was a chance he was going to find her irresistible as well. He hesitated, watching her as she stroked Arthur, still recounting the reasons he ought to let her mount herself—and then with carefully concealed purpose, he did the opposite.

When they had been riding some time, with the rooftops of Avery within their sights, they dismounted. Settling themselves on the grass in a bower of murmuring, shadowy leaves, they were content to sit and breathe in the scents of the undergrowth and to feel the warmth of the sun on their faces.

Francis rested his back against a tree trunk, one knee drawn up, his eyes on Jane as he idly twiddled with a stick. The ride had done her good, he thought, looking at her sparkling eyes and glowing complexion, her cheeks as pink as the campions growing in the long grass.

Jane caught her breath. She could almost feel his warmth, could feel the vital power within him, indeed could almost feel again his lips on hers. Sensations of unexpected pleasure flickered through her at the memory, making her quiver. They remained as they were, both aware of the closeness of the other and deep in their own thoughts. The warm air blew against Francis's face, clearing his mind. A bank of cloud had arisen in the west and its shadow was advancing towards them. There was a faint chill now in the breeze.

'Look,' Jane said, sitting up straight. 'Someone is coming.'

They got to their feet and waited. Jane was still standing beside Francis, but she was no longer looking at the beauty of the surrounding countryside. She was gazing along the wide lane towards Avery. Francis followed her gaze. A horse and rider were coming swiftly in their direction. The wind was blowing his cloak back behind him like a pair of large black wings. The wide brim of his hat hid his face, but there was something about him that made them unable to look away. In fact, there was something threatening about him that gave Francis an odd feeling in the pit of his stomach.

The rider drew to an abrupt halt only a few yards from where they stood. He rode a fine animal, a bay stallion, suited to a wealthy man. He lifted his face in Francis's direction, and although Francis could not see his features clearly because the brim of his hat cast a dark shadow across his pale face, he felt his stare. There was a stillness about him, a silence, that was entirely menacing. The man cast a shadow as long and black as the finger of Satan.

'Who are you?' Francis asked, stepping forwards.

Raising his head a little more, the stranger looked directly at Jane. 'I am certain you will know me after a moment. In the meantime, ask your companion. Mistress Lucas and I are well acquainted—is that not so, Jane?'

He spoke in a low silky voice. It was not one that Francis recognised, and yet…there was something. A sudden coldness claimed him.

The cruel talons of dread clawed at Jane. Her heart pounded so hard she thought it might run out of control and stop beating. 'Yes, we are,' she replied. She had hoped and prayed she would never have to lay eyes on this man again, but deep inside her she'd known he would come after her. He was a man close to fifty, tall and thin but solidly built. His face was clean shaven, his features clear cut. He would have been handsome but for the unattractively sardonic grimace and the scar that lifted one corner of his thin lips.

Atkins! Francis's sense of foreboding grew. He had not heard that name in a very long time, except in his nightmares. He sensed nausea rise within him and a sudden gruelling pain in his head. It was eight years since he had been captured when he and the men under his command had been attacked when on reconnaissance a few miles from Avery and Atkins had wreaked his vengeance on him. Every cruelty and every indignity of that event was as fresh in his mind now as on the day they had been inflicted.

The spasm of fury that passed through him caused him to break the stick that he clenched in his hands. For a moment he wanted to confront Atkins and break him as completely as he had broken his stick. But it was one of his great strengths that his lifetime of hardship and learning had taught him—never to act rashly. He was a master at keeping his feelings under control until the moment was right. The man's head turned, and Francis saw that it was indeed the same Captain Jacob Atkins. The shadow his hat cast across his face found a sinister echo in the black leather patch that hid his right eye, and the long silver scar that emerged from beneath it, ending at his jutting chin.

Upon settling his yellowish single eye on Francis, Atkins lifted a brow and leaned back in the saddle. His expression was hard to decipher. It spoke of arrogance, conceit and an underlying cruelty. Their eyes locked tight as a lover's embrace, neither man moving for a moment or relaxing their coiled tension.

It was Atkins who eventually let out a long sigh and said, 'Well, well! Colonel Russell! I did not expect to find you back in Avery. I thought I'd dealt with you and good riddance! Your hand healed after all, did it? And now I find you with my late sister's stepdaughter. I never expected to find the two of you together. How touching. It would appear you have formed an attachment.' His expression hardened, his gaze remaining fixed on Francis. 'So, Russell, we meet again.'

'So it would appear, Atkins,' Francis replied, his tone level. 'I am not the dead man you intended me to be. How galling it must have been for you to find I had escaped your henchmen, depriving you of the pleasure of shooting me.' He glanced at Jane. Her face was white with shock. 'Jane? Are you all right? You look as if you'd seen a ghost.' And then he realised that she had seen a ghost or someone out of her past that was as frightening as one, and he sensed an underlying fear. 'Mr Atkins and I are already acquainted, Jane,' he remarked, speaking out loud what she already knew, but this she kept to herself.

Panic was gripping her. She had a great desire to flee as fast as her legs would carry her, but they would not move. She was frozen, paralysed with fear. But she couldn't stand there, trying to make words come from her mouth. She had to speak. 'Yes, I know,' she replied through a stricture in her throat.

The penetrating coldness of Atkins's expression continued to convey his loathing for Francis. His expression had turned dangerous and his eye a deep muddy brown. When Francis Russell had taken out his eye with one thrust of his sword, he had learned to hate him with a deep, implacable and very personal hatred. There would be no appeasement until he was dead.

By now Jane had sufficient command of herself to speak. 'Mr Atkins has come to see me,' she told Francis with a nervous tremor, subconsciously having moved closer to his side, her expression not at all welcoming as she looked at her stepmother's brother. 'What are you doing here? What do you want with me?'

'Your departure from my house was furtive, Jane. I was disappointed to find you so lacking in courtesy that you could not tell me to my face that you wanted to leave my house.'

'Would you have allowed me to leave?'

He smiled thinly. 'Allowed? I was not your gaoler, Jane. We could have discussed the issue together.'

'I left you a note.'

'A note! After I had given you the comfort and protection of my person and my home, provided for you, is that the way to repay my kindness? No, Jane, I think not. I promised my sister that I would take care of you. As my charge you had a duty to stay and obey me.'

Jane watched him and her eyes glittered with such contempt, such hatred, such loathing, that another man might have looked away in shame. But not Jacob Atkins. He was no ordinary man in his behaviour to any human being.

'You are no blood relative of mine and I thank God for it. You have no legal claim over me and you will not treat me in the same vile way in which you treat your own daughters.'

'When you are underage and residing under my roof, I'm naturally responsible for you.'

'Your roof? I no longer reside under your roof. If you demand that I return, then I shall refuse.'

Atkins's face darkened to an ugly, mottled red. 'In which case I shall have to decide which course of action to take—which is not something I can do in a few minutes.'

'You don't say,' Francis uttered with irony, lifting his dark brows, his eyes as cold as his terse smile. 'What's the matter, Atkins? Invention failed you, has it?'

'No. Far from it.' His gaze rested on Francis Russell, remembering the day he had captured him as if it were yesterday. He remembered how, when the vice had crushed his hand, he had not cried out or begged for mercy, or struggled to try to save himself. He'd just set his back hard against a post and stood there. He'd flinched when the lighted tapers had been placed between his bloodied fingers, but nothing more. Jacob doubted that he could have done that, nor anyone else. He'd been fair put out to find he'd escaped, depriving him of the pleasure of shooting him after allowing him to suffer the pain of his injured hand and to contemplate his fate.

His gaze shifted back to the prim beauty and casually caressed the soft, enticing curves that the plain gown gently moulded. Her back was straight, her head elevated, conveying an undaunted pride. 'I would like to speak with you in private, Jane.'

'That is not possible,' Francis said, taking it upon himself to answer for her. 'Do you want to go with this man, Jane?'

She shook her head, her features tense. 'No. Never.'

'There you are, Atkins. You have your answer. I fail to see how you can make any claim on her.'

Atkins curled his lips in an angry sneer. 'Obviously you didn't hear me. Jane hasn't yet come of age whereby she can do as she pleases. She was a legal ward of my late sister. On her demise she became my responsibility. I am duty-bound to provide for her care.'

Francis smiled derisively. 'Knowing you as I do, I know how you treat others in your care, Atkins. That is hardly an act of solicitude.'

Atkins scoffed in rampant distaste. 'I'm sure the chit gave you quite a tale to win your sympathy, but that will hardly dissuade me from complying with the wishes of my sister.'

'That is not true,' Jane retorted icily. 'I am not your responsibility. I was there when Gwen died and she made no mention of any guardianship being transferred to you. Nor was there anything in writing.'

'I am a man of wealth and position, and if you don't want things to go badly for you, you'd better consider complying with my wishes. In the meantime I shall have to think it over and examine the various possible solutions to this difficult problem you have presented me with in peace and quiet. I would be grateful if you would see to it that I am lodged in suitable rooms at Bilborough.'

'I'm afraid I cannot do that. The Bilborough estate no longer belongs to me. It was sequestered by Parliament in my absence and sold. It now belongs to Colonel Russell.'

Atkins went deathly still except for his racing thoughts. Keeping his voice low and calm, he said, 'Why is it that I do not believe you?'

The muscles in Francis's lean cheeks tightened progressively until they fairly snapped. 'Jane speaks the truth, Atkins. Bilborough is mine, but it changes nothing where she is concerned. I give her my protection, and with God's grace she will remain unharmed—so do not speak to me of what you will do to her.'

Atkins's eye surveyed the girl who had defied him at every turn, narrowing as it took in her dishevelled appearance and bright, uncovered head and wanton mouth. His face darkened as he glanced from Jane to Francis and back to Jane. His lips curled with contempt. 'Look at you—your appearance is unseemly— you whore,' he breathed. 'This man has taken your inheritance and yet you cavort with him freely. Where is your self-respect, girl? What else has he taken from you? Have you no shame?'

Francis took exception to the slur; taking a step forwards, he raised a clenched fist. 'You bastard, Atkins.' His voice was low and deadly. 'Insult her one more time and I'll drag you off that damned horse and carve you into so many pieces you won't be fit for dog meat.' He stepped closer. 'Now take your mouldy presence from my land and my sight, you scurvy lump of dung, and keep the stench of your foul person from its gates, or I *will* set my dogs on you—although no matter how brutally you are mauled will hardly placate me as suitable recompense.'

'I shall keep your words in mind, Russell, but you'll regret this!' Atkins warned as he backed his horse away. 'I still have a score to settle with you, and now this. I'll make you sorry you ever laid eyes on Jane Lucas.'

'I doubt that,' Francis scoffed. 'Now get off my land before I throw you off myself, and if I catch you in the immediate vicinity of Jane, I will arrange for your judgement to be on a higher level than mine.'

The two of them stood and watched Atkins ride away.

Looking down at Jane, Francis captured her gaze. Plumbing the dark depths as he said, 'You didn't tell me Atkins was your stepmother's brother, Jane.'

'No.' Feeling awkward and absolutely terrified following their encounter with Jacob Atkins, her eyes chasing off in the direction of the horses, she mumbled, 'I—I never thought...'

'Of course you did. I recall telling you the name of my torturer. Why did you not say anything then?'

She shook her head dejectedly. She had deliberately not told him because in doing so she would have had to reveal that she was Tom. For some reason she could not explain even to herself, she was shy about doing so and preferred him to remain in ignorance. Perhaps it was because he was a fiercely proud man and she didn't think he would want to know how she had seen him as a captive—brought low, degraded and humiliated.

'Knowing how you must feel towards him—that you had just cause to despise him as much as I did, I thought that if you knew of my relationship to him, through Gwen, you would have insisted that I left Bilborough. That was why I—I didn't want you to know that I knew him—that he was Gwen's brother.'

Pain sliced through Francis that by his actions she'd had so little faith in him she truly believed he would have done that to her. 'I would never have turned you away from Bilborough.'

'I know that now, but I didn't then, when you told me he was the man who had inflicted your injury. How you must hate him.'

Grim-faced, Francis helped her into the saddle.

Looking into his eyes, Jane quickly averted her gaze. Something had moved in their depths, just for a moment. It was gone in a flash, but she did not want ever to see it again.

Chapter Seven

It was a silent, tense ride back to the cottage. With all her emotions bottled up inside her, Jane rode a little ahead of Francis with her lips pursed tightly as she tried to come to terms with their encounter with their mutual enemy. On reaching the gate they halted the horses, neither making a move to dismount.

Putting aside his fury at coming face to face with his most bitter enemy, Francis was deeply concerned for Jane. What had Atkins done to her to put such fear in her eyes? He had seen it when she had first set eyes on the man and she had let the mask she had so carefully kept in place slip, revealing a very frightened, vulnerable young woman hiding a damaged heart, a young woman who was in desperate need of protection.

Francis gave her a careful scrutiny. 'You're quiet, Jane. I can sense Atkins's appearance has upset you.'

She stared at him through terror-and hate-filled eyes. 'Upset? Yes, I am upset,' she said fiercely. 'I am upset that he has come here looking for me since I hoped and prayed never to set eyes on him again. He was and still is a horrible man—a monster.'

'Did he hurt you very badly?'

'It was more than that,' she answered quietly. 'The first time I met him was when he came to Bilborough during the war, before my father was killed. When I went to live in his house in Northampton he told Gwen that I was the most wicked and obdurate girl he had ever allowed under his roof. I half-believed him, for I felt only terrible things about him.'

She was about to dismount when he said firmly, 'Don't get down. I want you to come back to the Hall with me.'

She stared at him. 'But I'm not, Francis. I shall stay here at the cottage.'

'Don't be ridiculous. You are coming home, Jane, and you are staying there until this matter is resolved. I will not have you here alone while Atkins remains a danger to you.'

Still she resisted. 'No, I will not. I will not run from him again, Francis.'

'You will. You will stay where you are safe under my protection. I will not allow you to stay here.'

She glared at him, her face bright with indignant pride. 'You will not *allow* it? I cannot believe you said that. I can decide for myself what I will and will not do. I am outraged that you seem to have taken it upon yourself to protect me, which, I recall, is what you told Jacob Atkins. I never asked for your protection. I certainly don't expect you to protect me. And I definitely don't want you to.'

As indignant as she was, Francis's jaw tightened. 'I can see my concern for your welfare has displeased you, Jane. It was not my intention. Understandably you are distraught—which I must assume is why you are being unreasonable?'

'Unreasonable?' she flared. 'Because I don't want to be protected by you or by any man? When I left Northampton after four years of abuse at the hands of a monster, I swore that from that day on I would look after myself and nothing has changed. I prefer it that way.'

A gleam of anger showed in his eyes. His face became hard

and there was a visible menace in the set of his mouth. He turned his back to shut out the lovely vision she presented, of the child-woman who was now exhibiting such alarming self-possession. 'Damn it, Jane! Do you have to be so—difficult?'

'Unreasonable! Difficult!' She lifted her head in that defiant way Francis was beginning to know so well. 'Yes, if it suits me I shall be anything I please.' She turned her blazing, defiant eyes on him, but Francis was not fooled. Inside he knew she was hurting very badly. 'I thank you for the chivalrous feelings you possess towards me, but they are not necessary.'

'In the light of our encounter with Jacob Atkins I beg to differ,' he bit back harshly, feeling that they were in danger of losing something of their former intimacy with Atkins's arrival.

'And I will not be dictated to. Have you no principles or sense of fairness where women are concerned?' Jane bit back in frustration.

Urging his horse close to Arthur and leaning forwards so his face was close to hers, Francis's voice dropped to a low, icy whisper. 'You're mistaken if you think I care a damn about the kind of principles you speak of. Don't bother lecturing me on principles and don't mistake me for a gentleman, because I'm not. I am anything but. I have just fought a war in which I have done things that would offend and shock your maidenly sensibilities.'

'I doubt it,' she bit back. 'I had not been in your presence one minute before I made up my mind that you were the most conceited and arrogant upstart I had ever met.'

'And you are nothing but a silly, foolish girl who has no idea what you are up against when you try and pit your will against me and a sadistic murderer like Jacob Atkins.' He leaned back and yanked on the reins, causing his horse to shy away from Arthur. 'Now, if you are determined to stay here, kindly dismount and I will take Arthur back to the paddock. I think enough has been said between us for one day.'

Still angry, but also feeling confused and hurt by Francis's attack, which she had foolishly and unwittingly provoked, so that she could scarcely think, without saying a word and feeling tears welling at the backs of her eyes, Jane slipped from the saddle and looked up at him, faltering a moment, her anger diminishing by the second. 'Francis, I'm sorry.'

He looked down at her, his own anger melting at the sight of her tear-bright eyes. 'So am I. It is only this present danger and my concern for you that made me speak as I did.' Leaning down to her, with his hand he tenderly cupped her cheek. 'Have it this way if you must, Jane. I will leave you with your independence since it is clearly so important to you, but I shall not leave you alone. Jacob Atkins is our mutual enemy and we will shoulder this together. I will speak to Isaac and have men patrol the grounds. He will probably stay at one of the taverns in Avery so I shall have someone watch him.'

Jane watched him ride away. Not until he was out of sight did she turn and go into the house. One thing was uppermost in her mind. Despite their differences, both she and Francis had been deeply shaken by Jacob Atkins's arrival, both knowing he was not going to go away and neither of them knowing what would happen next.

It was Brutus, one of Frances's wolfhounds, that sensed all was not as it should be. Francis came awake with a start—not that he slept deeply, his years as a soldier had taught him to sleep with one eye open. He was alert, all his senses focused. He felt rather than saw Brutus prick his ears and lift his head from the carpet beside the bed. Pulling himself upright, he lit a candle and, looking at the clock on the mantelpiece, verified the time.

It was midnight. A frown drew his dark brows together. Getting up from the bed, he put a hand on the dog's neck, and felt the hair there standing up with warning. The animal's head swivelled, following something unseen. He was growling, a low and constant rumble that Francis could barely hear, but he could feel the vibrations travelling up his arm and arousing all the nerves in his body.

His heart beating fast now, Francis padded across to the window and looked out. The moon hung low over the tree tops, casting an eerie grey in the cool but oddly tense night. There was an urgency in him that made him uneasy. The night was calling, the shadows beckoning. Slipping into his linen shirt and breeches, he left the house with Brutus close on his heels, as silent as the wolf who had fathered him. The moon slipped behind a cloud, but Francis could still see the faint silhouettes of trees and outbuildings.

The steward's house drew him. Its shape squatted a little way back from the lane. He stood looking at it, wondering at the reason for his unease. Suddenly a glow appeared from the buildings at the back of the house, a glow that was fast becoming brighter. Sprinting round the house, he was just in time to see two dark figures running out of the yard and become swallowed up by the night. Were it not for the squeal of the terrified horses in the stable next to the building where the fire had been started, and the speed with which the flames were taking hold of the straw and hay stored there, he would have given chase, but the urgency of getting the fire under control was paramount to all else.

Isaac, who had been woken by the squealing of the horses, had led them outside and was tethering them to a post away from the fire. Together they began trying to damp down the flames with water from the horse trough. When Jane appeared in her night attire, having had no time to dress, with so much dry tinder in the small stable, great whorls of flame were shooting out of the door and through the roof, sending a shower of sparks into the sky. The smoke filled their nostrils, stung their eyes and scorched their faces, nearly driving them back. With no time to ask Francis what he was doing there or to enquire how the fire had started, unable to think of anything but the urgency of the moment, she snatched a bucket and began pumping water from the well and passing them to the two men to pour on the flames. With her hair flying out all over the place, she resembled a mad woman.

Thankfully they had caught the fire early and together the three of them soon had the blaze under control.

Isaac went to calm the two horses straining to be free. Jane lifted her head in a vague semblance of the girl she had once been. Grim-faced, soot smeared and unkempt, Francis stood beside her, staring at the smouldering remains of the stable.

'Who has done this to me?' Jane whispered, her throat aching with the smoke she had breathed in. 'Someone who hates me. It has to be someone who must want me to suffer to perform this terrible act of vandalism—to set fire to my home.'

'I don't know who did this, but I have my suspicions.'

'Had you not arrived when you did, they might have set fire to the house.' She clasped her hands to her cheeks in despair. 'I can't bear it. I can't bear to think about it.' Somewhere in the far spaces of her mind she felt the first stirring of awareness. It was an awareness that she hadn't quite grasped yet, but it was on the edges of her consciousness and soon she would find it. 'I have a dreadful sense of foreboding, of vindictiveness, for whoever is to blame for this crime against me harbours an implacability that is remorseless.' Wrapping her arms about her waist, on trembling limbs she moved away from him.

In her distress, Jane was unaware how Francis watched her

with carefully hooded eyes. He could not pretend that he was not worried by what had happened, yet only the jagged pulse that had leapt to life in his throat attested to his own disquiet as he stared after her, with mingled feelings of regret and concern.

As Jane looked around at the devastation, her eyes fell on a bucket of whitewash Isaac had left against the wall of the house. He was in the process of whitening the passage in the house that opened on to the yard. Slowly her eyes moved on upwards and the cause of her unease was made plain. She stood as one stunned, staring at the bold, ugly letters that had been painted on the wall of the house, deeply shaken by what she saw.

Witch.

That single word had been daubed on the stones, the watery liquid having run down the wall so that the statement looked grotesque. They had all been so absorbed in putting out the fire that none of them had noticed it.

Francis came to stand beside her, his face troubled. A trickle of sweat streaked his neck and his thick hair was tousled and flecked with bits of charred straw. Jane could feel her heart beating painfully in her chest and a small shudder ran through her. Unconsciously she stepped closer to Francis, taking comfort from his nearness. The night was warm and her nightdress clung to her with humidity and damp.

'Whoever did this will be found and punished,' he said, his voice quivering with a low, quiet anger.

'It's why they did it that worries me,' Jane whispered. 'That word has followed me. It's a nasty word to have hung around your neck.' Her spirits struggled beneath the weight of judgement against her. 'I have been condemned as a witch by the people of Avery without the benefit of a hearing. That single word bears out their verdict—they will kill me if they can. Alice was right. Some people don't forget.'

Francis didn't disagree. How could he when the evidence was starkly painted before his eyes. 'Atkins is still in Avery, staying at the White Hart?'

Jane was not surprised. Ever since he had presented himself there had been a prickling sensation at the base of her neck and she was for ever looking over her shoulder. 'I knew he wouldn't be far away. I know him too well to know he will not meekly go away and leave me alone.' She looked at Francis sharply. 'Do you think he is behind this?'

Seeing Jane's white face tight with shock and dark, fear-filled eyes, anger swelled suddenly in Francis's chest, a huge, solid thing, pushing hard enough to burst it. 'We can't know for sure. We can't be certain of anything where that devil is concerned.'

'Perhaps this is his way of punishing me. I can't help thinking…'

Francis felt the tension running through him snap like a broken wire. He'd been strung up like a puppet since he'd left the Hall. He knew that while ever Atkins was within the area Jane would not be safe. He knew Atkins. He knew how the man worked. He was a man who held grudges, a man who would not come out into the open and face his adversary alone. He would work behind the scenes, making things as unpleasant for his victim as he possibly could.

'Atkins is capable of anything, Jane. If he is responsible for this, he'll regret it. I meant what I said. I'll kill him.'

Jane turned her thoughts away from this new and dangerous direction and said, 'How did you know to come here—what did you see when you arrived?' she asked.

'I sensed something was not right—and my dog Brutus was uneasy. When I got here the straw in the stable had just been lit. I saw two men dart into the woods. I would have given chase, but my immediate concern was to put out the fire.'

Jane looked towards the lane that ran by the yard. The woods beyond were dark and seemed full of mystery and threat. She turned to the stable when a beam collapsed and sent flurries of ash and soot ghostlike over the ground.

'Do you think whoever did this will come back?'

'I don't think so, but I'll keep watch out here just to make sure. I'll send someone over in the morning to sort out the stable.'

Realising that she was still shaking from the incident, she managed a tremulously grateful smile before sinking on to the protective wall that circled the well, feeling exhaustion pulse through the quivering muscles of her legs. 'Thank you. I would appreciate that.'

'It's the least I can do under the circumstances.' His eyes narrowed as he regarded her with troubled scrutiny. 'Are you all right?'

'A little shaken, but I'm fine,' she answered firmly. 'Perfectly fine.'

Unconvinced, Francis sat beside her. 'Of course you are,' he said, taking her hand and raising it to indicate a slight cut on her wrist. 'You look like you've fought a battle.'

'Well, yes,' she said. 'Other than that. I cut it on the bucket.'

He rubbed a thumb over the smear of blood, erasing it. 'How do you feel now?' She had drawn away a little at his touch, but her eyes, live in the lantern light, were still fixed on his. He had the feeling that she was looking far beyond him, through him, but then the focus of her gaze came back and she looked directly at him for the first time since he had arrived.

'Better,' she whispered and closed her eyes. She took one deep breath and her body relaxed, going limp.

Fearing that she might fall backwards into the well, Francis gathered her to him, both arms wrapped around her.

Jane turned her face into his chest. 'When I left Bilborough, not knowing when I would come back—and fearing that I might not—all the horror and anger connected with that time still lurks in the back of my mind like a great dark shape under thin ice. The fire brought it all back—the feeling of being hunted,' she whispered into the linen of his shirt. He reeked of sweat and horses, of weariness and of a man who has laboured. 'Can you understand what I am saying?'

'More than you realise. When war broke out and I went to play my part, in all that time I never thought I might lose. I never thought I would be taken prisoner. I never thought I would die. It's strange and you will think me foolish. But in all that time when men were being killed around me—friends and acquaintances—I never thought it would happen to me. I thought myself unbeatable, invulnerable—until I met Atkins. Only then did I realise I was not invincible. I was not brave, I was just lucky. That day I felt fear and I could not flee from it. I had to stay and face it.'

Jane tilted her head back and looked into his strained face, seeing the ghost of his past in his eyes. 'Thank you for sharing that with me, Francis. Every man is afraid sometimes, and it's a brave man who will admit to it. I, too, have been afraid—of the same man. He has terrorised us both, but not any more—not if we don't let him.'

'Those are brave words, Jane, and we will endeavour to do just that—together.' Francis held her close for a moment longer, then put her away from him a little and looked down into her face. Tenderly he drew her hair back and tucked it behind her ear. 'I think you should go to bed. You look all in. Time enough in the morning to put things to rights. I'll ask Isaac to get rid of that,' he said, gesturing towards the painted wall.

She nodded, and without a word rose and left him. Deeply concerned, Francis watched her enter the house, a pale silhouette against the dim glow of the lantern. She was not safe in this present danger, not even within the confines of Bilborough. He would have to keep a better watch on the cottage, just in case whoever was responsible for the fire should try again.

When Jane went outside the morning after the fire, it was quiet. She stood looking at the burned-out stable, assessing the damage. The ashes were cold and already scattering in the light breeze, but the smell of burning filled her. It could have been worse, she supposed—the whole collection of outbuildings could have gone up in smoke, the horses, too. A shadow detached itself from the corner of the yard and came to her. She smiled when Scamp came to sit at her feet.

'Hello, Scamp.' He looked up at her and wagged his tail. 'What a mess it all is.' Scooping him up into her arms, she placed an affectionate kiss on his silken head. 'Come along and I'll give you your breakfast. Some meat and potatoes should fill you up nicely.'

Seeming to know it was time to have his belly filled, Scamp proceeded to lick her face. Laughing lightly, she put him down, watching as he bounded towards the door. About to follow, she looked across the yard to find she had a visitor—not a welcome visitor. Having left her horse at the gate, Alice strolled towards her. At the sight of her Jane distantly wondered what mischief she was brewing. She contemplated what pleasure she would gain from asking her to leave.

'Good morning,' Jane greeted coolly. 'Forgive me, but I didn't expect visitors so early in the morning.' Of a sudden she wished she had worn one of her better gowns and paid more attention to her hair instead of quickly sweeping it from her face and leaving the mass to curl in carefree abandon around her shoulders.

Alice's fair hair was neatly arranged beneath her bonnet, and she was gowned in costly good taste.

'Who were you talking to?' Alice asked, looking around. 'I heard you speaking to someone.'

'Oh,' Jane said, rather embarrassed. 'No—I was talking to Scamp.'

Alice turned a gaze of suspicion from the dog waiting in the doorway to Jane. 'Your face is wet.'

Jane wiped her face on her sleeve. 'Scamp is an excitable little dog and is in the habit of licking one's face when he's about to be fed.'

Reading what was going through Alice's mind, Jane gave her a wry look. 'Scamp is not my familiar,' she uttered tartly. 'He's a dog. Talking to him is less ridiculous than talking to myself.'

An expression of surprise flitted across Alice's face—perhaps surprise that Jane had read her mind, or surprise at her idiocy, and the creases of suspicion remained. She took in the scene with a snide smile.

'I heard you had a fire last night. I was riding this way so I came to see for myself.'

'As you see, someone set fire to the stable. Are you going anywhere in particular?'

'I'm on my way to Bilborough to see Francis. Do you think the fire was started deliberately?'

'I am certain of it. The perpetrators were seen running away.'

'Your return to Avery does seem to have provoked antagonism towards you. A witch hasn't been hanged in Avery for several years and considering the accusations directed against your stepmother before she fled the town, because of your close association with her and the suspicion that you were involved in what she did, your sudden arrival is enough to rouse fear in the hearts of every man, woman and child.'

'But I am not a witch, Alice,' Jane stated calmly. 'There are mischief-makers in every town and village and Avery is no different. I have no doubt the scandalmongers are revelling in all sorts of conjecture about my return, but I pay them no heed.'

'So they are—especially those who really do believe you are possessed by the devil.'

Jane laughed, scooping Scamp up into her arms when he bounded back to her. 'Which is quite ridiculous and concerns me not at all. And as for setting fire to the barn, well…' she shrugged '…I will not be frightened away by such things. It will take more than a fire to make me leave Avery.'

Alice's green eyes became piercing, like those of a hawk that had just spotted prey, except that Alice was beginning to realise that this quarry would not be frightened off by mere threats and was much too securely ensconced at Bilborough and under Francis's protection to attack outright.

'I met an acquaintance of yours the other day when I was out in Avery with my father—an interesting gentleman who is currently staying at the White Hart. A Mr Atkins, who was facially mutilated in the war.' Alice bestowed a taunting smile on Jane, noting how the colour had drained from her cheeks. 'He is to dine with us this evening. We were interested to know that he is acquainted with both you and Francis.'

Jane was conscious of a sinking feeling. 'Mr Atkins and I do know each other. He was my stepmother's brother. I lived in his house for a while in Northampton, and I assure you, I have few worthwhile memories of that time. Mr Atkins has few, if any, endearing qualities.'

'He told us how you left Northampton in something of a hurry. He also told us you were a bad influence on his daughters and that you deserved to be punished for your misdemeanours.'

'My, my,' Jane jeered coldly. 'What an interesting conversation you must have had with Mr Atkins. You really have no knowledge of the man whose acquaintance you have made do you, Alice? Jacob Atkins is a dangerous man and you and your father would be well advised to avoid him. You have no idea how cruel he can be. Francis has had dealings with him in the past and will confirm what I have said.'

Alice's eyes hardened. 'Francis?' Her curiosity to know more surfaced.

'Oh, yes. Francis is very well acquainted with Mr Atkins. Ask him, but I cannot promise he will tell you everything, of how Mr Atkins imprisoned him and tortured him. If someone hadn't gone to his aid and made it possible for him to escape from the vestry in the church in Avery where he was being held, then Mr Atkins—or rather Captain Atkins as he was then—would have killed him. If you are going to Bilborough, then I am sure Francis will be delighted to see you—or maybe not. You might well find him in bed.'

'I don't think so. Francis is an early riser.'

'Not today. It was Francis who alerted us to the fire. He's been here all night—keeping an eye on things. He hasn't been gone an hour.'

Seeing no point in going to Bilborough, Alice decided to return home. She would see Francis the following day when she visited Elizabeth at Russell House. Francis was to be their guest overnight so she would see him then. Her mouth twisted in an ugly sneer.

'How very cosy for you, Jane. Are you using witchery to make Francis want you?'

Jane suppressed a smile. 'I don't think I have to resort to charms and potions to attract his attention, Alice. And anyway, why would I?'

'You would do it for what you stand to gain—and Bilborough

rates high on your agenda. You may think it is to your advantage to use your charms and cast your spells, but believe me, if he favours you with any attention at all, it is because he feels sorry for you and partly responsible for the situation you are now in. That is all it is.'

Jane smiled. 'Well, then, if that's all it is, you have no need to concern yourself, have you? But have a care, Alice. A woman with a tongue as loose as yours may well find herself charged with slander.' Her smile became mischievous. 'Although with all this talk of witches that seems to have erupted in Avery since my return to Bilborough, should you assist the mischief-makers in spreading rumours about me, then I may well put a curse on you.'

Alice paled and glared with abhorrence at the hungry, squirming dog Jane still held in her arms, as if she could smell sulphur from the very depths of hell. She stepped back, and Jane could see the fury gather on her face before she turned and walked out of the yard. Utterly surprised at herself, Jane asked herself what she thought she was doing. Had she not just given Alice reason to believe there was considerable truth in the accusations that she really was a witch?

Later that day Jane was at work in the little flower garden at the front of the house when she heard sounds of someone approaching. She straightened and looked over the gate just as a horse and rider came into sight, the latter being Francis, the man who haunted her every waking moment and her dreams. He drew rein beside the hitching post on the other side of the gate and dismounted.

'Good afternoon, Jane.'

She shoved her hair out of her eyes and, after giving him a

smile, continued tending the flowers. 'Why, Francis. You are the last person I expected to come calling,' she greeted calmly.

His brows gathered in a lopsided query while a smile touched his lips. 'My apologies. I didn't mean to startle you. Can you stop that now? I'd like to have a talk with you.'

Though her mind was not on her labour, Jane continued to dig around a clump of deep pink stocks. 'Whatever it is you have to say to me, then it can be done while I am working.'

Francis came and stood over her, looking down at her bent head. When he spoke his voice was flat and devoid of any expression. 'Tell me, Jane, do I bother you?'

She paused and took a moment to look up at him, squinting her eyes in the sun. She dared not reveal the truth. Since their parting, this man had played too much on her mind. She had considered resorting to her earlier strategy and batter his defences with an assault on his emotions in order to regain Bilborough, but since Jacob Atkins's arrival in Avery, she had other problems at hand.

'Yes, you bother me. You bother me every time you are within my sights. You bother me when you speak to me, and what you say bothers me.'

'And do thoughts of me bother you when you are in your bed, Jane? Do thoughts of me keep you awake, and if you do chance to sleep, do thoughts of me bother your dreams?'

'You think too highly of yourself, Francis. When you are away from me I think of you not at all,' she lied.

'Now why is it that I do not believe you, Jane? I have come to talk with you privately, and I would be grateful if you would spare me a few minutes and go for a stroll with me and listen to what I have to say.'

She stopped what she was doing and stared up at him for a long, indecisive moment. His lips were pressed tightly together and she saw now that his expression was grave. She got to her feet. 'Very well.' Taking off her broad-brimmed sunhat, she wiped her forehead on the back of her hand, and pinned a loose lock of hair behind her ear. Removing her apron and gloves, she left them on the wall. 'I'll walk with you a little way, but I mustn't be too long. I've promised Isaac an early supper.'

She fell into step beside him, and together they strolled away from the house. She tipped her head to the sun. It was so good to feel the heat on her face. 'I do hope your intentions are honourable, Colonel,' she said, trying to sound flippant. 'I seem to be at your mercy. Are you determined to compromise me?'

He gave her a slow smile. 'Soothe your fears, Jane. That is not my intention. And have a care. You'll get freckles,' he teased.

'Then it's as well I'm not vain about my looks.'

They carried on walking, neither of them speaking. Giving Francis a sideways look, Jane noted that he looked thoughtful. It was clear he had something on his mind. The more she saw of him and got to know him, the more she became attuned to him. She could feel the vibration of some strain in him, and she was beginning to think she had something to do with that.

'Francis, what is it?'

'What?' He raised his eyebrows in question.

'What aren't you telling me?' she asked with what patience she could muster. 'Why have you come to see me?'

'Because I am deeply concerned about you—more so since the fire, and to tell you there are threats being made against you.'

'Threats—against me?' She sighed deeply in exasperation. 'I have to confess that I too am worried. Any day now I fear someone will set a torch to the house, or that some other disaster might befall me.'

'There you are then—you are afraid.'

He fell silent. Jane felt a qualm of unease. He really did seem troubled. 'Tell me what they're saying about me in the town.'

He narrowed his eyes at her, obviously trying to guess her reaction when he told her. 'Atkins has been busy stirring up trouble for you. Clearly he feels cheated out of both you and Bilborough, so he is spreading malicious gossip in the hope that people will listen to him.'

'And are people listening to him?'

'Unfortunately they are.'

'What has he been saying?'

'He is making you out to be a monster, a witch, blackening your character, carefully prejudicing any potential jury members by making sure your guilt is spread in every scandalous detail. Your relationship to your stepmother—or corroboration, as people prefer to call it—does not help matters.'

'But that's just slander—poisonous talk. Is there anything that can be done?' she asked, sickened by all this nonsense.

'Apart from going before them and looking as little like a depraved monster as possible, very little.'

With a sigh she shook her head. Now more than ever she began to feel the stricture of her situation. 'None of this surprises me. I have lived long enough to have a fairly cynical view of human nature and to know how directly public opinion expresses itself. And yet I am still shocked. My name is on everyone's lips, for they are certain I am as much a witch as Gwen was. How cruel the lie that shames my family name,' she said bitterly. 'My fate does not bear thinking about if those who think me guilty take matters into their own hands. We all know how witches are dealt with—but I'd prefer not to have to dwell on that aspect of the matter.'

'No,' Francis agreed, 'neither do I. They've approached Justice Littleton to have you examined, but since I made a point of having a word with him, implying that I would withdraw my funding for the new orphanage that's being built if he appre-hends you in any way, he's reluctant to do so.'

Jane stopped and faced him. 'You did that for me?'

Francis nodded. 'My influence is strong in Avery. In any case, despite Justice Littleton's puritanical outlook on all things, he has little stomach for trying a witch. However, I doubt it will change anything. The so-called witch hunters are determined to have their pound of flesh.'

'If they are as determined as all that, then they are not going to change.' Jane looked at him, a cold shiver running up her spine. 'Do you think I'm a witch?'

He looked at her incredulously. 'Give me some credit. I am an educated man. I do not believe in witches. It's just supersti-tious nonsense.'

'I'm very much relieved to hear it—although being a witch would have some compensations. I would have turned Jacob Atkins into a toad at first sight,' she remarked crossly. 'What can I do?'

'As to that I have two suggestions.'

Interest kindled in her eyes. 'And they are?'

His blue eyes became fixed on hers, warm but serious. 'First, for your own safety I think you should leave Bilborough. Have you thought any more about going to London?'

'I have, but that's all I have done. I would like to go to pres-ent my case—to have Bilborough returned to me, but I'm afraid my funds are rather limited just now.'

'If you are hellbent on doing that, then I cannot prevent you and would not dream of trying. It is your God-given right. However, I can provide you with funds to stay elsewhere,' he said slowly. 'I can arrange for you to leave Avery. I have friends in London you could go to.'

Jane stared at him in bemusement. 'But why, when I might use the funds against you? I might even succeed in having the estate returned to me, in which case you would be made to vacate Bilborough. Forgive me, but I am confused.'

'The money I would give you would be for your keep and nowhere near the amount you would need to present your case.'

'I see. Please do not think me ungrateful, but I cannot accept your offer. I will not take money from you or accept your charity. In short, I will not be obligated to you, Francis. I am fairly self-sufficient. I prefer it that way.' She had her pride and she was adamant. Falling into step beside him when he walked on, she looked at him askance. The gravity on his face alarmed her. She stopped walking and grasping his arm, forced him to face her. 'You said you had two suggestions that might help solve my predicament. You have told me the first. What is the second?'

Francis glanced down at her small hand resting on his arm. Heat was seeping through his clothes, desire already tightening his loins—and *that* with just her hand. He didn't understand why she had such a volatile effect on him, but he understood that he wanted her. He wanted her in every way it was possible to want a woman—by his side, in his bed, warm and willing in his arms. And to accomplish that he was prepared to do the first irrational thing he had done since he had first laid eyes on her.

'Very well. My concern for your safety goes beyond the handful of witch hunters. Atkins is at the White Hart, hoping to raise public fury to the point that a mob might be stirred up to seize you and hang you out of hand, thus resolving the problem of having a witch in their midst. As much as I would like to have him run out of Avery, he has done no wrong and Justice Littleton will not hear of it. Atkins's very presence threatens you, Jane. I would like to know you are safe.'

He stood before her, tall and powerful, his face austere.

Knowing he was right, Jane found no worthy retort to offer. 'Then what can I do?'

Prey to a desire stronger than reason, he fixed her with burning eyes. 'Since you won't leave Avery, I'd like to offer a solution to the problem. There is a way you can return to Bilborough where you can live out the rest of your life in safety.'

The dark eyes under the disturbingly intelligent forehead were suspicious. 'But how? How can I do that?'

'I am not usually a man of hasty decision when it concerns a lasting relationship, Jane, but I am asking you to marry me. Return to Bilborough as my wife.'

He was moving towards her as he spoke, drawn irresistibly by her beauty. Jane stared rigidly at him in disbelief, momentarily lost for words. He looked so cool and dispassionate, and completely self-assured. She wondered what had made him offer such a drastic solution to her problem and was not feeling particularly complimented by his offer.

'I see!' she replied caustically, feeling more hurt and degraded than she cared to admit. If she married this man, then she would be mistress of Bilborough Hall, in her rightful place—and that was all she had ever wanted, but at what price to herself? Her ravaged pride rebelled at the thought.

Any self-respecting woman would have turned from the man who had stolen her home and reviled him for it. But that wasn't what she had done, Jane thought with bitter self-revulsion. No, indeed. With no preparation for an attractive man working on her emotions, she had used all her female powers of persuasion to get under his skin, and he had tried seducing her in turn. She had been taken in by him, had liked being with him and had lowered her guard and allowed him to soften her with conversation and kind words—worse, encouraged it and even invited him to kiss her and touch her, enjoying the things he had done to her, when she should have been repelled at being handled by a man whose very name was associated with her downfall.

'Coming from you, I find your proposal quite outrageous. You cannot be serious.'

'I am perfectly serious. Why is it outrageous?'

She was amazed by his question, but determined to discuss the matter calmly and frankly. 'Because I don't want to marry you.' Even as she issued that statement, it was beginning to ring a note of insincerity in her own mind.

Francis's eyes hardened. 'Perhaps you should think about it before you make any hasty decisions.'

'I don't need to think about it. You must have a poor opinion of me if you think I can be bought so cheaply. I won't marry you.'

Francis considered her a moment before he said, 'Cheaply? Oh, no, Jane. For you, marriage to me would be advantageous indeed. Although, it could prove beneficial to us both.'

'It could? How?'

'Your life is in danger. You need protection and somewhere to live that is safe. I can defend you. Under my protection there isn't a man in Avery who would dare threaten you.'

'Thank you for your concern,' she said tightly, 'but I'd rather not inconvenience you. I can live without your protection.'

'Come now, you cannot even leave the house without Isaac to accompany you. If you marry me, you will be able to live at Bilborough Hall. It will be your home.' He smiled. 'You see, Jane, I'm not completely selfish.'

'And you? How will marriage to me benefit you? What will you get out of it?'

Jane was so humiliated by his reference to her plight that it took a moment for what he said next to register.

'I want a son.'

She was so surprised that she stared at him in disbelief. 'A son?' she echoed. 'You want *me* to give you a *son*?'

'Marry me and give me a son, and in return Bilborough Hall will be your home again.'

Chapter Eight

Jane continued to stare at him, finding it impossible to believe what he had asked of her, that he wanted a son. Perhaps beneath his cool and unemotional façade his life was as empty as hers was and he needed her. But then again, perhaps she was fooling herself. Her lips curved in a wry and bitter smile.

'At least you're not asking me to marry you for my money.'

'It would not be a fitting prelude to a marriage that is to be entered into for cold monetary reasons and no other, Jane. You do like children?'

'Of course, and I long for children of my own.'

'Then at least we have that in common. Apart from wanting a son, there are other reasons why I want to make you my wife.'

Jane's disconcerting dark brown eyes gazed into his. 'I know you are a wealthy man, Francis, and in these uncertain times you cannot be asking me to marry you to gain social position and power.'

'And if times were different and King Charles was still on the throne, would you marry for one of those reasons?'

'No,' she replied. 'I would not. I will marry because I love someone, and am loved in return. I will not settle for any other kind of marriage.'

The softly spoken words had been filled with such quiet conviction that Francis simply stared at her before he finally sighed. She looked so beautiful, so young, that the armour of cynicism that had surrounded him all of his adult life began to melt, leaving him feeling very much alone.

'I think,' he said softly, 'that it will be more a question of whether you will ever be safe. You see, you need me rather badly, although you don't yet realise it.'

'I don't need anyone, and are you really as cold and heartless as your proposition makes you sound? You have asked me to be your wife as if you were discussing a common business arrangement—without feeling or emotion. I appreciate the sincerity of your proposal, but my answer is no, Francis, I cannot accept such an offer. I will not marry you.'

Francis's face hardened and he fell back a step. 'I do not ask you to make up your mind this instant, Jane. Think on my offer carefully before you decide.'

'I don't need to. I will never forget how tormented I have been ever since I became aware that my home had been taken from me and sold to you. You cannot imagine how I have craved revenge—and now you have the audacity to ask for my hand in marriage as if what you have done can be ignored.'

'Jane,' he countered, his mien softer now. 'My mother was the daughter of a staunch Royalist, but my father did not hold it against her. I have friends who fought on the opposing side. They did their duty as they conceived it must be done. But I know well that they bear me no personal animosity. Things were strained, I admit that, but at the end of the day we are all Englishmen wanting naught but the best for our country.'

His words were words of reason, but Jane was not prepared to listen to such calming talk. 'I hear what you say, but for myself I cannot feel the same.'

'Why will you not listen?' Francis exclaimed angrily, combing his hair back from his forehead with his fingers in frustration. 'Forget your opinion of me.'

'I cannot,' she cried passionately. 'How can you be so arrogant to believe that I would fall at your feet in gratitude after all you have done to me? Yes, I want to return to my home, but I will not tie myself for the rest of my life to the man who took it from me and has done nothing to ply me with a promise of love or devotion, a man who wants to make me his wife for no other reason than to give him a son. Please don't ask me again. You will be wasting your time.'

So saying, she turned on her heel and began walking quickly back to the house. It was a difficult moment for her. Knowing he was following her, she wanted to maintain an air of cool disdain, to walk away from him with calm defiance and her head held high, but her mauled pride and an aching distrust of the future assailed her senses. Momentarily blinded by a rush of tears, she stumbled on the hem of her gown. A supportive hand came to her aid. Long fingers grasped her elbow and held her firmly until she regained her balance.

Francis leaned forwards so his face was very close to hers. 'Why do you run from me? I am not a patient man. When I see something I want I will use any means at my disposal to posses it. And I want you, Jane. I want to protect you. But then, you know that, don't you?'

Jane could not move. His whisper was hypnotic, he was luring her into a trap she could not foresee. 'Don't. Please don't say these things.'

'Why? Do I tempt you,' he asked softly, 'as you tried to tempt me to get me to give you back your home? Can I not tempt you now with Bilborough?' He saw her eyes darken, as if with desire.

'And pleasure,' he went on. 'Can you not imagine the long dark nights of pleasure with me, Jane?'

Furious with herself that she should display such weakness, she raised her chin and found the brilliant blue eyes resting on her with something akin to compassion or pity. It was too much to bear.

'Please remove your hand,' she said meekly.

Francis's hand slipped away and he stopped and watched her go, surprised and more than a little disappointed by her response. A proposal of marriage from a man as rich and as powerful as he was would surely have overwhelmed a young woman in such dire straits with surprise and delight. But that such an offer would be rejected so positively and spiritedly stunned him. He set off after her and, drawing level, took her arm and halted her, forcibly turning her round to face him.

His eyes were brittle. 'Forgive me if I sounded *businesslike*, Jane, but my proposal was well meant. And, yes, I do want a son, but I am not entirely heartless. I would be equally as proud should the child be of the opposite gender. Think about it. You could do far worse. After all, what have you to offer—apart from your own charming self?'

Angry tears of humiliation stung Jane's eyes. 'What you say is true. I have nothing to offer any man—and for that I blame you.'

'Jane.' His voice was flat, hard and biting. 'Accept things as they are.'

'Never,' she cried fiercely. 'I will never accept it. I cannot.' In her anger and frustration she lashed out and struck his chest with her clenched fist.

'Enough, Jane,' he bade sharply as he pulled her body towards him.

His embrace tightened and she lay against him, gasping for

breath. His mouth swooped down upon hers, twisting, hurting, his tongue thrusting through her lips, searing, moving, possessing her. Jane struggled weakly against him, trying to summon some logic from the confusion in her mind, but unable to do so. Pleasure battled with her will. The crush of his lips on hers, his iron-thewed arms holding her pressed to his hard frame felt almost comforting, and she was answering, not fighting any more, growing warm.

As suddenly as Francis had clasped her to him he released her and she stumbled free of him. His eyes were puzzled as he stared at her for a moment, then filled with anger. He took her chin between his finger and thumb and forced her to meet his eyes.

'Do you honestly believe you can hide your feelings behind your hostility like a child afraid of being a woman? Continue to fight me if you must, but arm yourself well, Jane, for nothing you may say or do will see you safe from me.' Dropping his hand, he took a step back, but did not relinquish her gaze.

Jane tore her eyes away, hoping to hide the effect he truly had on her. Something had changed between them—or maybe something had changed inside her. Fear rose up within her, not of him, but of herself, for in spite of all the hostile words and accusations she had thrown at him, she wanted to draw him to her, to show him just how much she wanted him, how much of a woman she really was. She struggled to revive her will, but, failing miserably, whirled and ran from him, not pausing until she was back inside the house, hoping and praying he had not seen the naked desire that must have shone in her eyes. Warm confusion came from the haunting sense of pleasure that she felt on just being close to him, and at the thought a hot, searing excitement shot through her body. What spell had Francis cast on her that she should desire him so?

Francis watched her go in silence, his warrior instincts stirred by the depth of his passion for her, his desire to possess and protect her now stronger than ever. He would have gone after her and argued with her, but his short experience with Jane Lucas had taught him to recognise intractable stubbornness when he saw it. He would let her mull on his proposal for now, and once she had got over her repugnance at the idea of marrying a Roundhead, maybe the pull of living in her beloved Bilborough would make her change her mind.

In her anguish Jane could think of nothing but Francis's proposal. He wasn't just any man. To her he had become something else, something special, and he did things to her emotions and her body she did not understand. Her confusion came from the haunting sense of pleasure that he gave her, that every time his visage appeared in her mind's eye her heart beat with a sweet wildness that stirred her very soul.

What spell had he cast upon her that she should desire him so, that if he were here now she would cling to him and beg him to give her that which she yearned? She had never felt so fully a woman as when she was with him, and she was amazed that no shame or guilt rose to condemn her for the kisses they had shared. Could she bear it if he were to disappear from her life completely?

Alarm rose inside her, as if something infinitely special, something elusive, was escaping her. If I never see him again, if I lose him now, I will wither and die, she thought wildly. Scalding tears pricked her eyelids so that everything around her grew hazy. Resolutely she fought them back. In a sharp moment of perception, she knew a loss so strong it seemed to squeeze the breath from her body.

It took her some moments before she could compose herself enough to realise that she should give his proposal some thought, for she could not go on like this.

Jane spent the following morning alone in the surrounding countryside with a basket on her arm. They had few medicines and salves in the cottage and with time on her hands she was collecting useful herbs to begin her own dispensary. Her search took her through a coppice of silver birches, their leaves shimmering in the summer air. The hedgerows and low stone walls were a treasure trove of useful plants: yellow stonecrop, which was helpful for staunching bleeding and to cure ulcers and sores, pink-flowered valerian, useful as a sedative and to sooth the nerves, common sorrel, standing tall against the grass, the yellow-flowered fleabane, which, when dried and burned, gave off a vapour that drove off fleas and many more.

Gradually she worked her way back to the cottage, dropping to her knees occasionally to dig up roots with her little stick. Satisfied with her morning's pickings, she stood and stretched her aching back. As she did so she saw a young woman coming towards her from the direction of the cottage, the brim of her bonnet shielding her face from the sun's rays. A wide smile stretched Jane's lips when she recognised Hester Atkins and she hurried to meet her.

'Hester! How wonderful!' she cried, embracing her warmly. 'But what are you doing here? I never expected you.'

'When I received your letter informing me of your loss of Bilborough, I was shocked and so worried about you that I had to come. Father is away so he could not stop me—besides, I thought you could probably do with a friend. A kindly woman at the Hall—Mrs Preston—told me where to find you.' She glanced at the basket on Jane's arm overflowing with greenery and smiled knowingly. 'Still collecting your plants, I see.'

'But of course, Hester. You should recognise most of them since you accompanied me on my expeditions when I lived with you in Northampton. It also gives me something to do. You must stay at the cottage with me. You can tell me all about Northampton and your sisters. I've missed all of you so much, Hester.'

Linking arms, they headed for home.

'What will you do now, Jane? Of course you could always come back to live with us.'

'No, Hester. I can't do that,' Jane answered quietly. Hester nodded, understanding more than anyone else Jane's reasons for not doing so. 'Colonel Russell—the man who now owns the Bilborough estate—has asked me to marry him.'

Hester stopped walking and stared at her. 'Good gracious! How fortunate. And? Will you?'

Her face expressionless, Jane nodded. 'I have given it much thought since he asked me—and I think that I might very well become his wife.'

'Why, Jane? To return to Bilborough? It will be like a dream come true.'

'Yes—and also,' she murmured, giving vent to her feelings and knowing a soft flush was spreading over her cheeks, 'because I—I believe I am falling in love with him. I have been trying to stop myself, but it's impossible.'

With happiness shining in her eyes for her dear friend, Hester hugged her fiercely. 'But—that's wonderful, but—isn't it all rather sudden? I am astonished.'

'Indeed I cannot believe it myself, and I have much to think about. The worst of it is that he fought against the King during the war—but,' Jane said, remembering the tender moments they had shared, 'he is an honourable man, and if I thought it possible that he harbours some loving thoughts for me, that he could love me above all others, that he would take me in his arms and caress me as a lover would, that he would find me all he should ever want, then I think I would be a devoted and loving wife and put the past behind me.'

'Then if he is an honourable man, and knowing you as I do, Colonel Russell will be unable to resist you. He is a lucky man.'

Jane smiled softly and squeezed Hester's arm affectionately. 'Bless you, Hester.' They walked a little way in silence, broken when she spoke on a sombre note. 'Your father is here in Avery. Did you know?'

Hester's face fell. 'No, but I am not surprised. He will be disappointed that Bilborough no longer belongs to you.'

'That is an understatement. As you know he intended to marry me and claim it for himself—regardless of my wishes—and already he is punishing me for its loss.'

'Punishing you? But it is hardly your fault that it was sequestered—although he will not see it that way and I can imagine how angry he must be. While ever he lives he will never forget, Jane—not this, nor the man who took out his eye. It was done in war, but to my father it was personal.'

'I know. The man who maimed him was Colonel Russell—the same man who now owns Bilborough—the man who has asked me to be his wife.'

'Then the grim reality is that Father will do his twisted best to destroy it all.'

'He's already started. He's determined to destroy us both. Already he is blackening my name in the town—putting it about that I meddle in witchcraft.'

Hester paled, appalled. 'No, Jane, not you. I know Gwen fled Bilborough because of the accusations against her—but you…'

'The worst of it is that people are listening—how long before they believe it and take action?'

* * *

Jane found out the following day when her beloved Scamp was found dead outside the cottage gate. Isaac, his face grim, said he'd been poisoned, for it was the only explanation he could think of for the animal's sudden death—and also the fact that some strange-smelling meat was found nearby and there were traces of vomit around the little dog's mouth, giving truth to his suspicion.

Jane was devastated. When she stared down at her loyal pet's lifeless body, his eyes wide open and glazed, she felt the blood draining from her face. Why would anyone want to poison a harmless, lovable little dog? What harm had he done to anyone?

Trying to come to terms with the pain of losing Scamp, for the next twenty-four hours she was edgy, starting at noises, looking at shadows.

Confused, muddled and frightened, her fears were realised the following morning by the sound of voices and movement outside the cottage. Looking out of the window, she saw a large contingent of people. Squinting into the sun, she couldn't see their faces, nor even tell how many there might be. Only one man was mounted—Jacob Atkins. He hovered beyond the gate at the back of the crowd.

Responding to a loud banging on the door while wiping the palms of her hands on the skirts of her dress, on leaden legs she slowly moved towards it, terrified at the thought of confronting the mob. She glanced at Hester. 'It's your father, Hester. Please stay out of sight. If he sees you here it will only inflame him.'

Hester shrank into the shadows when Jane opened the door. Mr Atkins had come to the front of the crowd and dismounted. Boldly Jane faced the mob, her head raised proudly.

'What do you want?'

Atkins's hand shot out and he grabbed her chin. His fingers dug into her flesh and he forced her to look into his cruel eye. 'Still defiant, Jane? You won't remain so proud. Before they've done with you your wits will have flown. You see,' he told her piously, 'this is what comes of not being sensible. It is your own fault that I have been obliged to do this.' He let go of her.

Jane ignored his taunts, knowing he was trying to frighten her. She kept her stare defiant and controlled, even though she did feel the need to kick his shin. If sheer blind rage could kill, Jacob Atkins would have dropped dead on the spot.

A spokesman stepped forwards and thrust his ugly face close to Jane's. 'You're coming with us.

There was an unmistakable look of gloating on his face and seeing it, the hair on her body rippled with cold. 'Would you mind telling me why? I have done no wrong.' Trying to keep a firm grip on her nerves, her gaze shot to Jacob Atkins. He smiled in the most unpleasant fashion.

'Ah, now, there you are mistaken, Jane,' he said, his voice full of threat. He was aware of the reason why Gwen had fled Bilborough and sought sanctuary in his home—although he had no time for such nonsense and didn't believe in witchcraft anyway. But he was not against using the same methods on her stepdaughter for daring to stand against him, for spurning him. 'We've come to take you into Avery to answer to the serious charge of witchcraft.'

'If Justice Littleton has any questions he wishes to address to me, I will most respectfully respond, but I owe none of you an explanation.'

'We've got to take care of this matter ourselves if we want to see justice done,' someone shouted.

'That's her. That's Jane Lucas—stepdaughter to Gwen Lucas,' a woman's voice called, high and shrill and malevolent from the back of the crowd. 'What woman would do such wickedness as to wantonly poison a woman and her unborn babe but a witch?'

A high shouting of condemnation greeted that. Jane could feel the current of hysteria and violence in the air. In fear and desperation she took a step back, her eyes fixed on Jacob Atkins. 'Can you not see that what you're doing is foolish? Can you not realise the futility of your revenge against me and Francis?'

Atkins's face darkened and, with a scornful curl to his thin lips, he said, 'Don't waste your breath, and don't think I can be so easily swayed from my intentions, for in spite of the revulsion I feel at you and him together, I shall learn to overcome it. As far as I am concerned nothing has changed—only that Francis Russell has one more thing to lose that will make my revenge sweeter.'

Jane shrank back, for the man before her was a stranger and the single eye that bored into hers was that of a madman, and she knew, with a sinking heart, that this was indeed what he was, for only a madman would behave this way.

'You are out of your mind. You have lost your senses. Leave Avery before you regret your actions.'

'Regret?' He laughed insanely. 'I shall regret nothing I do where Russell is concerned.'

Jane swallowed hard. 'Then there's nothing else to be said. You have descended into the very realms of evil so you know nothing else.'

Atkins stepped away from her when a heavy man with cropped dark hair and a greasy leather jerkin reached out and seized her arm in a vice-like grip and jerked her forwards, dragging her towards a wagon.

'Let go,' she cried. 'What are you doing?'

She kicked out at him and attempted to drag herself free, but he got hold of both her wrists. He shouted for help, and several eager hands hauled her up inside, where someone tied her wrists behind her back.

'Where are you taking me?' she demanded.

'The gaol,' Atkins said, with a note of grim satisfaction. 'And then, thank God, you'll get what you deserve.'

She stared at him in defiance. 'Not until I have been tried. I have faith in Justice Littleton and English justice.'

Atkins laughed maliciously. 'Just wait until you've experienced it. I can guarantee the examiners will not be gentle with you, Jane. Far from it.'

Jane shot a look at Isaac in the doorway. He was stiff and staring and deeply ashamed because he was unable to help the mistress in the hands of the mob. At that moment Jane could think of only one person who could help her. 'Find Francis, Isaac. Tell him what's happened—I beg of you… He'll know what to do.'

'Much good he'll do you,' Atkins growled, mounting his horse.

Jane hated being helpless in many ways, but the armour of righteous fury was wearing off, and while she kept a fierce face for Jacob Atkins, he knew she was afraid. Not without reason, either. He was not stupid. And clearly he realised that his strategy of spreading gossip and scandal concerning her in order to endanger her had worked.

As the mob made their way to Avery with their captive in their midst, Hester came to stand beside Isaac on the doorstep. His lips were clamped together, but strangely Hester was calm.

'We'll do as she asked and go and see Colonel Russell, Isaac. Try not to worry. Everything will be all right. Jane will come to no harm. We'll think of something.'

By the time Jane reached the courthouse she was holding on to her temper and sanity by a thread. With her wrists tightly bound, she was completely drained from the sheer physical exertion of trying to remain upright in the wagon as it jolted over the rutted road.

Her cell beneath the courthouse was small, the walls beaded with damp and the straw on the floor foul. When the door banged closed on the world outside, that was the moment when she began to fully comprehend the ramifications of what was happening.

Her wrists had been untied and she rubbed at the flesh where the bindings had cut deep. Earlier she had not been able to think straight for anger; now there was fear of the evil being planned against her, that she might not have the energy or the strength to fight. She sagged against the wall. Already she had faced public humiliation, and now possibly death because of Jacob Atkins's spite.

Her thoughts turned to Hester and Isaac and how worried they would be, but gradually their images faded to make way for another, this one with deep blue eyes and a haunting smile. Francis would not be smiling when they told him what had become of her. Imagining how he would react made her tremble and gave her courage. However much she had insulted him, and whatever else he was, at her darkest of moments, Francis was a strong, unwavering gleam of hope for her to cling to in this, her darkest hour.

The light was fading when the bolts on the door were pulled back. Pushing herself up from the pallet Jane bit her lip to stop it trembling, loath to show any sign of weakness. A man with a long face and a lantern jaw stepped into the cell. It was Justice Littleton. He was neatly attired in a fur-trimmed robe and velvet cap. He had been a good friend of her father's. He was also a dour Puritan, but he was a fair man.

'Mr Littleton, I'm so glad to see you. I do hope you can clear up this misunderstanding. In the eyes of the law I have done no wrong.'

'I'm just as upset about this as you are, Mistress Lucas. Originally there was no intent to arrest you, but you were taken because of your association with your stepmother, Gwen Lucas. There are those who suspect you of practising witchcraft.'

'And I tell you it is utter nonsense. I am not my stepmother.'

'No, but in the light of Mr Atkins's accusations against you—and the evidence he has that could incriminate you—there is some danger to you. There are some people in Avery who remain loyal to your father and have no desire to see you examined on the charge of witchcraft, and those who shout the loudest are those whipped up by Mr Atkins's rantings. I remember him of old and I hadn't much time for him then. He is not like his sister.'

'No, not at all.'

'It is unfortunate that she made herself unpopular. The climate of opinion in Avery is none too favourable to you at present. There is a certain amount of hysteria driving those who believe you are guilty. It has been claimed that you have a dog—a familiar—and that on occasion it has been seen to…to…'

Jane elevated an eyebrow. 'What, Mr Littleton? What has my dog been seen to do?'

He appeared flustered suddenly and wiped his perspiring brow with his handkerchief. 'Why—to—to lick you, as though he were…'

'Sucking me? Dear me. I think I know where that damning information has come from,' she uttered drily, thinking that Alice Merton's association with Mr Atkins must be closer than she realised. 'It is utter rubbish, of course, and for your information, Mr Littleton, my dog was poisoned yesterday.'

'I'm sorry—I didn't know, but it proves nothing. You must understand that people are suspicions of such things.'

'People are always suspicious of things they don't understand.'

'I am sure you are right, but I would like the atmosphere to die down before you are tried.'

Jane went cold. 'Tried? I am going to be tried?'

'I'm afraid so. I cannot ignore what I have been presented with. I would not be doing my duty if I were to do that. However, if you were to be tried in this present climate, there is a danger of the evidence being disregarded for the sake of satisfying the lust for blood. The longer it is drawn out, the less inclined anyone will be to act in haste.'

Lust for blood? Jane paled. Those three words captured exactly the emotion emanating from the faces of the crowd when she had been brought in to Avery. Some had shown signs of sympathy and doubt, but it would be a brave man who would dare to stand against the majority.

'It would appear that common sense has taken flight before the onslaught of fear and prejudice,' she uttered firmly. 'Where is the justice in that? My father was a revered and respected landowner in this town who all his life lived in honour, whereas, during the years of conflict, Mr Atkins gained a name for savagery. For the short time he spent in Avery there were several cases of his brutality. Ask Colonel Russell. He will confirm that.'

'Your father, John Lucas, was an exceptional man. We may not have seen eye to eye over the years, but he was a man of honour.' He turned towards the door. 'For your own safety you must remain where you are. In the meantime I shall speak to Mr Atkins.' With a curt nod he went out.

Jane's heart sank when she heard the key turn in the lock and she shuddered at the thought of spending the night in that vermin-infested hole. She sank down on to the pallet, her head dropping into her hands as the hopelessness of her situation overcame her.

Gradually the cell darkened. From the depths of her cell, she heard laughter; in fact, the voices sounded unusually joyful. She reflected bitterly that it was probably her imminent trial that they were happy about. She remembered all too vividly the jeers and cries of hate that had followed her to the gaol, and yet, on reflection, she had seen a few friendly faces, and some who had glanced uncertainly at their neighbours and measured Jacob Atkins with doubtful eyes.

Stunned by fear and fatigue, she collapsed on to the pallet and slept the sleep of a hunted animal.

When she woke it took her a moment to convince herself that she wasn't trapped in some bad dream, but as she emerged from the mists of sleep, memories of the previous day's events came back in all their dreadful clarity.

It was mid-morning when she heard footsteps approaching the door. When she heard the key turn in the lock she got dizzily to her feet. The door opened and Francis was there with Justice Littleton. Justice Littleton had been in the courthouse meeting with several aldermen. They were concerned about the arrest of Jane Lucas—no one had been tried for witchcraft in Avery for five years. He had left when Colonel Russell arrived demanding to speak to him and to be allowed to see to the prisoner.

Francis had arrived back at Bilborough after spending the night at his brother's house. Alice had been present and much of what she'd had to say had been about Jane and made no sense. Alice had told him in detail of her conversation with Jane when she had called on her the morning after the fire. She referred back to the time he had spent in Avery as Atkins's prisoner, sympathising at the treatment meted out to him and going on to say how fortunate it was that someone had gone to his aid and made it possible for him to escape from the vestry in the church where he was being held.

Francis was perplexed. How did Jane know that? How could she? He had told no one that he had been imprisoned in the church. Only one person knew the details of his escape and that person was Tom since he was the one who had made it possible. No matter how hard he had thought he could make no sense of it.

To clear his head he had walked to the paddock. Resting his arms on the fence and watching Arthur grazing across the paddock, he recalled how he had stood and watched Jane that day when they had ridden Arthur together. He remembered how she had looked, how the breeze had toyed with her hair, and how animated her expression had been. He remembered the moment when she had turned in his direction—and her face became frozen in his mind.

Suddenly it hit him why she was so familiar. 'Tom!' He had said it out loud. 'Good Lord!' Why hadn't he seen it before? The black hair framing the creamy visage, eyes as dark as two shining blackberries, the soft and sensitive lips. Even with the undisguised fullness of womanhood, the features were unmistakably Tom's.

A chuckle started deep in his chest. 'Well, I'll be damned.'

As quickly as it had come, the moment of amused astonishment had left him. From the moment he'd laid eyes on her he had known she was familiar, but when he had returned to Avery to thank the one person responsible for making possible his escape, he had been looking for a flat-chested lad with short cropped hair—who was not a lad, he had just discovered, but a girl, an untried girl with a spirit he'd admired and honoured, a spirit that had not been broken by whatever had happened to her since. The girl who had risked her life to save his had become a full-grown woman—a woman who now had just cause to despise him and to regret what she had done for him that day.

He was enlightened by this new-found knowledge, but found he didn't quite know how to deal with it, for Jane must know who he was and for some odd reason wanted to keep it to herself.

When a distraught Hester and Isaac had arrived and given him an account of Jane's arrest and imprisonment, he was engulfed with a fury such as he had never known. His visage grim, he had lost no time in heading for Avery, for he was not prepared to wait for the culmination of Atkins's sadistic plans for Jane. Jane's plight shocked him more than he cared to admit, and the thought of her in some stinking cell shocked him to the core.

Jane saw Justice Littleton say something to Francis, heard the deep half-audible answer, and she felt something that had been knotted inside her for a long time release itself at the sound of Francis's voice. At the sight of him her relief made her weak in both her knees and her senses. He stood for a second, looking at her. Then, very slowly, he moved towards her. He towered above her, and when she looked up at him she thought she had never seen him look so tall—or so pale. Or was his pallor and those deep lines at the corners of his mouth due to some trick of the light? He was wearing a plain brown jerkin over his white linen shirt, and as far as she could see he was not armed. She felt her blood pounding in her temples. Taking her hands, he drew her close, searching her face.

Seeing her in such distress tore at Francis's heart, but not so much that he had not already assessed the situation fully. The evidence brought against her by Atkins was flimsy. It was unlikely she would be tried for witchcraft.

'Jane. Are you all right? Are you hurt?'

She shook her head, touched by his concern. After all her

angry words on their last encounter, and the way she had thrown his marriage proposal back in his face, he had not abandoned her. 'I knew you'd come,' she whispered. 'I—I hoped you would.'

He looked into her face. 'How could I not? I'm only sorry it's taken me so long. I was not at home when Hester came to the hall. I was staying with Richard and Elizabeth. I only got back this morning. I had left men guarding the cottage, but they were outnumbered by the mob.'

Shivering inwardly from the gruesomeness of her situation, she said, 'I'm sorry if you've been inconvenienced, but I—I didn't know who else I could turn to. It would seem that everyone in Avery hates me.'

'Only those who have been taken in by Atkins.'

'They—they poisoned Scamp. Did you know?' She spoke softly, her eyes awash with tears of grief and anguish.

He nodded. 'Isaac told me. I'm sorry, Jane. I know how much you loved that dog. You did right to send for me.' Behind him, Justice Littleton coughed and Francis turned, his features grim. 'I regret that you have taken Mistress Lucas into custody. Is it correct that Jacob Atkins had her forcibly taken from her house?'

'Mr Atkins insisted that he was being a good citizen and was concerned about the possibility of Mistress Lucas being involved in witchcraft and what dangers the people of Avery were in.'

'Atkins has nothing better to do than cause whatever trouble he can. Since when did Atkins—a man who does not live in this town—acquire the position of authority to enforce the law in Avery?' Francis demanded, trying to contain his fury. 'Does it not strike you as odd that he has taken it upon himself to represent every member of the community?'

'Mr Atkins was Gwen Lucas's brother who therefore considers himself a good authority on the matter. He has revealed that on her deathbed, his sister confessed her guilt to the crime of witchcraft, and that Mistress Lucas was involved. Mr Atkins considered it his duty that she be delivered into the hands of the authorities to be examined.'

Unable to believe what he was saying, Jane gasped. 'That is not true. Gwen said no such thing. I was with her to the end—as was Mr Atkins's eldest daughter Hester. He is lying. There was no confession.'

Francis's eyes hardened imperceptibly as he stared at Justice Littleton. 'You alone have control over the custody and disposition of any prisoners, and Mistress Lucas has been in your custody long enough. You therefore have also the power to release her.'

'I do, but to make such a decision may complicate a situation and make it more difficult while tempers are so inflamed.'

'She has not been committed for trial, and, in fact, there is no evidence whatever against her,' Francis stated firmly.

'Mr Atkins has made accusations against her and insists she must be examined for heresy. She must be investigated.'

'To hell with Atkins,' Francis fumed. 'There is no merit to the charge. Along with thousands of other women, Mistress Lucas is a herbalist. She does not practise the black arts. Atkins is acting on purely personal resentment.'

'There is malice against her,' Justice Littleton said levelly. 'For reasons unknown to me the witness dislikes Mistress Lucas. If she is indeed accursed, then it will show in her behaviour.'

'She will not be judged,' Francis uttered angrily. 'I believe in none of this—witches, curses and spells. Witchcraft is the gravest accusation a woman can face. A woman mired in sin, a woman given over to the devil—I have seen women accused of such take ordeals where strong men have turned away sickened. If that is what Atkins wants for Mistress Lucas, then I will see him in hell first. What does he hope for—to see her swim, or to see her burn? The man gained a name for savagery and looting in the early days of the war, and dealt his own kind of brutal justice to those who opposed him. Surely, having known Mistress Lucas's father, and having her acquaintance for the time that you have, you will have drawn your own conclusions as to her character?'

Mr Littleton had narrowed his eyes, and appeared to be thinking intently. 'Your arguments are not entirely without merit, sir,' he said with formal courtesy, his gaze falling on the prisoner. 'Yet I find it strange that as her stepmother's brother, who gave you shelter when you left Bilborough, Mr Atkins has brought the charge of witchcraft against you. However, the crime of which Mistress Lucas stands accused is of a serious nature. For me to release her must necessarily cause public outcry—and I would prefer to avoid public unrest.'

'I quite understand your reservations,' Francis agreed fairly. 'Perhaps some form of surety might be offered, which would overcome them?'

Mr Littleton bristled, more than a little offended. 'What do you suggest, sir? Do you have the impertinence to try to *bribe* me?'

'I had no intent,' Francis said, keeping his voice level, his eyes direct. 'What I offer is my word that Mistress Lucas will not leave Bilborough until this matter is cleared up.'

'And how will you do that? Mistress Lucas no longer lives at Bilborough.'

'She will. For her own safety I shall offer her my protection. She will reside with me at the Hall. I give you my word that there she will remain. When you have found out what you want to know, if you need to question her I shall provide her with a good defence lawyer.'

'Pardon me,' Jane interrupted gently. 'I have no need of a

lawyer. My innocence and good faith should be defence enough. I have not committed any of the crimes of which I have been charged.'

'That still remains to be proved.' Justice Littleton looked from Francis to Jane and then back to Francis, rubbing a finger slowly across his upper lip, considering.

Jane's pulse was beating fast while she waited. She was trying to think logically about the situation, as a means of distracting herself from the crushing disappointment that Justice Littleton might not agree to Francis's offer, that Francis might go away and leave her in that awful place. For an overwhelming instant she thought she could not bear it.

Francis glanced at her and caught a glimpse of her face. He put out a hand and gripped her forearm. 'Calm yourself, Jane,' he said softly.

Justice Littleton cast a wary look at them both, before his eyes became fixed on Jane and he studied her once more. Her beautiful face was framed in a halo of dark hair. It was a soft beauty that stirred even his cynical heart. He looked at Francis.

'I am not a stupid man, Colonel Russell. The accusations against Mistress Lucas are unlikely in my mind, but that does not mean to say that I do not believe in witches. I do,' he said fairly and with complete matter-of-fact seriousness. 'I have known some, when I was the magistrate at the Sessions held in Cambridge some years ago. Two women—they were both condemned. I just do not believe Mistress Lucas is one. She does not look capable of such wickedness. Assisting her stepmother in poisoning a woman—if that is indeed what happened—'

'She was innocent,' Jane objected fiercely. 'I swear she was.'

Justice Littleton regarded her with thin-lipped disdain. 'Then why did she run away? As I was saying, assisting a person in harming another is a serious crime that cannot be acted upon without proof. There is little chance of Mistress Lucas being brought to trial in any sort of timely manner—if at all—in which case I shall agree to your offer. Perhaps it would be better to wait until dark before you leave. It will be safer then.'

'I shall go now,' Jane retorted, stepping closer to Francis. 'I have done no wrong. I shall not hide.'

'Very well, if that is what you want. It just so happens we have a villain in the pillory who is attracting a good deal of interest—so maybe you will be able to get away without being apprehended. Did you bring anyone with you?'

'Just another horse for Mistress Lucas.' Seeing the tension in her strained features, Francis took her hand and squeezed it reassuringly. 'Do not be afraid. No harm will come to you while you are with me.'

Chapter Nine

They were making their way to the front of the Court House, where Francis had tethered two horses when they found themselves confronted by Atkins. He stepped out of the shadows. Two burly men hovered at the back of him.

'Colonel Russell? And where are you taking the prisoner?'

Francis's eyes turned icy with the loathing he bore the other man. 'She is not under arrest. She has committed no crime and you know it. Stand out of our way, Atkins,' he said with calm deliberation, 'and go back to Northampton.'

Atkins faced his old adversary with all the hostility and antagonism that this man had aroused in him from the moment he had taken the sight of one of his eyes. They had fought actively in the Civil War, both escaping violent death by the narrowest of margins, seeing their fellow countrymen captured and slaughtered and an England crumbling around them into ruin. They had seen sights they would never forget for as long as they lived, but for this moment they could forget it all and stare at each other with deep loathing, the greater issues giving place to an instinct as primeval and as animal, which drives two stags to fight come spring.

'I thought you'd try something like this,' Atkins hissed. 'As you see, I have taken precautions.' He made a gesture with his arm to the men behind him. 'Return Mistress Lucas to the gaol before I have her forcibly taken back.'

'On what charge?'

'Witchcraft—which you know well enough. She was condemned by my sister on her deathbed, when she confessed all.'

'Jane was with her to the end. There was no confession.'

'She's a liar.'

Francis's eyes hardened. 'You are the liar, Atkins. The lady whom you have so callously slandered is to be my wife, and you should know me well enough by now to guess that I am not partial to having anything taken from me by force, especially when it's something I treasure.'

Atkins's brows shot up. 'Your wife?'

'You heard, so you see, Atkins, you are in no position to insist on anything. I am taking Mistress Lucas to Bilborough.'

'How very cosy,' Atkins jeered.

A cold shiver of dread had settled on Jane's chest and she was almost paralysed by fright, but she had a reflex of self-defiance, and before Francis could answer, she had stepped forwards. 'For God's sake, stop this cruel game. Haven't you caused enough misery? Does it not occur to you how hateful and unjust all this is?'

Looking at her, Francis thought she had never looked more beautiful. The silver rays of the sun stretching out across the sky touched her hair and set the dark strands aglow, the soft grey of her high-necked gown created a soft and lovely setting for her delicate beauty. Her striking comeliness caused the onlookers to debate the wisdom of Mr Atkins, for it was clearly evident that this was no raving wicked witch, only a pale and frightened young woman.

Taking her arm, Francis drew her away towards the horses. 'Come, Jane. Let us be away from here.'

'Return her to the gaol before I make you,' Atkins demanded, refusing to let all his scheming come to nought.

'You're welcome to try,' Francis challenged. 'But if you harm either of us, you will be risking getting yourself locked up.' Having reached the horses, he released the first from the post to which it was tethered.

Atkins sneered. 'I'm sure my men will be anxious to help.'

'Do they do everything you say?' Francis probed.

'Always,' Atkins boasted. 'I have no doubts concerning their loyalty.'

When Francis turned his back on him, totally ignoring him and his henchmen while he assisted Jane up into the saddle, Atkins thrust a hand inside his coat and brought out a thin-bladed knife. On turning, too late Francis glimpsed the evil glint of the knife being drawn back to strike a death blow. Jane screamed as Francis went reeling backward, but he did not fall. He grabbed for his shoulder with his gloved hand as blood oozed from the wound down over his arm and chest. He grinned evilly and, unhindered by the wound, knocked the knife from Atkins's grip. It clattered to the ground and Francis placed his boot on it when Atkins bent to retrieve it.

'Leave it,' Francis hissed, 'if you value your life.'

With a cry of horror, Jane slipped from the horse's back.

Having witnessed the incident, before Atkins's henchmen could move to finish what Atkins had started, a furious Mr Littleton with two of the gaolers stepped between them.

'Mr Atkins, enough, I say.'

'Damn you, Atkins,' Francis hissed, fixing his gaze contemptuously on his old adversary. 'I could kill you for what you've done, but I am not a murderer. Lock him up, Justice Littleton,' he ordered, as Atkins's henchmen shrank into the shadows and disappeared. 'This man assaulted me without provocation and for that I demand that you arrest him.'

Atkins was white-faced and visibly shaking with savage temper. 'Like hell you will.'

'Perhaps the time spent kicking your heels in that stinking gaol to which you consigned Mistress Lucas while you await trial for attempted murder will make you rue the day you ever set foot in Avery. You have long believed yourself to be above the law and you may live beyond this day, Atkins, but I warn you. If the powers that be see fit to release you, you will leave Avery, otherwise I won't rest until I've seen your carcass buried in a slime pit. You are now the hunted. You have ceased to be the hunter.'

Justice Littleton gestured to the gaolers. 'Arrest Mr Atkins,' he ordered. 'Lock him up.'

The gaolers took Atkins's arms and dragged him, protesting loudly, towards the gaol. Inwardly he seethed. All of his plans, his revenge, were falling into ruin around him. But he gathered the last of his strength as he was dragged away and shouted, 'You're a traitor, Jane Lucas. A traitor.'

Jane was dazed and feeling sick. The shock of seeing Francis reel when Jacob Atkins had lunged at him with the knife had almost been too much. She turned from the prisoner's departing figure without so much as a pitying glance. She was satisfied that he would pay for the crimes against herself. Yet her satisfaction was marred by the fact that he had attempted to kill Francis and almost succeeded.

Justice Littleton turned to Francis, who was clutching his wounded chest with his gloved hand. 'Atkins is in no position to trouble anybody for some time. Go home and get that tended.'

'It's nothing,' Francis said with confidence. 'A flesh wound—nothing more serious than that.'

Jane immediately withdrew Francis's hand from his wound and, opening his shirt, examined it. He winced slightly as her gentle fingers touched his torn flesh.

'Justice Littleton's right. We must get you home. The wound isn't deep, but it needs cleaning.'

He managed a grin. 'I'll go willingly, Jane, as long as you promise to tend it yourself.'

And so Jane found herself riding out of Avery at Francis's side. She was not afraid of Jacob Atkins any more. Since Francis had held her and kissed her and asked her to be his wife, she had lost every scrap of fear she had ever known. He would be her husband. He had just saved her from a dire fate and would transport her back to Bilborough and teach her the joy of marital bliss and fulfilment as a woman. As she rode beside him towards Bilborough Hall, which because of him she would be able to call home once more, there was a warmth and lightness about her as if she would never fail to fear anything ever again.

Francis rode easily, but he continued to hold his chest where Jacob Atkins's knife had penetrated the flesh. He said nothing, and her woman's instinct warned that he was far too proud to admit to the pain it caused him, especially to her. The knowledge of his fierce pride and strength warmed her in a deep and unfamiliar manner.

Jane's release from gaol was greeted with great relief and excitement at Bilborough Hall. Hester's heart was sore. How close her dear friend had come to being charged with witchcraft, how close she had come to paying the ultimate price for a crime of which she was completely innocent—a charge trumped up by

Hester's own father. How she hated him. How she wished he were dead so he could hurt them no more.

'Thank the merciful heavens you're safe,' she said as she embraced Jane. 'I've been nearly beside myself, not knowing if Colonel Russell would find you dead or in what condition you'd be.'

'I have suffered no harm that a hot bath and some decent food won't put right, Hester,' Jane assured her. 'The same cannot be said of your father. He has been arrested for attacking Colonel Russell.'

Hester accepted her father's arrest without emotion. 'I see. Then if he is locked up he will be unable to harm anyone else. I shall go into Avery to see him. In the meantime I think Colonel Russell is in need of attention.'

Jane turned her attention to the wounded man, and no one noticed when Hester slipped quietly from the hall.

Leaving Bilborough behind, Hester strolled through fields and followed hedgerows fragrant and lush with cow parsley, Sweet Cicely, celandine and wild celery. But it was none of these that she sought. Shading her eyes from the sun's glare, she paused now and then, peering into undergrowth thick with nettles until at last she found what she was seeking.

It was a sticky, hairy plant that was found scattered throughout the land. It had stout stems and leaves with large teeth. It had pretty, long spiky flowers, the petals yellow with violet veins. But its attractiveness was deceptive, for this plant was called henbane—also called Devil's eye—often used in small doses as a sedative to help relieve a variety of afflictions. Given in large quantities it was deadly poison.

Picking a large bunch, she placed it in her basket and, light of heart, sauntered back to the house. When she had dealt with the plants as Gwen had shown her how to and she had poured the end product into a jar, she would walk into Avery, to the gaol, to visit her father.

Jane looked at the blood oozing through Francis's shirt. 'Francis, allow me to dress your wound before you bleed to death.' She looked at Mary, whose alarm-filled eyes were fixed on the wounded man. 'I don't think it's serious, Mary, but the wound needs to be cleansed. Please fetch me some hot water and clean dressings, and ask one of the maids to prepare me a bath.' She smiled at Francis. 'I know I should bathe first, but I'm sure you won't mind the stench of the prison while I tend your wound. I can't in all conscience leave it to fester while I languish in my bath.'

'Do you think I have not smelled worse? Besides, I consider myself fortunate to have such a skilled healer to tend me.'

'As to that, we shall have to wait and see. I can only hope it will not fester. It is the very least I can do, for if it were not for you, I would still be in gaol and you would not have been wounded.' And so she squared her shoulders, drew a deep breath, and reminded herself that Gwen had taught her how to tend wounds, and this was not the first time she had been called on to use her skills. 'I shall do what Gwen has trained me to do. I would do the same for any man, woman or child in need of help.'

The fact that he was Francis Russell mattered to her not at all—at least, not until she found herself alone in a room with him and he put his back to the closed door. His brooding gaze sought hers across the room and suddenly the fact that he was Francis Russell did indeed matter, very much. Being alone with him was worse than unwise, it was downright dangerous. To her chagrin, she found she was unable to speak or breathe or look away. Damn him for the way he could so easily turn her composure to melted butter. She needed to think and to endeavour to gather her wits about her. She needed to steady her heart.

'Where would you like me to sit?' Francis asked softly, his eyes not having left her face for a moment.

Dragging her gaze away from the bloodied fabric of his shirt, Jane looked around the room. 'Over here,' she managed to say finally, 'close to the table, where I can have the bowl and dressings to hand.'

He did as she asked, unbuttoning his shirt as he crossed to the chair.

'What are you doing?' she asked.

He peered at her, his dark brows raised. 'Surely if you are to treat my wound, you cannot do so through my garment.' His eyes held a devilish gleam. 'Unless my nakedness unnerves you,' he enquired soberly, as if that were perfectly acceptable.

Jane bit her lip and weighed the awkwardness of having him naked against the difficulty of trying to tend him with his shirt on. 'No—of course not. Of course you must remove your shirt. I will help you,' she said when he winced on trying to pass it over his head, endeavouring to sound brusque and efficient, rather than reveal her true state of apprehension and feeling strange inside.

She moved close, close enough to feel the heat of him and his breath on her neck as she helped him remove the blood-soaked garment. It was a slow and laborious task as she helped him slide it over his head, but eventually he was free of it and was left standing before her, naked from the waist up. As innocent as she was, Jane was woman enough to deduce the sudden heaviness of his breathing was not entirely due to the pain of removing his shirt. He was as disturbed by their nearness as she was—she saw it in the heat of his eyes.

Though there was an ugly wound above his right breast that

continued to bleed slowly, she could only see his wide chest and the smooth, curving slopes of his muscles. She knew he was looking at her, but she dare not meet his gaze.

She stepped away from him while he sat in the chair, relieved when Mary appeared at that moment carrying a bowl of hot water and clean dressings and ointments, which she placed on the table beside Jane. Mary bent forwards to peer at the wound and shook her head. 'Deep as it is, it looks clean enough, although it's going to need a stitch or two to close it.' She glanced sideways at the young woman. 'Are you up to it?'

'I am, Mary. It won't be the first wound I have stitched.'

'Then I'll leave you to get on with it while I prepare you some hot water for a bath.' She stepped away from Jane and wrinkled her nose distastefully when the stink of the gaol assailed her. 'I'll get you a needle and thread.'

Trying not to look at Francis, Jane dipped a clean cloth in the warm water and wrung it out. It was necessary for her to stand close to him, and because of the way he was positioned, she was forced to lean against his outstretched thigh. There was a dangerous gleam in his eyes and Jane knew he was thinking about how close she was. She wanted to curse the blood of her bold ancestors that coursed through her veins, rendering her incapable of tamping down her desire.

Taking a deep breath, she proceeded to cleanse the wound. Her touch was gentle as she wiped away the blood, not unduly concerned as it continued to bleed freely. She pretended he was just another person she was treating, one of many she had treated in the past, but the ruse did not work. Touching Francis's warm, naked flesh with her fingers made her feel things no innocent maiden should feel. She could hear his breathing, smell the manly scent of his skin, and see a pulse throbbing in his neck.

'Mary was right, it will need a stitch or two.'

'You could cauterise it,' he suggested matter-of-factly, shrugging when she looked appalled. 'Why not? I've had it done to me before.'

'No, that is the easy way and the most painful.'

'Right. Needle and thread it is then,' he agreed, smiling gently.

Jane was thankful for the rare light-hearted moment, hoping to hide the effect he was having on her. From the moment he had entered the gaol to rescue her, something had changed between them, or maybe it had happened before that, that changes had been taking place inside her from the moment she had laid eyes on him. It would take more to sort out than she could hope to summon just then, with his expression of undisguised interest on his darkly handsome face.

When Mary had brought the needle and thread and left to prepare Jane's bath, after passing the needle through a candle's flame she looked at him. 'This will hurt,' she said, moving closer still to him.

'I've suffered worse,' he replied, his tone warmly reassuring.

She looked at him, conscious as always of an unwitting excitement. Flushing hotly, she bent her head, the movement sending a shiver of sunlight slanting through the window over her bright, dark head. Then, raising her head, she met his look with a little frown, her body taut, every muscle stretched against the invisible pull between them. Becoming absorbed in her task, aware that his gaze was fixed on what she did, Jane hesitated a moment before she pushed the needle into his flesh, but he didn't even flinch or utter a sound, so she pulled it quickly through.

'Why did you say what you did to Justice Littleton?' she asked softly, hoping to distract him from what she was doing.

'And what might that be? Remind me, Jane.'

'You told him that I was to be your wife. I don't recall accepting your proposal—indeed, I remember telling you most adamantly that I would not marry you.'

He grinned down at her bent head. 'I was hoping you might have changed your mind. Besides, it added logic to my proposal that you stay with me at Bilborough. As my future wife Justice Littleton will assume you will be safe under my protection and will not attempt to leave until the charges have either been dropped or acted upon.' With his gloved hand he tipped her face up to his, forcing her to pause in her task. 'Have you changed your mind, Jane? Will you be my wife? Will you give me leave to hope?'

She flushed and lowered her eyes, a gentle smile curving her soft lips. 'I might—but I would be grateful for a little more time. So much has happened to me since our last meeting that my mind is all confusion. Do you think this is the end of it—that I will not be put on trial for witchcraft?'

'I very much doubt it. Justice Littleton is a shrewd and clever man. I think he has the measure of our friend Atkins and will drop all charges against you.'

'I pray that will be so. It seems impolite of me not to have uttered one word of thanks to you for coming to my rescue.'

'It was the least I could do. After all,' he murmured, gazing down at her shining head, his words full of meaning, 'one good deed deserves another.'

Something in the tone of his voice made Jane pause without taking her eyes off the wound. She took a moment to consider his words before realisation hit her. Apprehensive, looking up she met his steady gaze. 'You know, don't you?'

'That you and Tom are the same?' He nodded, warm, tender light in his eyes and a teasing smile tugging the corners of his mouth. 'I should have realised sooner, but when I returned to Avery I was looking for a lad, not a lovely young woman called Jane.'

'And a witch by all accounts,' she teased softly, pulling on the thread, having completed the second and final stitch.

'You are the most beautiful witch I've ever seen.'

The soft flush deepened on her face and she turned away to concentrate on selecting an ointment. She spread pungent-smelling paste over the wound, before winding clean strips of fresh linen about his chest. 'Dressed as I was at the time it was natural you would think I was a boy. I often wore breeches. It was easier for me to ride dressed like that—and no one took any notice of me.'

'And your father didn't mind?'

'He was away. He didn't know, and Gwen was so engrossed with her plants she hardly noticed.'

'I was well and truly taken in.'

'How did you find out?'

'Something Alice said about my escape that day I was Atkins's captive. She mentioned that I had escaped from the church vestry in Avery. Only Tom could have known that.'

'Alice paid me a visit before riding on to Bilborough to see you, the morning after the fire. I think I may have said too much.'

'I'm glad you did. At least it put an end to the mystery of Tom. Why didn't you tell me, Jane? Was it because since returning to Bilborough and discovering I had taken your home, you had cause to regret saving my life?'

'At first,' she told him truthfully, and then an impish smile twitched her lips, 'and then I thought I would have a little fun and keep you guessing. But it would have made no difference at the time.' Her expression became grim. 'Mr Atkins tortured you for what you had done to him previously, and I knew he didn't intend letting you leave Avery alive. I have no time for personal vendettas. Mr Atkins didn't care about winning the war as much as attacking you.' She sighed. 'It would appear Mr Atkins is still after your blood—and mine, too, for daring to disobey him.'

'Now he's locked up he cannot harm us, Jane. So—you were concerned about me even then, all those years ago.'

'I'm concerned about fairness,' she answered simply.

'There's nothing fair in war, Jane.'

'But that wasn't war.'

'It's always war to men like Atkins. All part of the game they play.'

Jane stopped what she was doing to stare at him. 'How can you take it all so blithely, when you could have been killed?'

'And would you have grieved for me, Jane?'

'As I would for any soldier,' she told him. 'Enough blood was being shed without that kind of thing. I would have tried to help anyone who was in such dire circumstances. There,' she said, securing the bandage. 'It is done.'

'I thank you,' he said, getting to his feet and taking a moment to adjust the bandage.

'Will you remove your glove?' she asked, seeing it was soaked with blood. When he cast her a dubious look she smiled. 'Nothing I see can shock me, Francis.'

A wry smile touched his mouth, but it did not reach his eyes. 'You're sure about that, are you, Jane? People shy away from deformity.' There was no self-pity in his voice, just bitter resignation.

Jane shook her head. 'Are you worried that I'll swoon at the sight of it? I'd like to think I am made of sterner stuff than that. Please.'

He did as she bade, his eyes never leaving her face as he watched her reaction. His hand was badly scarred from the burns he'd received and two of his fingers were shrivelled and fused together. When she looked at the mutilation her heart ached for the pain he'd been made to suffer, but she managed to smile as she gently wiped away the blood that had seeped inside the glove.

'I've seen it at it's worst, don't forget, and I have to say that it's healed better than I expected. At least you haven't lost the use of it completely.'

'No, and you're always so practical. It's thanks to your careful ministering that infection was kept at bay.'

'I did what I could with what little I had at my disposal and the limited time. You escaped. That was the main thing.'

As Jane began to tidy everything away, something dark and unsettling was beginning to form in her mind, and she felt that what he had said—that one good deed deserves another, needed explaining further. 'Why—why did you ask me to marry you, Francis?' she asked hesitantly.

Unaware of her unease, a slow, tantalising smile spread across his firm lips and his eyes raked her before gazing into the depths of her dark eyes. 'Ever since I first laid eyes on you you've tormented me in one way or another. Once met, you are not the kind of woman it is easy to forget.'

'But you did. You didn't remember me when I turned up at Bilborough.'

'No—but there was something about you that was familiar and it baffled me for some time. I remember telling you when you left me that day that I was indebted to you for what you had done for me. You see, I have not forgotten what I said.' With eyes that glowed he acknowledged the depth of his feelings. 'When you befriended me that day, not only did you put yourself in danger, but in all probability you saved my life. And now, if I am to have issue, then I am in need of a wife, and I could think of no other woman who would do.'

Jane tilted her head to one side, looking at him intently, unsmiling, for she didn't care for the dark thoughts and doubts that were forming in her mind. 'Pray tell me, Francis, how do I torment you? In what way? Do you see me as some kind of temptress—a witch who pricks you sorely for the sake of amusement? How can I, a mere woman, trouble you so?'

Grinning lazily, he perched his hips on the edge of the table. 'You're a witch all right, Jane. What other explanation can there be for this strange yearning that seizes me whenever you are in my thoughts? You must have cast a spell on me.'

Despite the tension building inside her, she managed to smile. 'Please don't let Justice Littleton hear you speaking like that. He'll have me back inside his gaol before I can protest.'

Reaching out with his good hand, Francis took her fingers and drew her closer. 'Aye, but you're an angel too, Jane, when you look at me as you did in the gaol—all soft and warm and clearly glad to see me.'

She gave a strained laugh. 'Relieved, more like. I was beginning to think I had been abandoned.'

'Not by me. Never by me,' he murmured, bending his head towards her face, his breath stirring the tendrils of her hair that covered her ear.

He placed his lips on her fingers, his gentleness causing her breath to catch in her throat. Gazing up at him in soft confusion, she was unable to fathom the tenderness that she suddenly felt for him. Recognising the quickening of her own pulse, the effect of his burning blue eyes was total and devastating.

Yet she no longer felt complimented by a proposal that she was beginning to suspect had been given to return a favour, and suddenly she felt more hurt and degraded by this man who haunted her dreams than she cared to admit. When he had asked her to be his wife he had told her there were other reasons why he wanted to marry her. She hadn't asked what they were, but now she knew. Feeling that everything was moving too quickly and conscious of a need to sort out her thoughts, placing a trembling hand flat against his chest, she pushed herself away.

'I'd better go. My bath will be getting cold.'

Francis pushed himself away from the table and went with her to the door. His hand rode on the small of her back as he escorted her across the hall. They were, for that moment, aware only of each other and did not see Mary and Isaac standing across the hall. In unison, their brows lifted in thoughtful surprise as they observed the master raise his hand and make so bold as to gently caress Jane's cheek. Jane looked up and smiled at him. Instead of the stinging slap the two servants expected, the intimacy was accepted without an attempt to brush away his hand.

'Well, I never,' Mary gasped. 'It would seem Colonel Russell has caught Jane's eye. What say you, Isaac?'

'Aye,' Isaac agreed. 'So it does, Mary.'

Jane went to her room where she could think things through more rationally. When she had taken her bath and scrubbed the filth of the gaol from her flesh and dressed in clean garments, as darkness descended she stared out of the open window into the star-filled night, wrapped in the aura of a melancholy mood. She realised she had been too hasty in her decision to accept Francis's proposal of marriage, for the more she thought about it the more convinced she became that he had asked her to marry him to repay the debt. The thought struck at her heart like a lash, making her cringe with humiliation and hurt that was almost beyond bearing, until blessed, cold numbness came over her, until she felt nothing at all.

She felt that she was being propelled into a loveless marriage with a man who didn't want her, but was prepared to do the honourable thing because he was in her debt. Francis pitied her and played the saviour's role most heartily. But it wouldn't do. Not for her.

Focusing on her reflection in the glass pane, she scanned the pale, strained face looking back at her, at the eyes that were filled with a kind of hunger. Francis had seduced her with a mere touch. He had caught her and she was ready to own it at last. She wanted him. She was sick to her very soul with longing for him. She was indeed trapped—just like that little fish that had taken the bait. She loved him more than her heart and soul and wanted him more than life itself. She was dragging herself into hell with desire for him, but it wasn't enough. The man she married must love her in return, otherwise what hope did they have of happiness together?

Gazing at Bilborough's surrounding acres, she waited for the comfort that this blessed place always gave her. But the old easy magic of her home did not work, did nothing to ease her sadness.

When Francis knocked on her chamber door hoping to speak to her, she told the chambermaid to tell him she was resting.

'Is she ill?' he demanded of the maid in alarm.

'No, sir, merely resting.'

An hour later, when Francis knocked again, he was told the same thing.

The following morning when he tried to see her again, he was informed she was having a bath. Annoyance now replaced his worry.

'Tell Mistress Lucas,' he ordered in a dire warning tone, 'that I will not enquire after her again, but I expect to see her downstairs within the hour, fully rested, clean and amenable to me.'

Feeling listless and very unhappy, Jane was in no hurry to leave her room as she tried to find a way out of the dilemma for Francis's sake and her own. After tormenting herself in this way until she thought she was going out of her mind, she left her room to go in search of Hester, only to find herself confronted by Francis in the otherwise empty hall, waiting for her to emerge from her room.

He looked so swarthy and formidable, the heavy muscles in his shoulders swelling beneath his loose-fitting white shirt in such a way that she was unable to look away. He seemed to radiate a force that made her feel weaker than she was.

'Francis!'

He gave her a long, cool look, his eyes as bright and as sharp as the teeth of a trap. 'Aye, Jane, none other.'

'I—I'm looking for Hester.' She would have fled, but Francis stepped in front of her.

'Easy, Jane. Spare me a moment of your time.' The blue eyes flinted like hard metal. 'We have a matter to discuss.'

'I'm listening.'

'Will you not sit down?'

'I might. It all depends what you have to say.'

His brows snapped together and his eyes narrowed, and when he spoke his voice was carefully controlled. 'Would you mind telling me why you've been avoiding me? Every time I knocked on your door I was told you were either resting or taking a bath.'

'I—I haven't been avoiding you, Francis.'

'Yes, you have.'

She thought quickly for an answer that would soothe and placate him. 'It—it's just that so much has happened of late—everything moving so fast, I—I was confused. I have so much on my mind—that is why I may have seemed…'

'Cold and uncaring,' he provided harshly, studying her face closely.

'If I did, then it was not intentional.'

'I am relieved to hear it.' He breathed an inner sigh of relief that the skirmish was over. Believing they were in complete accord once more, tipping her chin up, he touched his lips to hers and felt the gasp of her indrawn breath at the same time as her body seemed to tense. Puzzled by her rather extreme reaction, he raised his head and waited for what seemed a long time for her to open her eyes. When her long lashes finally fluttered up, she looked bewildered. 'Is something amiss?' he asked cautiously.

She looked away. 'No, not at all,' she replied, but it seemed as if the opposite were true.

Francis looked at her in waiting silence, but before she could say anything else, Hester came into the hall to inform them that a carriage carrying Colonel Russell's sister-in-law and her sister Alice had drawn up in the yard.

With an exclamation of annoyance, Francis brusquely excused himself and with long purposeful strides left the hall.

Later, knowing the confrontation with Francis could not be put off any longer and that she must tell him she would not be his wife, Jane went in search of him. Unfortunately she came face to face with Alice as she was leaving the house. Alice showed no surprise at Jane's sudden appearance, and there was a hard, venomous glint in her green eyes. Jane was tempted to turn and go back inside, but it was too late. Alice's voice rang out coolly, halting her on the steps.

'Why, Jane. You are still here, I see.' She sauntered towards her, her dislike obvious and the thin smile on her lips insincere. Her eyes shone ruthlessly like those of a cat, her claws coming out to play. 'I trust you are suffering no ill effects from your short imprisonment in the town gaol. How unpleasant that must have been for you.'

Jane faced her coldly, intending to remain calm, refusing to be intimidated. 'As you see, I am well and free,' she retorted pointedly.

'I hear Mr Atkins has been arrested.'

'You heard correctly. He attacked Francis—indeed, he tried to kill him. Mr Atkins deserves to be locked up. Being as concerned about Francis's well-being as I am, then I am sure you will agree.'

'Of course—and I have taken note of your concern for Francis, since without him your precious Bilborough is denied you.' She tossed her head haughtily. 'I have just seen Francis. He tells me the two of you are to be married. I congratulate you—not on your marriage, but on managing to secure him. What a clever, conniving woman you are, Jane, and how well you have played your game—and how fortuitous that because of what I said, he recalled that you were Tom, the lad who saved his life.'

Jane looked at her sharply, angered that Francis was so certain they had struck an agreeable bargain he had told Alice. 'Secure him? Conniving? I don't think so. Francis—'

'Is marrying you for no other reason than to repay you for aiding him in his escape from Mr Atkins,' Alice exclaimed, a fierce surge of pleasure shooting through her when she saw Jane's face whiten. 'Don't deceive yourself. Francis doesn't love you. He feels that he owes you, and he can think of no other way to repay you for saving his life than by making you his wife, so that you can return to live at your precious Bilborough.'

'If it suits you to think so, then do,' Jane said coldly.

At that moment Elizabeth appeared from the garden. With a quick look at both their faces and Jane's hands clenched by her sides, she took in the situation at once. Giving Alice a harsh, reproving look, she said, 'Alice, it is time we left. Go and get your things.'

Throwing Jane a final glare, reluctantly Alice stalked into the house, but she left her resentment behind like a draught of cold air.

'I must apologise for my sister, Jane,' Elizabeth said. 'She has a tongue that would put a wasp to shame.'

'Please, think nothing of it, Elizabeth. I'm sorry you have to leave before we've had a chance to talk properly.'

'I shall stay longer next time, I promise. I am staying with Father and Alice for a few days and we only called in passing. I wanted to tell you myself how horrified both Richard and I were to learn of your imprisonment and to express our relief when we heard you had been freed.' She smiled warmly. 'I saw Francis earlier. I hear congratulations are in order. I'm so happy the two of you are to marry—and I know Richard will be.'

'Francis—told you?'

'Yes, and I shall be delighted to have you as a sister-in-law.' On seeing Jane's downcast features and the bleakness in her eyes, she frowned. 'Why, what is it? Has Alice said something to upset you? I admit there have been times when she has angered and frustrated me beyond bearing, but she is my sister and I owe her my protection. She is a woman like you, Jane—full of desire and longing like you. She may be greedy, but she is not a bad woman. But I can see that, while ever she remains close to you and Francis, there will always be discord. Which is why Richard and I—with Father's permission—have decided to take her to London for a few weeks. Hopefully in that time a suitable husband can be found for her, so you and Francis will be able to wed without any interference from her.'

'Nothing has been decided for certain, Elizabeth,' Jane said tentatively. 'I—I'm thinking of returning to Northampton with Hester. After everything that's happened of late, I—I feel I need a time to recover.'

'Why, of course you do, and you are right to do so.'

When Elizabeth and Alice had left, Hester received Jane's

request to go with her to Northampton with a mixture of delight and puzzlement.

'But of course you may, Jane,' she said without hesitation. 'You know we'd love to have you, but—I am sorry—this is all rather sudden. Why have you decided against marriage to Colonel Russell?'

'Because—though it grieves me to say it—I—I cannot trust his motives for marrying me. I was just going to look for him—to tell him.'

'I think he's ridden into Avery,' Hester informed her. 'He had a message—something about my father being taken ill. I am to go myself as soon as Isaac has brought the carriage round.'

Jane stared at her in astonishment. 'He—he is sick? Is it serious?'

Hester looked at her steadily. 'I really can't say.'

When Francis and Hester returned from Avery they brought with them the news that Jacob Atkins was dead.

'Dead?' Jane felt a small shiver creep down her spine.

'Yes, Jane,' Hester said. 'He is dead.'

Jane was stunned by the news, but not sorry to hear it. 'But—how? What caused it?'

'We're not sure,' Francis answered curtly. 'And of course there will be an inquest as there is on any sudden, unexpected death that occurs in gaol.'

'But it looks like his heart,' Hester was quick to explain. 'I told Justice Littleton that he has suffered with his heart for years.'

Jane stared at her in stupefied amazement. 'He has?'

'Indeed. Why, there was a time when he had such a seizure that we thought it was all over for him. It was obvious to me that he had suffered another such attack.'

'It was? I see.' Jane realised as she said it that she didn't see at all. It was as if, although she had nothing to do with it, she knew there was more to it than was immediately obvious. But then, why should she care? Jacob Atkins deserved to die for the wickedness, the pain and the fear he had inflicted, not just on her and Francis, but on his three children. 'I cannot pretend to be sorry, Hester. I owe him nothing but humiliation and imprisonment. Your father was a monster and I'm glad he's dead.'

Hester reached out and squeezed her hand, and Jane was somehow not surprised to see that she was smiling in a strange but loving way. 'I know. All our lives can now be lived in peace—without fear.'

Chapter Ten

Jane found Francis in one of the paddocks checking a newly delivered horse. On seeing her he crossed to the fence and climbed over, wearing what could only be a mask of composure, for which she could hardly blame him after she had kept him at arm's length since she had tended his wound.

As she stood cool and composed, he nodded politely. 'So, Jane, you deem to speak to me at last. I trust you have recovered from the news of Atkins's demise.'

'Yes, and I do not grieve for him. How can I, after what he has done?'

'And you know Justice Littleton has dropped any charges made against you?'

She nodded. 'You must know how relieved I am. H—how is your wound? Better, I hope?'

'It's healing.' He looked at her hard. 'I don't think you've sought me out to speak to me about my wound, Jane. What is it?'

'I—I've come to tell you that I shall be leaving with Hester for Northampton in the morning. There is no reason for me to remain any longer. Now that Mr Atkins is dead, I am no longer in any danger—so I have no need of your protection.'

'Leave? You are leaving? Just like that?' he said in an awful voice.

'Yes, I feel that I must. I have made my decision. I...'

'What?' He moved closer, putting his fists into his waist, glowering at her. 'What the hell are you talking about? From what you said when you tended my wound, I was under the impression that you'd given the matter some thought and would say yes.'

She stepped back from him. It was hard to think with him so close, looming over her, so big, so male. She recognised the threat of her emotions welling forth in greater volume and sought to turn aside, but his hand, firm and unyielding, caught her chin and forced her to face him, refusing to allow her to escape his close inspection. She could do nothing but submit to his probing gaze.

'What is it, Jane?' he demanded. 'What has happened to make you change your mind about becoming my wife? Do you feel threatened in some way? Is that it?'

'To tell the truth, Francis, only one person dares to threaten me at this moment,' she said pointedly, knocking his hand from her chin and turning away, leaving him no doubt to whom she referred.

'Since I have never threatened a woman in my life, I can only think it must by your peace of mind I threaten.'

'Perhaps intimidation is a better word.'

'You feel intimidated by me, Jane?'

'No. I do not feel in the least intimidated by you,' she lied.

'Then why are you leaving? Since I suspect my proposal of marriage has something to do with your decision, I would be grateful if you would enlighten me.'

A disconcerted shake of her head was her response. 'Please don't pressure me, Francis. It's not important.'

Her casual words fired his anger even more. 'On the contrary, it *is* to me,' he countered, 'and if I am angry, it's because I am unable to fathom your decision to leave Bilborough. I can understand that events of the past few days and Atkins's death has obviously distressed you, but a time of quiet here at Bilborough will soothe you.'

'No,' she cried. 'I dislike this pretence we're going through, and I have decided that it would be best if I release you from your commitments.'

His eyes narrowed. 'Pretence? Are you telling me that when I kissed you you were only *pretending* to like it? I do not pretend what I feel, Jane.'

His icy tone hit Jane like a bucket full of freezing water. 'No, maybe not, but henceforth from this moment, you may live your life without worrying about marriage to me. I have no wish to marry—not you, not anyone—and I want no more of it. Indeed, I can bear no more of it, and I cannot continue.'

'For God's sake, Jane, you're not making sense,' Francis argued. 'Surely you must realise why it is that I don't want you to leave. Why I will not let you leave.' His voice had gone low and deep, almost hoarse. 'Since the first moment I saw you I've longed to have you for my own.'

Feeling hot and cold, Jane looked about her in fear. A hawk hovering above her in the sky caught her attention and she watched it as if fascinated. She wished she could look him in the eyes, but she knew she would be unable to control her heated emotions. How could he lie to her so blithely, when the truth was that he wanted to marry her to repay a debt?

'Please don't say that,' she cried softly, feeling the pain of knowing he would deem her unworthy were it not for the debt.

Her disappointment should not shock her, but somehow it did, and deeply, and she felt the pain of a woman who did not know if the man she yearned for could love her just for herself. The full force of the emotions churning within burst from her.

'When you asked me to be your wife I had nothing. When I came to Bilborough I was an orphan who had come in out of the darkness, a stranger, an intruder in what I had always believed was my home, the home I had been coming towards since the day I left. It was where I belonged. I had loved it and missed it and needed it, and when I stepped inside I came into the very heart of it.'

She breathed in deep a breath of wind blowing softly off the land. She breathed in the smell of it. She could almost taste the soil and the grass, studded with flowers, where violets and pale yellow primroses and cowslips grew in early summer. She knew it was her home and she wanted to belong here again, even though she knew it was too late.

'But then,' she continued, looking beyond him, 'I saw it through new eyes and I saw you. I soon saw that this private world was being run perfectly well without me, that I was not a welcome heir, finding my way home at last.'

'Nothing is the same, I grant you, but Bilborough can still be your home—and I can be the family you no longer have.'

She shook her head. 'I have no family,' she said coldly, meeting his gaze directly. 'When I dreamed of Bilborough I did not dream of you. All the family I had are dead. You need not worry about me, Francis. The life I thought of as bleak has surely taken a turn for the better now Mr Atkins is dead. I shall go away and try to find somewhere that I can be myself.'

'Stop this, Jane,' Francis argued. 'Stop this nonsense.' Reaching out a hand, he rested it gently upon her forearm as he sought to calm her. 'You'll feel different in a few days.'

'No, I won't! I'll feel exactly the way I do now,' she cried, throwing off his hand. 'I'm freeing you from your commitment,' she declared resolutely. 'There is no more to be said.'

He caught her hand and held it fast within his grasp. There was an ache in the pit of his belly that would not be appeased by denials and rationalisations.

'There are some things that cannot be put aside so easily, Jane. You may turn from me if you wish, but I can promise you it will change nothing.' Taking her by the shoulders, he forced her to face him. What he saw in her eyes was in complete variance with what her lips conveyed, and there was a trembling in her slender body that belied her words of denial. His lust overcame his common sense. If he could silence her protests, perhaps her heart would follow. Drawing her tightly, to him he covered her mouth with his.

Jane stepped back from him, all her grief and anger and frustration boiling over at once. 'You may force me, Francis, if that is your desire, but I will never be yours.'

'It is not over, Jane,' he said. 'I intend to delve further into this until I get this matter settled between us. I have no intention of simply letting you walk away from here—from me—unless I have reason to believe that your contempt for me is beyond the measure I can bear.'

Jane backed away from him. 'That is your prerogative, Francis. Think what you like, but I am still leaving with Hester in the morning.'

'Aren't you forgetting something? Bilborough! I don't know what game you think you're playing,' he said, low voiced, 'but I stupidly thought you wanted to be back at Bilborough more than anything else. Like a fool I promised myself I'd see you brought safely back to your home the only way I knew how—without losing out myself. I thought you needed advice. I thought you

might need me. More fool me,' he said bitterly. 'I now see you
don't. Go to Northampton. I'll leave you to your ruin. You'll be
gone and will never see Bilborough again.'

For a moment there was a rage so hot and so burning that
Jane could see nothing, not even his face, for the red mist that
was in her head and behind her eyes. She breathed deeply, to
try to slow the rapid thudding of her heart. She was so angry.
She wanted to punish him, to hurt him, to cut him to the heart.
He was feeling nothing, though her life was over. She glared at
him with angry fury.

'I will take Bilborough back,' she cried, her eyes black with
unsatisfied anger. 'This is my house. My land. If I decide to wed,
then I'll find someone else. Someone who is wealthy enough to
help me buy back Bilborough. And then you can get off my land.
Then we'll see who gives the orders around here.' She was final
in her dismissal of him as she turned on her heel and walked on.

Francis came after her in one fluid movement, faster than
Jane would have thought he could move. He was at her side in
an instant and grabbed her by the shoulders and shook her so
that her head rocked on her shoulders.

'Don't be ridiculous,' he shouted. 'What are you saying?'

She blazed back at him, angry, unafraid of his violence. 'That
I will wed a rich man and have you off my land. You see if I
don't.'

His blue eyes burned at her for one moment longer, then he
flung her from him so that she stumbled backwards. 'The devil
you will,' he hissed.'

The shocked look on his face made Jane wish she had never
flung those empty, careless words at him to taunt him. He looked
as if she had stabbed him in the heart. But she could not, would
not weaken before him, and tossed her head haughtily.

'Yes, Francis, the devil I will. Just watch me.'

'Then it is right that you go,' he said coldly. His hard eyes raked over her, and then he turned and walked away. He was tempted to turn back, but he caught himself up short, wondering if he really had made a stupid, blundering mistake in asking her to be his wife. But the hollow feeling in his chest removed any doubt from his mind that he could no more live without Jane Lucas than he could his own heart.

Jane watched him go, her throat choked with anger and her cheeks wet with tears. She hated to see him striding off in a rage like that. She wanted to speak to him, to take back the awful things she had said and that she had not meant.

Francis looked up from his correspondence to see Hester hovering in the doorway to his office. Whenever he was in the presence of this lovely young woman, he found it hard to believe she was the spawn of Jacob Atkins.

'What is it, Hester?'

'If you could spare me a moment of your time, I—I would like to talk to you. It concerns Jane.'

Francis threw his quill down onto the desk. 'I thought it might.'

Hester moved further into the room and perched nervously on the edge of the chair, facing him across the desk. 'I believe she has told you she has decided to come with me to Northampton in the morning.'

'She has,' he said, getting to his feet and beginning to pace the floor with his hands clasped behind his back, unable to understand why Jane was behaving so strangely. 'I am surprised. Yesterday she agreed to be my wife, and then she changed her mind. I cannot for the life of me understand why and she has given me no sound reason for doing so.'

'I have tried to dissuade her. She cannot leave this house. Bilborough is life's blood to her. Without it she will wither away.'

'What do you expect me to do, Hester? What can I do?'

Hester got to her feet. Colonel Russell was so very tall and male, and excessively masculine men always discomposed her. 'You must make her realise that she will never be happy away from here. You have to try.'

Francis laughed, unable to conceal the bitterness he felt by Jane's decision to leave, her rejection of him. 'Me? You know how headstrong she is. I've asked her to be my wife and she has turned me down. Why would she listen to me?' He stopped pacing and looked at the nervous young woman. 'She doesn't know you're here, does she?'

'Dear me, no. I know she would never forgive me if she knew.'

His face softened. 'I think she would. Jane is very fond of you.'

'I know, and I'd do anything in the world for her, which is why I'm here now. You have just told me that she has given you no reason for deciding to leave Bilborough—and I beg your pardon if you think I am intruding, but she must have good reason for declining your proposal.'

'If she has, I'm damned if I know what it is. She was upset—and very angry—but for the devil of me I cannot remember her giving me a valid reason.'

Hester smiled and resumed her seat on the chair. 'Then if you will spare me a moment of your time, I will tell you.'

Following her confrontation with Francis, utterly miserable, Jane had sought sanctuary in her room. When Hester came to tell her that Francis would like to speak to her and that he could be found out in the paddocks, having no wish for a repeat of their last encounter, she was tempted to ignore his request, but, knowing she would have to face him some time, she reluctantly acquiesced.

Francis was leaning on a fence, standing with his back partially to her, calmly watching two of his splendid horses grazing. His broad shoulders were squared, his jaw set with implacable determination, and even in this pensive pose, he seemed to emanate the restrained power and unyielding authority she had always sensed and feared in him. The closer she got to him, drop by precious drop she felt her confidence draining away. How could she have deluded herself into believing that she could turn her back on this man and walk away?

'You wanted to see me?' she said in a flat, emotionless voice.

He turned at the sound of her voice and looked at her. For the past half an hour as he had waited for her to arrive he had been struggling with his feelings as he told himself that Jane had been hurt and humiliated, and that when his summons came she would undoubtedly demonstrate her rebellion against him by doing something to defy and provoke him. He reminded himself that no matter what she said or did, he would be patient and understanding. But when he looked at her, at her chin held defiantly high, it was all he could do to bridle his temper.

'I'm glad you could spare the time to come and see me,' he remarked curtly. 'I thought you might refuse.'

Jane lifted her head, her anger draining slowly away. Although a trace of defiance still shone from her glorious dark eyes, they were sparkling with suppressed tears, shining with the pain of their imminent parting. The translucent skin beneath them were smudged with shadows, and her normally glowing complexion was drained of colour.

'I couldn't do that. I wanted to see you to apologise for my anger earlier. It was uncalled for and I'm sorry.'

Francis shrugged himself away from the fence, stretching languidly, and Jane watched the way his muscles seemed to ripple beneath his shirt. He stopped in front of her, looking down at her solemnly. She looked beautiful and proud and aloof, all part of the contradictions that made up this lovely young woman.

'You are a difficult woman to win over, Jane Lucas. I would be sorry to see you leave—separated by a chasm of misunderstandings and anger. Does the thought of being my wife bring you such misery?'

Jane was shocked by his unexpected gentleness and completely at a loss as to how to answer. She wanted to appear haughty and remote, cold—anything but weak and helpless. It was on the tip of her tongue to retort that the last thing she wanted was to be his wife, and yet, on the other hand, she owed it to him to be truthful.

'No, the idea doesn't make me miserable.'

'Then I think we should discuss why you decided to reject my proposal. Perhaps then we may be able to resolve the issue. I have been speaking to Hester and she's made me see things more clearly.'

With anger stirring afresh, Jane stared at him, sarcasm quirking the corner of her mouth. 'She has? And you are so certain that we have things to sort out between us?'

'I am. I see your pain. I want to take it away, to see you happy. Jane, did you really believe that you were so undesirable to me that I would take you for my wife merely to repay a debt?'

She stared at him. 'Hester told you that?' He nodded. 'Then, yes, I do think that. I did not think you wanted me for the woman that I am.'

'And you held that against me?' He smiled faintly when she nodded. 'Then you do not know me, Jane. Will it change how you feel if I tell you that I did not know you were Tom until after I asked you to be my wife? I did not see or speak to Alice until the day they came and took you away.'

Jane stared at him, beginning to realise that her fears were all of her own making. What Francis had just revealed was humbling. She was mortified when she remembered how she had misjudged him, even though she'd had every reason to suspect his motives. 'Is—is this true?'

He nodded. 'It is.'

Suddenly she found she was speaking past a lump in her throat. 'Why didn't you tell me? Why did you let me go on thinking those—those awful things? You have no idea how I have tortured myself over this.'

Reaching out, he traced his forefinger along the curve of her cheek, relieved when she didn't draw back. 'How was I to know what thoughts were in your head? I wanted you to come to know for yourself the kind of man I am and to trust in me. But I had doubts of my own, Jane. There was Bilborough, you see. I thought that was what you wanted.'

'Yes—I—I did—more than anything.'

'Careful, Jane,' he said warningly. 'You are sounding to me like a woman who would use me to leap to the top of the tree. Whereas I would have taken you in love.' When she turned her eyes on him and searched his face, he nodded, his expression sombre. 'Aye, Jane. I do love you. I think I've loved you from the moment I first saw you standing so poised and brave on the day you returned to Bilborough. I thought that you were the loveliest, most enchanting creature God ever created. I love you enough to trust that together we can solve whatever life offers us. I desire you and were I the meanest beggar I would still want you. It would make no difference. But what of you?' he queried. 'Must I doubt you? How could I ever be sure it was me you wanted— or your precious Bilborough? Is it me you want?'

So torn about her emotions was Jane that tears sprung to her eyes. For a moment she held herself stiff, then when he opened his arms she moved into them, feeling them close about her. It was like coming home. 'You,' she said. 'Without you nothing matters. Not Bilborough—nothing.' He held her tight and the ice and the pain in her heart melted in a rush of desire. 'It is you I want. Please believe me, Francis. It is you I love—for your honour and your courage—and your persistence, for I did not make it easy for you.'

His voice came soft, husky, almost a whisper. 'You have my heart, and I can only pray you will trust me with your own, to keep and cherish it for ever. But must I ever court you, Jane, destroying the barrier you have built around yourself stone by stone, tearing down your resistance until you yield to me—that tears at the roots of my very sanity?'

Standing back in his arms, beneath his gaze, Jane quaked, and when he drew his fingers gently along the bare flesh of her jaw, they seared the ends of her nerves until she ached to be drawn to him once more. The steady eyes, the resolute, firm mouth had not been so close for a long time. She remained still, drawn into those eyes. Her lips were parted, her breathing rapid in anticipation of his kiss. But it did not come. Instead he chuckled deeply in his chest and, seeing the bemusement in her face, stepped back from her.

Sorely offended at the thought that he was playing with her, irately, she said, 'You are a beast, Francis Russell.'

There was more than a trace of laughter in his tone when he said, 'Aye, Jane, I agree with you, and no doubt of the most irksome sort.'

Jane stared at him, and, sensing the lightness of his mood, a delicious smile broke upon her lips. 'And it is an accepted fact that I am a witch.'

'It is,' he agreed. His smile broadened.

'Then are you not afraid that some day I might take your heart and rip it to pieces?'

'That, my love, you have already done. What about the rich man you told me you are to marry? The rich man who will give you everything your heart desires?'

Jane looked puzzled for a moment and then laughed out loud. 'Oh, you idiot, Francis Russell,' she exclaimed. 'You poor deluded idiot. I told you that in a rage, when you were so certain I would marry you, and I thought you only asked me to repay the debt. I was angry. I wanted to hurt you back.'

'Then if it's a rich man you want, I have money—so you will want for nothing. Everything your heart desires shall be granted. Although as my wife you must be prepared to be answerable to me for all things—but I promise not to beat you,' he murmured, a playful, teasing gleam dancing in his eyes.

Jane looked at him in exasperated, mischievous amazement. 'And *that's* your definition of a good husband, is it?'

Frowning, in jest he said, 'What else might you want?'

'What else?' Jane was so taken aback she stared at him a moment before saying, 'Well, if your definition of a good husband is one with wealth and position—who does not beat his wife—what does that make you?'

He shrugged, sitting down on the grass beneath a spreading oak and pulling her down beside him. 'Never having been a husband I cannot answer that, so I cannot say if I will be good or bad. If you become my wife, you will have to decide. Already you have called me a brute—a conceited jackanapes, a buffoon and a few other things along the way, which I won't repeat for the sake of decency. But I would promise to do my best.'

A little smile curved her lips and she looked at him from between narrowed eyes. 'And you wouldn't beat me?'

'No, never that. But it's not uncommon for a man to beat his wife—with a stick, mind, not his fists—if she's done wrong, that is. It's often necessary and his affair.'

'With a stick?'

'A stick—or his belt.'

'And you would condone that, would you?'

A look of disgust crossed his face, but there was a distinct glint in his eye. 'I'll have you know that I am the very soul of good nature. It's not something I would do.' He grinned when she raised an eyebrow, plainly not convinced. 'I've never laid a finger on a woman in my life and I don't intend to start. But you can't ignore the fact that a man's wife is legally his property.'

'And that gives him the right to beat her?'

'If she has no notion of what constitutes wifely obedience. But then one never knows what goes on in a marriage—some women might be pleased for their husbands to beat them.'

'Pleased?' Jane gaped at him in astonishment, almost choking on her laughter. 'How can you think that any woman would ever be pleased to submit to such an indignity?'

The glint grew brighter in Francis's eye. He was clearly enjoying himself. 'Some do—and many men who do it wouldn't unless their wives bedevilled them into it with their sharp tongues and needling ways.' He smiled. Jane was giving him a hard look. It was impossible to imagine any man trying such a thing on this feisty young woman. If he did, he'd have the devil of a fight on his hands, as stubborn and wilful as she was. Should anyone raise their hand to Jane Lucas, she would fly like a banshee.

Still smiling a little, he got up and pulled her to her feet, then took her wrists, which he lifted gently over her head and pinned against the trunk of the tree she had been sitting under so that she was obliged to lean back flat against it. 'A husband would not beat his wife to hurt her, you understand, but to show her who is master.'

'To humiliate and degrade her, more like—to own her.'

'You I would like not only to possess but to own, Jane.'

'And what is your definition of that?'

'Exactly what I say.'

'The man I take for my husband I, too, will own, but not in the way you mean.'

'My meaning is not so very different, I know that very well. It will have nothing to do with money or position, but feelings and emotions.' There was still a gleam of humour in his eyes, but his voice was serious. 'I want to make you mine, Jane. I will do anything I must to make that happen.'

She glanced at him askance, a little smile playing on her lips. 'Including beating me on a regular basis?'

'I will never hurt you—not intentionally,' he said, speaking softly. The corner of his mouth lifted slightly.

'Good. Then I wouldn't feel obliged to poison you.'

'And if you were so tempted, how would you go about doing it?'

'I am knowledgeable about herbs and things, as well you know—especially about mushrooms—the common kind that are delicious to eat, and the lovely-to-look-at kind that work fast in killing a person when eaten.'

'Then if you were so tempted to do such a thing, I might reverse what I have just said. Given time before I finally expired,' he said with a low chuckle, bending his head and nuzzling his lips in the warm hollow of her neck where a pulse was beginning to beat erratically just below the surface of her flesh, 'I just might be tempted to take a stick to your very attractive backside—which, as I recall, is soft and round and very pretty. You will recall…when…'

Blood flared abruptly in her cheeks and she gasped. 'When what? How do you know?'

Raising his head, he glanced at her, raised one eyebrow, then she, too, recalled the incident when she had nearly knocked him over on the landing at Bilborough when she had chased after Scamp.

He grinned, his eyes bright with mischief. 'I see you haven't forgotten.'

'No indeed,' she said, extremely embarrassed. She had succeeded in putting that very humiliating episode to the back of her mind, and did not appreciate having it recalled. Francis, on the other hand, was plainly enjoying the recollection. He eyed her in a manner she found absolutely insufferable.

'Your nightdress didn't leave much to the imagination. Do you always go to bed like that?'

'Like what?'

'Scantily clad.'

'I was not,' she flared, her face hot with indignation.

'You were when you clung to me for support.'

Jane began to feel the throbbing of blood in her veins. 'I had to hold on to something, otherwise I would have fallen. You happened to be the nearest thing.'

'Oh, yes,' he said, and the grin widened. 'So I was. It was your own fault, mind, that you bumped into me.'

'My fault?'

He nodded. 'Although I recall you blamed it on your dog at the time. Still, I didn't mind you falling into my arms the way you did. If you hadn't slipped, you'd never have got so close to me.'

'Close? And you imagine I enjoy being that close to you, do you?'

His eyes gleamed. 'Are you telling me you don't?'

'It is conceited of you to assume I do.'

He caught the sudden pique in her voice. His eyes sharpened and fixed on her face. 'You prevaricate, Jane.'

Jane pulled against his grip by sheer reflex, but the pressure of his hands on her wrists increased. She realised that pinned to the tree like this, defenceless and exposed, he could do anything he liked to her—and would. She squirmed against him, trying to escape the memory of how it had felt to be in his arms, but to no avail—and she knew she didn't want to escape it, but to experience it once more. His free hand caressed her cheek—it was no more than a featherlight touch, but that was all it took to make her realise that if he had a mind, he could touch her anywhere, in any way.

She had stopped pulling at her trapped wrists. She felt the sudden breeze blow across the land, but did not feel its chill. She felt desire, hot and dangerous and exciting. She bit on her lower lip, but she could not stop it trembling. There was only one cure for that, and it worked when Francis pressed his mouth on hers. His tongue was insistent until she met it with her own, first with hesitancy, then with welcome, then with passion.

The wedding of Jane and Francis was attended by a select few. Richard and Elizabeth were in London with Alice, and much as Jane would have liked Francis's brother and his wife to be there, she was glad Alice was absent. Apart from Mary and Hester, who had decided to stay for the wedding, there were just a few of Francis's friends who lived in Avery.

Because of the new regulations governing marriage under the Commonwealth, they were married before the justice of the peace in Avery, where the formalities were of the simplest kind. When he repeated his vows, Francis smiled as he gazed down into Jane's eyes, and when it came for her to speak her vows, her heart was so full of love she could hardly make herself heard. But the civil rite did not satisfy Jane or Francis, and wanting to feel it had been lawfully done, afterwards the wedding party entered the church in Avery to receive their blessing by a minister.

Many people turned out to see the happy couple, and Jane was heard to comment cynically how strange it was that those who would have happily seen her tried for witchcraft and hanged for a witch, should have forgotten so soon and were at the forefront of the crowd to wish them a long and happy life together.

Everyone returned to Bilborough, where a feast had been laid on for the guests. It was a quiet affair and when they had taken their leave, Francis drew his radiant bride towards him and lifted her gently and carried her in his arms up the stairs to their bedchamber, where the windows looked out over the gardens and the fields beyond. There he undressed her and laid her down on the soft bed. When he joined her, naked in her innocence she turned and faced him and closed her eyes, letting the warmth of his body against her cool skin wash over her. His warm breath stirred shivers along her flesh, and a curious excitement tingled in her breast.

His hand and his lips, skilled and knowledgeable, wanted to know and taste every part of her. He caressed and stroked her and found the core of her so that she sighed and moaned between her kisses. Holding her close, his hard-muscled chest pressed against hers, he entered her and she clung to him, feeling pain that made her gasp, followed by a warmth deep inside that made her sob with pleasure. She was devoured in a searing, scorching flame that shot through her like a flaming rocket. The warmth spread until her skin seemed to glow.

Never had she felt such delight as they gave and took their pleasure of each other, moving and seeking, their need for each other a hunger beyond sanity. Jane writhed in a sensuous fire, consumed by its flames, their sighs of ecstasy muffled by ardent kisses, their bodies demanding and contented in a frenzy of loving until she cried out loud. And then there was nothing but their laboured breathing as Jane lay in the fold of her husband's arm.

Leaning on his elbow, Francis looked down her, his blue eyes smiling and radiant with love. Jane could feel the glow of it on her flesh. 'If I could, I would make time stand still for this one night,' he murmured, brushing aside the ebony curtain of her hair and placing his lips in the warm softness of her neck.

Nestling into him, she sighed. 'We have a whole lifetime to be together, every moment of it, but I doubt even that will be long enough. So love me again, Francis—my husband.' She raised her hand and caressed his cheek. 'You cannot know how good it feels to say that.'

He grinned and rolled her on to her back. 'You cannot know how good it feels to hear you say it. Nearly as good, in fact, as…' His mouth was taken in a gently arousing kiss, and he did as she asked and loved her until the sky lightened with the dawn.

Jane awoke to the sound of birds. She turned her head to the man who was still asleep beside her, as snug and warm as a wolf in its lair. She smiled as she remembered the night past, already anticipating the moment when he would wake and they would begin again.

Cautiously so as not to wake him, she slipped out of bed and padded across to the window, pulling back the heavy curtains from the lattice window. The room was suddenly filled with bright sunlight. Every detail of the scene that met her eyes was familiar to her, but never had it affected her as it did at that moment.

She heard a rustling behind her and a floorboard creaked, and then two strong arms came around her and her husband lifted her hair and kissed the nape of her neck. She leaned against him and sighed and together they stood at the long window of their bedchamber overlooking the gardens, golden edged with brilliance, the sky so blue and so large it filled the empty window.

'Thank you,' she whispered.

His arms tightened around her. 'Thank you? What is there to thank me for?'

'For bringing me back to this. This house—this peace—this world that will be ours. Bilborough is a gift indeed, but the greatest gift of all you have given me is your love.'

'For ever, my darling,' he murmured, and as he said it, Jane's precious Bilborough, the day and the world were all around them, new with hope and possibility.

* * * * *

UNTAMED ROGUE, SCANDALOUS MISTRESS
Bronwyn Scott

Notorious Crispin Ramsden is captivated when faced with self-made Miss, Aurora Calhoun. She's a woman whose impetuous nature ignites a passion that is as uncontrollable as it is scandalous! Can these two wild hearts find a place to belong?

HONOURABLE DOCTOR, IMPROPER ARRANGEMENT
Mary Nichols

Dr Simon Redfern has risked his heart once before and is shocked when he longs to make the compassionate young widow Kate his wife. Faced with family disapproval, Kate must fight her growing attraction to the man she can't have but so desperately wants.

THE EARL PLAYS WITH FIRE
Isabelle Goddard

Bitter Richard Veryan was left heartbroken after beautiful Christabel Tallis jilted him before their wedding. But when he and Christabel meet again, years later, temptation hangs in the air. He wants to prove he can still command her body and soul—then *he'll* be the one to walk away...

HIS BORDER BRIDE
Blythe Gifford

Clare, daughter of a Scottish lord, can recite the laws of chivalry. She knows dark rebel Gavin, illegitimate son of an English prince, has broken every one. Clare is gripped by desire for this royal rogue. Could he be the one to unleash everything she's tried so hard to hide?

Mills & Boon® Hardback
Historical

*Another exciting novel available
this month:*

HIS COMPROMISED COUNTESS

Deborah Hale

The scandalous wife!

When his beautiful, flirtatious wife scandalises Almack's by being caught in the arms of his enemy, Bennett Maitland, Earl of Sterling, finally ends his unsuitable marriage. He banishes Caroline to his remote childhood home— only to end up trapped there with her!

Having lost the love of her cold husband, Caroline is outwardly defiant, yet her wounded heart aches for what they once shared. If she dares, she has one last chance to break through Bennett's icy reserve—and rekindle the fiery passion that once consumed them!

HIST0112 HB HCC

Mills & Boon® Hardback Historical

Another exciting novel available this month:

THE DRAGON AND THE PEARL

Jeannie Lin

The most beautiful courtesan of them all…

Former Emperor's consort Ling Suyin is renowned for her beauty, the ultimate seductress. Now she lives quietly alone—until the most ruthless warlord in the region comes and steals her away…

Li Tao lives life by the sword, and is trapped in the treacherous world of politics. The alluring Ling Suyin is at the centre of the web. He must uncover her mystery without falling under her spell—yet her innocence calls out to him. How cruel if she, of all women, can entrance the man behind the legend…